BLOOD DOMINION

Book Two of the Blood Saga

MAQUEL A. JACOB

MAJart Works

Oregon, US A

MAJart Works

2001 NW Aloclek Dr #211

Hillsboro, OR 7124

www.majartworks.com

Publisher's Note: This is a work of fiction.

Names, characters, places, and incidents are a product of the author's imagination. Locales and public names are sometimes used for atmospheric purposes. Any resemblance to actual people, living or dead, or to businesses, companies, events, institutions, or locales is completely coincidental.

Cover Design by Dar Albert

www.wickeddesigns.com

Illustration by Nelli Valova

https://www.dreamstime.com/blackmoon979_info

Blood Dominion/ Maquel A. Jacob -1st ed.

ISBN 978-0-9979564-7-4

ACKNOWLEDGEMENTS

Big thanks to NIWA (Northwest Independent Authors Association) for letting me be a part of a great community. To NaNoWriMo for supplying an awesome platform that drives writers foward. For all the tragic souls who volunteered to beta read my first vampire novel and gave me uncensored feedback. My gratitude is infinite.

I cherish you all.

ALSO BY MAQUEL A. JACOB

THE CORE TRILOGY

BOOK ONE: CORE OF CONFLICTION

BOOK TWO: SEEDS OF CONVICION

BOOK THREE: BONDS OF CONTRITION

A CURVE OF HUMANITY

BOOK ONE: ORIGINS

BOOK TWO: SHADOWMEN OBJECTIVE

BOOK THREE: PURGE SEQUENCE

WELCOME DESPAIR

A COLLECTION OF SHORT STORIES

*****COMING SOON*****

CRIPPLED EARTH

BOOK FOUR OF CURVE

CHAPTER ONE

HIGH CLASS MERCHANTS

The rhombus shaped transporter jetted from the main passenger cruiser as it neared the grey planet's atmosphere. It was a personal ship chartered for the Jaubro merchant family onboard. The trip had taken eleven moon cycles and they were finally heading home. As it passed the sun, dark shields covered the windows. Out in the darkness it was a blinding curse. The ship punched through the atmosphere and slowed its descent. A cluster of cities came into view, covering most of the landscape. A few humble abodes scattered within the open spaces could only be recognized due to their property's floodlights.

Up ahead was the docking station, it's many highways connecting to the markets and waterways. Aboard the transport, a young Eterina Jaubro stood at a window watching the scenery go by. The shields had risen to reveal her homeworld.

"This is merchant convoy beta. Please prepare docking area for landing," the pilot spoke into the commlink to the station controller.

"Dock station beta is open and ready. Proceed," came the reply.

Their ship did a half circle maneuver and positioned itself above the clamps on the landing pad. The giant claws grabbed hold of its body and pulled it down into place. A whirring sound emitted as the ship powered down and decompressed.

Steam hissed and blew out as the ship's hatch opened, the hydraulics straining against the weight of the hull to reveal the family of four. In vibrant robes, Mother, Father, daughter and body guard waited for the ramp to finish extending before walking down. All of them were tall, the daughter equal in height to her mother and a near spitting image. Where her mother's hair was dark, she had blonde hair that cascaded down her back in deep waves. Her eyes shone bright even in the gloom and her lips were stained with a touch of red.

Her father towered over the two women, his lean body packed with muscle beneath the robes. A black hat of stiff fabric sat atop his head covering dark blonde hair. Their body guard came from the bloodline of an ancient one, known as Volshins, that grew wings and could fly. His eyes glowed red, creating a stark contrast with his pale skin and black hair as he scanned the area for any signs of danger.

The sky was a muted grey from the stratosphere blocking most of the sun's rays. The planet had days of grey and total darkness at night with a constant chill in the air. Their heavy robes kept them warm. In the city below, heat mixed with the cold air forming wispy puffs that swirled around everything. Row upon row of buildings stacked close together seemed to sit atop each other. A crowded place, it housed most of the upper class. The peasants and royalty had it better by living on the outskirts. Behind the station sat the royal palace, looming over all, blocking the already dim sunlight.

It was still midday and the docks were bustling with business. Ships were being loaded and unloaded with merchandise. Merchants called out orders to the dock workers, making sure logistics went smoothly. Floodlights sat strategically around the strips, enabling everyone could see what they were doing. The mingled smell of products flowed in the air along with oil and metal.

As the group set foot on the dock, the head of the Endaga family greeted them. He was of the lower houses but still a profitable merchant whose family dealt with trade like them. He wore simple clothes dirtied from doing labor and short dark hair peeked from below a well-worn brimmed hat. His son, Tavelo, stood behind him in silence, taking quick glances at Eterenia. Hair black as night and cold blue eyes were the features that intrigued her most. Even though he was of equal profession, she still found him of no consequence and beneath her.

"Master Jaubro," Lord Endaga greeted her father. "How was your trip?"

"Uneventful."

Her father removed the handkerchief from his pocket and dabbed his eyes.

"Was the merchandise not up to standard? That

would be surprising knowing their reputation."

"Yes, well, they had bartered with some subpar corporation and the goods were not inspected properly. I had to forgo the deal."

"A pity. There is some other news that may not be to your liking."

"Oh?" Her father arched an eyebrow.

"It seems, there is strife in the palace."

"That does not bode well for commerce."

"Indeed." Endaga looked over at his son and leaned closer. "Is there room in your schedule for a meeting?"

A strange expression came over her father as he glanced at her briefly.

"I can arrange that. Wait to receive my courier."

"Of course. Good day, then. We have to finish inventory before the patrol comes around."

The two men tilted their hats to each other and parted ways.

On the boardwalk adjacent to the station, Eterenia caught a glimpse of some royal soldiers harassing another merchant on the docks. Their insignia identified them as servants to the Prince. It was no secret he wanted the throne now instead of later. She let out a huff. Patience was a virtue in her opinion. She would wait until her father said she was ready to take over the business accounts.

The stroll to their home took a little under an hour, giving them time to enjoy the scenery and engage with the rest of the community. Stoned streets twisted and turned between narrow areas to form driveways. One of the buildings on the far cluster jetted out a tad farther than the rest. A golden hue covered it from top to bottom with minimal accents around the windows. They walked up the cobbled steps to the large double doors and the body guard opened it using his handprint on the sensor located on its side.

A long, wide foyer spread in front of them and they walked down it to the lift sitting open at the end. It too was a golden color inside and out. The body guard made sure everyone was on board before pushing the button for the top floor.

When they arrived, Eterenia took off down the second corridor to her room. She wanted to get her travel clothes off and put on something more comfortable. The heavy garbs were fine for outdoors but inside the hearths kept the whole floor toasty warm. Her chambermaid met her at the threshold of her bedroom.

"Welcome back, my lady."

"Thank you. Please help me out of these."

Eterenia begin to struggle her arms out of the sleeves.

"Hold on," the chambermaid chided. "No need to rush. You can relax soon enough."

"The trip was so long," she said, breathless.

"Stand still."

The chamber maid finally got her arms out and lifted the first robe over her head. The second one was a wrap which she undid and let fall away. Lastly was the straight long sleeved sheath that tied in the front and around the neck. She loosened it and it too fell to the floor. Stark naked, the daughter ran to the washing room and turned on the water. She sighed with pleasure as it gushed out onto her head then soaked her whole body.

A knock at the door made the chamber maid stop from picking up the discarded garments. Count Jaubro stood in the doorway and gave her a certain look. Her smile turned into pursed lips and she nodded. As he left, she went into the other room and made a cup of hot drink. From her pouch, she pulled out a small vial and let a few drops land in the cup.

"Hurry up and get out of there. I made you something warm to drink."

"Oh, thank you!" Eterenia called.

The water was turned off and grabbing her robe, Eterenia came back into the main room. She took the cup from her chambermaid and smelled its aroma.

"Mmm, smells delicious."

She began to take small sips. The chambermaid watched her the entire time.

Lord Endaga and his son, Tavelo, walked up to the doors of the golden house and waited to be recognized by the security cameras. Small lights mounted on the sides of the building illuminated them for that purpose. Residents leisurely walked the streets as evening set in. Dark grey clouds covered up the already dim skyline and the chill deepened.

The doors opened and there stood the body guard looking put off as usual. He looked down on them like garbage and slowly stepped aside to gesture them in. Tavelo frowned with disdain at how his family was always treated. They were not as wealthy but had the same clout as any other top merchant on the planet.

Inside on the main floor, he half marveled and half disliked everything around him. Expensive pieces were positioned in key areas and the floors were carpeted in plush rich colors. The windows went from floor to ceiling with heavy drapes cascading down like waterfalls. Huge mirrors hung on the walls in every room. He assumed it was for vanity sake.

Why else would one have so many all over their abode? He asked himself.

Ruby chandeliers dangled from above, the lights hitting them to give a pink glow, making the gold rose colored. The lounge area had a large table where crystal goblets sat on a golden tray. There were at least ten different liqueurs along with an ice bucket and water Carafe. The two older men immediately went to it while he lingered at the threshold.

Last time he was in that house, the two fathers argued about who was worthy of the man's daughter. It was laughable since everyone within certain circles knew he would give her to the highest bidder that in turn made his family more fortunes. He could tell by the way she looked at him, how she felt about him. Nervousness came over him as they walked further in. He could see movement in the guest library and caught a glimpse of bare legs being positioned on the large chaise.

"So, that's how you do it," his father said to Master Jaubro. "Does it not make you feel vile, having her knocked unconscious and not feeling a thing?"

"I'm not some monster," her father retorted. "She is merely relaxed to the point of submission. What kind of father do you take me for?"

"One who is not taking my proposal seriously."

"I will not play favorites. You will all get equal chance to sway her mind, and mine."

His father turned to him.

"Are you not ready?"

The question startled him. He stepped back a bit.

"I can go in?" Tavelo asked.

Her father held on to a half full glass of spirits while gesturing with two fingers towards the library.

"It only lasts for about an hour. You should get your fill while you can."

Tavelo went through the arched entrance and stopped at the edge of the chaise. Eterenia lay peaceful on her back, naked except for a necklace with her family crest laying just above her bosom. He stripped down, folding his robes haphazardly and set them on the floor. Approaching, he crawled on top of her. His heart was beating so fast it felt like it would burst from his chest. Heat rose up throughout his body and his fangs grew out past his lips. He could smell her, and it was intoxicating.

His hands roamed her flesh and she stirred from the feather light touches. He gently spread her legs and as he entered laid one arm flat above her for leverage. There was a sharp intake of air then she moaned softly but her eyes did not open. He went slow for fear of hurting her if he lost his state of mind. Each thrust put him in a state of euphoria and he felt himself shudder with ecstasy.

He made himself flat against her, so he could caress the side of her neck with his lips before sinking in his fangs. His eyes rolled back from the sweet tang of her blood filing his mouth. He only took enough to satiate his palate then sat back on hands and knees to watch while he moved inside her. His hair brushed against her face and shoulders, his own family crest necklace swaying with his motion.

This time her eyes fluttered open halfway and stared at him. At first, he contemplated what to do if she started to panic then decided regardless, she would have to endure it. He didn't want to stop and was on the verge of climax. Her body told him she was as well. He felt her walls tense around his cock, forcing him to come. Her back arched as he spewed his seed. A small strangled cry escaped her lips before she went limp and closed her eyes. He was left spent, sitting between her sweat drenched thighs trying to catch his breath. He too was covered in sweat.

"Well, look at his impeccable timing," he heard his father say. "With only a few moments to spare."

"He is, indeed, capable," Master Jaubro added.

Then it dawned on him that they were watching the whole time. Time. It went too fast. To him it felt like only a few minutes. He flushed with embarrassment and eased off the chaise in search of his clothes. He knew where he had laid them, but they were not there.

"Come," her chambermaid said. He had not heard her come in. Which explained his missing clothes. "You must wash yourself before the evening meal."

He looked around for something to cover himself. She seemed impatient, so he cupped his hands between his legs and followed her out. Naked as the dawn, he walked down the corridor amongst other servants who didn't give him a glance. They reached a single washing room the size of a bedchamber with cream colored tiles and a large ringed spout high above. There was a basin for quick clean up and a wash bench for sitting if one was so inclined. A drying robe hung on the peg near the entrance.

"I need to cleanse the lady," she said while leaving.

The way she glanced back at him with contempt conveyed that she felt he had desecrated Eterenia. Angered, he turned on the spout and let the warm water clean the sweat from his hair and body. It hid the tears of rage that fell along with it. On the settee by the window he found his clothes piled nice and neat.

Dinner was jovial and full of life as spirits were poured and meat delicacies filled the long table. A handful of merchants and their children had been invited and the dining room was packed. People leaned over the center to engage in hushed conversations about the latest gossip. Cups were sloppily waved about, spilling drink amongst the food. Tavelo sat two seats down across from Eterenia. He watched her eat, a longing tugged at him. She glanced up at him as if she had no idea he had been there before the other guests. An invisible shield surrounded her as no one jostled or bumped into her.

What kind of drug did they give her?

He was more upset by that. Letting her be defiled by others was no surprise but he didn't like her father's methods. She should be cherished more. At the end of the table sat her mother, just as beautiful and laughing with the men surrounding her. Son and daughter locked eyes. For a moment there was mutual silence then her eyes narrowed. She disengaged and continued eating.

I will have you.

He promised not only her but himself.

Another merchant fell into him, laughing; drunk. He shoved the man off and caught his glass of spirits before it fell over. Her father raised a glass and tapped it with the end of his knife. The entire table came to his attention. He waited until everyone was settled and gave a winning smile.

"To my fellow merchants. May we find more prosperous ventures this season and indulge like this always."

He raised his glass even higher and his guest did the same.

"To prosperity!" They all replied in unison.

A few of the merchants made sideways glances at Tavelo and his father. When there was eye contact, they gave forced smiles of encouragement. Tavelo tried his best not to frown. Out of the corner of his eye, he saw Eterenia look at the other merchants in disgust at their behavior. He wondered if she was really on his family's side. Not all of them were disrespectful. The lower class envied them of course and some of the middle class saw their potential. They just needed a break to get back the status their family once had over two centuries ago.

After having their fill of food and liqueur, Tavelo and his father were escorted out to a carrier waiting outside. The hovercraft was a standard model for residential commute. It would have looked odd to have them in a luxury one. Their host had already paid the fare. They got in and his father gave the operator their sector number and building. He looked them over and snorted, recognizing their crest. Even the workers were biased in the city.

Unlike some of the higher merchants who resided in elevated homes, they lived alongside the docks in a modest house set on the bottom. He could see it come into view as they approached and again, the difference was stark compared to where they had just come from.

The buildings didn't merely appear to be stacked atop each other, they literally were. Different sized structures were grafted onto others to conserve space within the city which meant the higher up and bigger, the better your view. The only scenery his family had was of the waterways. He didn't mind that. The water was calming especially on stormy nights. One day, his family would get more accounts and be on par with the others.

Each merchant family kept the same clients for generations. Th amount of business conducted was regulated by commerce and how much credit could be extended. If a merchant could get larger shipments with their clients, the more they could profit. There was a trust that defied politics and commerce laws. They only worked with them directly. The planet was richer than the others in the solar system solely because of that. Even though there were thousands of merchants, only ten families ruled over them. His was one of them yet they had a lack of respect from the rest. All because they didn't make large deals on a regular basis and came out last in revenue every quarter.

How could one gauge another's worth like that?

His mother came out of the house to greet them. Her hair and robes were disheveled from stocking inventory and bags puffed under her tired eyes. His temper flared.

We work harder than any of them.

"How was your meeting," his mother asked. She came up to her husband and gave him a soft peck on the cheek.

"Eventful. Of course, he had to throw party," his father answered.

"Are you drunk?" Her gaze was sly.

"Perhaps a little. You could take advantage."

He showed his fangs.

"Ugh," Tavelo let out as he turned his head in repulsion.

His mother smacked him beside the head.

"How do you think you were born?"

"That doesn't mean I want to see."

The three walked inside their home and Tavelo sat on the bench to undo his boots. His mother helped her husband with his. He could feel the mild warmth from their hearth and wished for a bigger upgraded one like the Jaubros. Because of that, they had to wear one of the heavier robes inside. The cooler season was in mid swing. They had another five moon cycles before they could turn it down and conserve energy.

Loud giggling drew him out of his reverie and he saw his parents tickling and necking each other as they headed for their bed chamber. He cringed and made his way to his own. Along the way, he pulled off the top heavy robe and draped it around his shoulders. There was a cold patch in the corridor due to a crack in the foundation. They hadn't the funds to repair it.

His bedchamber was dimly lit, the dark bedding make it seem even darker. He plopped down on his bed and removed the other layer of robes, keeping the bottom one on. Lying back, he stared at the ceiling thinking about Eterenia.

She was so soft and warm.

As he knew she would be. Her hard exterior was a ruse. He saw how late it was and decided to sleep. The number crunching would start in the morning and he was eager to see how well they had fared. What he did know was that they weren't going to be on the same level as the others, again.

The merchants meeting of the ruling ten houses took place in the commerce center at the docks. One of the rare buildings not made of metal, it breathed with life from natural materials. The hearth was massive kicking out steady heat. The mornings were always colder since the sun barely turned the sky grey. Servants employed by the center went about setting the drinks and food paid for by merchant dues. Not just the merchants came but their whole family to gloat over the numbers, ranking each other. The head of commerce did the calculations and ran through the data for the meeting.

When the servants were finished, everyone formed a line and filled their plates with the first round of snacks. There was no alcohol, it being morning and level heads were needed.

"Ladies, gentlemen, are we ready?"

The head of commerce sat down at the end of the conference table. His multiscreen was unfolded before him. Its clear quality let them see what information he was pulling. That way, no one could accuse him of fudging the data for one family over another.

As each family's current earnings were announced, there were congratulatory toasts and hand clapping. The Jaubro family was naturally the frontrunners. Towards the end with only three families left, the head of commerce cleared his throat.

"I want to give a special congratulations to the Endaga family. They have double their profits for the quarter. To your great success."

There was a silent pause around the room as the information sunk in. The claps built slowly until everyone was doing so and giving the family praise.

We're not last!

Tavelo fought back tears while his mother squeezed his thigh under the table. She too held back her joy. His father had a smug look on his face. From across the table, he saw Eterenia turn away with a shocked expression. Not being last meant they could negotiate for a new contract with their clients. There was no need to limit supply and demand because they would have increased credit.

By the end of the meeting, sprits had been brought out for a feast to celebrate the end of one quarter and the start of a new one. The bottom two families were curt towards the others, feeling disgraced. Eterenia and her family came up to his and shook their hands.

"I always knew if you applied yourselves, there would be no stopping your climb," Master Jaubro said to them. His tone was condescending, yet others heard it as genuine praise.

"Yes, well, we do work hard."

He saw his father's grip tighten and the two men stared at each other. When they released, so did the tension. The two mothers hugged and gave each other a kiss on the cheeks. Eterenia stayed away as did he. The festivities kicked into gear and before she could walk away, he grabbed her by the wrist then ran out the building.

A few streets down, she wrenched herself free and stopped.

"What do you think you're doing?"

"Getting us out of there," Tavelo answered.

"What?"

"Did you really want to be there around all those insincere egomaniacs?"

Her expression changed and seemed to struggle until a grin formed. She let out a small laugh. He sighed with relief. If she had demanded to go back, there was no way he could explain his actions. He looked up at the silvery sky, matted in color.

"It's the brightest time of day. We should enjoy it a little." Her eyebrow raised the same way her father's did. He held out his hand. "Come with me."

She stared at it as if he had offered something rotten before walking towards him to take it. Their eyes met, and he thanked the stars for not going into heat from her touch.

A New Reign

Searchlights from the palace swept across the dark skies intruding on the homes in the city below. This was the third time in the last few months that life was interrupted by an unforeseen incident involving the Prince. His officers were abusing their authority and many of the victims were merchants. Twice, he had proposed new laws and was shut down by his father, the emperor. He felt that the kingdom should have the reins on commerce, not the merchants themselves.

The head of commerce had been targeted multiple times to give up the data on each account. He refused regardless of the consequences. To add insult to the Prince, many of the clients came to his defense and any punishment was reversed. He gave the merchants fair warning when it looked like there would be trouble.

Tonight, it was a fire raging on the docks. The smell of burning oil and metal filled the region and workers scurried to douse it out with hoses connected to the waterway. Members of the merchant family affected were being rescued out of the debris by concerned citizens in the area. Workers from other docks battled to save the shipments.

Master Jaubro came up to the boardwalk and looked down on the carnage. His eyes burned red with rage. He had personally gone to the emperor to plead for an end to this madness and was assured the Prince would be reprimanded. It was now clear that the Prince didn't care what the emperor thought or wanted. Smoke, ash and steam engulfed the docks as the fires were finally contained. The head of the Callesi merchants came up behind him and rested a hand on his shoulder.

"All we can do now is regroup."

"This madness must stop!" Jaubro said.

"Yes. For now, we wait."

A worker came up the stone path. Jaubro decided to stop him.

"How much has been lost?"

"It's a miracle. Only twenty percent was destroyed."

"That's still too much," Jaubro replied.

The worker nodded and continued to the tavern across the bridge. The owner and his employees were setting out barrels of water and non perishable foods. Other businesses were doing what they could with supplies to help the wounded and volunteers.

Bringing his attention back to the docks, he caught a glimpse of Endaga's wife hauling a large sack of product. Her dress robes were filthy, hair in disarray. Behind her was the son pulling a crate carrier filled to capacity. Then he remembered. The Endaga family was always at the docks until closing, working themselves tirelessly. In that moment, he felt shame for how he viewed them over the centuries. None of the other top merchant families did that, not even his own.

He signaled for his body guard.

"Send a message to the Endaga family inviting them to dinner tomorrow."

"As you desire."

The body guard bowed his head and stepped back to stand near the transport.

"Makes you feel inadequate, doesn't it?"

Callesi gave him a sideways glance.

Jaubro turned towards him, angered.

"What do you mean by that?"

"No offense, Jaubro, but I have never seen your family do such things."

"Did you read my mind?"

Jaubro grabbed the man's shirt collar.

"I would never do that without permission. Is your conscience not clear? Feeling guilt?"

Jaubro let him go and continued to watch the recovery. His hands gripped the railings.

Exhausted and sore, the Endaga family entered their home and barely got undressed. They gathered in the lounging room and sat on the cushions near the hearth. The warmth settled them as they laid in silence for a while.

"What is happening?" Tavelo asked.

"The Prince thinks he's correct in his assessment. But he is still ignorant regarding commerce," his father answered as he sat up.

"The emperor rules with an iron fist but he is not

a dictator," his mother added.

"If he keeps doing this, there will be a collapse and our planet decimated."

Tavelo placed his hands behind his head and frowned.

"That is true, my son, and a sad fate if it comes to pass," his father said.

The entry bell dinged, and his mother got up to answer it. Tavelo and his father followed to make sure it wasn't one of the Prince's officers. A few merchants had been ambushed in their homes. A young servant appeared on the security camera screen and they recognized him from the Jaubro house. She opened the door and greeted him.

"What brings you here so late in the dead of night?"

"An invitation from Lord Jaubro. Please accept his humble request."

He held out a tablet with the RSVP on screen. There were two selections and she chose the one to accept.

"Thank you. We look forward to serving you."

The servant bowed slightly and returned to the transport awaiting him.

"Well, I guess we should find our best robes for tomorrow," his mother sighed.

She closed the door and headed back to the lounging room.

Tavelo resumed his position on the cushions and pondered what prompted Lord Jaubro to invite them. Anything that merchant family did he deemed suspect. He didn't consider they may have found a sense of comradery or even compassion. On the other hand, he would get to see Eterenia again. His groin tightened, and felt it heat up. He sat up in a hurry.

"I'm going to my bed chamber."

Without kissing his parents good night like he usually did, he half ran down the hall, an erection in full bloom.

The fancy transport arrived in front of their building and neighbors gawked when they emerged from their home wearing expensive robes. His mother wore silver while his father wore a deep purple. His robe was a royal blue that accented his eyes. The man servant had shined their boots to almost black mirrors. He felt out of himself and grimaced at the unwanted attention. They climbed into the silver bullet shaped hovercraft and were off to the Jaubro family merchant's home.

On arrival, they ended up in a queue for the entrance. Many other merchant families had been invited and it was requested that they enter last. Tavelo bit his tongue at the behest of his mother. He could not understand the man's thinking when it came to his family. After nearly a half hour wait, their transport pulled up to the golden doors and the family body guard came out to personally greet them. His blood red eyes were devoid of emotion.

"This way, please." He made a half bow and extended an arm towards the entrance.

Inside, they rode the lift to the main floor and was bombarded by cheers as the doors opened. Everyone was clapping and smiling with no forced cheer. Tavelo reared back whereas his parents happily went along saying thank you.

"Our guests of honor have arrived," Lord Jaubro announced. "Let the festivities begin!"

His father went up to him and whispered while grinning.

"What is the meaning of this?"

"A show of appreciation for all your hard work on the docks. That must have been a grueling ordeal," Jaubro answered.

"It was nothing compared to the atrocity itself. We only did what was right."

"Of course," Lord Jaubro said. "Now, come. Have a drink and enjoy the attention."

Tavelo fumed. What they did was nothing special. Anyone who saw the incident would have done the same. And then he thought rationally. No, not the other merchant families. To them, it was a lesson in humility and they didn't dare not praise his family for what they deemed heroic.

Farther off in the corner stood Eterenia drinking from a clear flute of exquisite design. She glanced over at him with boredom. He made his way to her and was stopped a few feet away by her mother. Lady Jaubro towered over him and he realized she was the same height as his father.

"Young Tavelo, that robe compliments you well."

"Thank you, Lady Jaubro."

"Are you prepared to entertain my daughter? She doesn't seem to be enjoying the party."

"That is not true," Eterenia balked.

"If she would let me, I will oblige."

He bowed to her.

Eterenia gave him a dirty look and drained her glass. Her mother smiled, caressing his cheek and went into the fray. A mug was shoved into his hand by a merchant passing by.

"Drink your fill, my boy!"

He turned his attention to Eterenia. She appeared to be waiting on him to do something. He had no idea what. Thinking it over, he pulled her to him. She pushed him away and glanced around the room to see if anyone had noticed. He chided himself for being stupid. Most of the merchants with sons were trying to get close to her as well and would not take his approach too lightly.

"Shall we take a stroll on the veranda?" He asked politely.

In answer, she turned and walked towards the double doors that led out to it. He followed in silence. The night air was cooling, and a soft breeze picked up. She leaned over the ledge, her body almost at a ninety-degree angle.

"Why do you hate me so?" He asked.

She turned to him, a horrified look on her face.

"I do not..." she stammered.

"Then why? Why do you treat me like a pariah, like them?"

This time she became angry.

"I do not treat you like them," she relied through gritted teeth. "I know you are not some pompous ingrate. But your family seems so fixated on being one of them."

"What would you have us do, then? We need the status for our sake, no one else's."

He moved away from her as his anger built. His breathing came hard and fast, so he forced himself to calm down. She stood straight.

"My apologies. I shouldn't have said that."

He stared at her for moment.

Without warning, he crossed over and took hold of her. His mouth covered hers in fervent hunger. Her hands hit him repeatedly to let go but he didn't until she relented. He felt her body relax, she returned his kiss. When they released, she slapped him hard.

"Don't ever do that again." She wiped her mouth with the back of one hand.

Tavelo fought the urge to slap her back, clenching his hands into fists. She gave him a smirk and leaned backwards against the rail.

"I need a drink," she declared.

Her golden hair flowed in the wind as she tilted her head sideways and smiled at him.

Taking a deep breath, he walked back into the main room to fetch one for them both. He needed one too, possibly three. As he perused the offerings on the various tables, her mother came up holding two glasses.

"Be careful, young Endaga," she cooed.

The glasses were handed to him and she left again. Tavelo stood perplexed before heading back out to Eterenia.

Screaming filled the city streets as word came through from the palace. The emperor's soldiers had fled into hiding at the request of their master, leaving only a squad of one hundred to defend him against the Prince. His son had declared war and within hours, slaughtered most of the people loyal to his father inside the palace. Those who managed to escape went into the city to warn the people. The first to hear were the merchants and they commenced an emergency meeting to plan for what could only be called an attack.

While they huddled in the Commerce building, the planet wide P.A. system kicked on.

"Emperor Mallen the Fourth is dead. I have secured my reign. You will all bend to my will."

The Prince's voice was strong, dripping with malice.

Royal transports zipped across the sky, some landing near the docks. The Prince's officers flooded the boardwalk as merchants and workers locked up their products. They would rather die before giving the unlock codes. The merchants in the commerce building shuddered in despair at the potential blood bath about to occur. Volshins swarmed around the ships, scaring away the workers.

A group of officers marched into the square and set up a barricade so no one could leave the docks without coming through them first. Their commander scanned the area with cold eyes. Each dock locker had four officers standing guard ready for orders. The first merchant was accosted, and an officer grabbed him by the neck. His cohorts kept the mother and two sons at bay.

"Open it," the officer demanded.

"Never," the merchant spat.

The officer dropped the merchant.

"Kill them and break it open."

As one of the officers slit the young boy's throat and the mother was stabbed, chaos ensued. The merchants went into a rage, attacking the officers with talons and fangs. The Volshins swept down to assist, snatching up merchant family members and draining them dry before dropping the lifeless corpses onto the streets. Blood flowed into the river.

A loud siren screeched across the land, making the officers and Volshins halt their attack. They all looked up and the sky rained tiny lights that landed harmlessly on the ground, disappearing.

"Move out!" The commander called. "We return after our new Emperor's coronation."

The barricade was left up but now anyone could get through. Officers on the docks gathered themselves, leaving a trail of carnage behind without a care. Inside the commerce building, the merchants and their families cowering in fear snapped out of it and became enraged. This was not how trade worked.

"Those monsters," a merchant father yelled.

"Hurry, we must tend to the dead and wounded," another said.

The Endaga family was already out the door with two other families in tow. At the first dock slip, they found the merchant, bloodied, kneeling over his dead wife and son while the surviving older son sat in shock. The locker was covered in deep dents but not compromised and the keypad remained intact. They were built to withstand attacks from far worse than Volshins.

Lord Jaubro stood in the doorway of the commerce building taking in the scene. A feeling of dread overcame him as he concluded that the new Emperor was insane enough to destroy the planet itself if he didn't get what he wanted.

Merchant clients arriving at the station were subjected to hostile inspections of their person and any product that they may have brought with them. Some of it even confiscated until further review. When it became clear that the clients would leave and not negotiate any trade, the new emperor had no choice but to change protocol and let them in on their terms. Past the barricade, the clients were met with their merchant counterpart and escorted away.

Lord Jaubro hurried his client and assistant into the transport and watched the barricade get smaller as they sped away. He didn't trust the royal officers not to follow. He ushered them out just as quickly when they arrived at his home.

"I am not pleased with these new events," the client said. "Is it true, he murdered the emperor? His own father?"

"Yes. He tossed his body from the top of the palace into the ravines below."

The client's eyes went wide in horror.

Jaubro continued.

"It was quite the ceremony. He made sure it was on the planetary feed for all to see."

"Montrous!"

"We use that term a lot these days."

"What will you do?"

"If we must, fight. Or die along with the trade on this planet."

"Will product be safe?"

"I will guarantee it," Jaubro said.

The group went into his home and the body guard made quick glances around to make sure no one was spying on them. To the left he spotted a royal officer in disguise, a different hooded robe covering his uniform. He made eye contact and the officer stepped back into the shadows.

❧

Tavelo saw the officers enter the station and tensed up. He was working the family dock by himself due to his mother falling ill and his father meeting with the other merchants. An important shipment for the Jaubro's sat ready to be delivered. By the way the officers moved he knew that's what they were after. He went over to Eterenia who was keeping watch on the product.

"You need to get rid of the shipment or get it back in the locker," he said in a rush.

"What are you talking about?" Her face scrunched up with impatience.

"There isn't much time," he seethed.

"This is not your dock or your product so..."

"Royal guards!"

Her face blanched as she looked around, realizing how vulnerable everything was. He stepped away to gauge how far the officers were.

"I don't know how to use the carrier," she cried out. "The locker was opened for me. I have no way of securing it."

Tavelo thought for a moment then went back to his dock. He came back with his family's carrier and proceeded to load the Jaubro shipment. She followed him visibly panicked. They got the shipment loaded in the Endaga locker right as the officers found the lot empty and spotted them. The first set of officers came up to them, his face contorted with anger.

"That shipment is from a Jaubro client and now the property of the kingdom."

He shoved the shipping dossier under her nose and jabbed her with it.

"Sign the release for us to take custody of the goods."

"No."

The other officer struck her down with one blow and before he could get a third hit in, Tavelo stepped forward.

"You are mistaken. This shipment belongs to the Endaga Merchants."

"You will stay out of this matter," the officer spat.

"Is it not in our locker?"

"This," the officer wagged the dossier, "is proof of delivery to the Jaubro dock. If it is in your locker then it is an act of theft." He kicked her while she tried to get up and she slumped down. "Sign this release!"

"Leave her alone! I already told you."

He didn't get to finish.

The other three converged towards him and began beating him. He could hear her screaming at them to stop. The first officer moved to the locker, instructing one of the others to grab the carrier. Tavelo managed to get loose and rammed the officer out of range. Wiping blood from his face, he hit the lock sensor on the unit and heard the mechanism slam the shield door into place. He was able to get in one cruel smirk before they brought him down again.

Suddenly it all stopped.

The head of commerce stood in the dock area with armed workers. He walked up to the officers and pushed them out of the way.

"Your warrant is for the Jaubro dock, is it not?"

The first officer stared at him. His fingers twitched.

"You have no authority to demand anything from the Endaga dock. I suggest you leave, or I will report you to the emperor's advisor."

In acknowledgement that he had been bested, the first officer gave the signal for his men to follow him and. Not before spitting on the ground near the two merchant children as they left the docks. The moment they were out of range, the head of commerce helped them to their feet.

"I guess we'll have to do a transfer of ownership as soon as possible. If not, they will come back and this time." He shook his head at the thought of them being hurt again.

"Father will be furious," Eterenia said between coughs.

"Yes, you don't look so good," Tavelo added.

She looked over at him and her eyes showed sadness. He wanted to hold her but knew better in the presence of others.

Her father was indeed angry although not for what Tavelo thought. Now he understood why she looked at him that way on the docks. All the man yelled about was the loss of the shipment. He had not heard from the head of commerce yet so had no idea it was indeed safe. His father was also angry about it. Not willing to stand by and hear their ravings any longer, Tavelo spoke up.

"We have it." The room went still, and both men turned to look at him. "It is in our locker."

"You stole my client's shipment?" Jaubro roared.

"What have you done?" His father yelled, incredulous.

"Is this how you get more revenue? How long has this gone on?" Lord Jaubro grabbed Tavelo by the front of his shirt. "Explain yourself!"

"That is not how we do things and you know it! How dare you accuse us!" his father countered.

"Did he not just confess?"

"Stop!" Eterenia covered her ears. "Why won't you listen?"

Their body guard came into the room with the head of commerce in tow.

"He says it is an emergency."

Jaubro let go of Tavelo and stood in a defensive stance. The head of commerce came further into the room. He had been waiting for the right time to intervene and relied on the body guard to let him know when.

"Your client is going to come and claim the shipment for distribution tomorrow morning. I did a transfer of ownership to the Endaga's. Once you get to the docks, they will release the hold and the original transaction will be complete. By the time the royal officers show up with a new warrant, it will be long gone."

"Then the shipment is safe?"

"You have the young Endaga to thank for that. At the expense of his well being, he made sure to secure it before they got their hands on it."

Lord Jaubro turned back to the Endagas.

"My apologies. I should have listened first."

For the first time, he took a good look at his daughter and sucked in a breath. His eyes turned blood red and he pulled her into his chest. He saw how beaten Tavelo was and felt a twinge of shame. His wife came into the room and cupped the young man's face.

"Let's get you cleaned up and comfortable."

Her smile made him do the same and he let her lead him away. Every bone in his body ached and the thought of warm water rushing down on him sounded heavenly.

Eterenia stood in a bright satin pink cloak over her robes and ribbons in her hair. The day was not so chilly, and she wanted to feel the air on her bruised face. Her chambermaid had put salve on it to reduce the swelling and her face looked normal enough. The pain still lingered. Her father and mother were behind her and on to the right was Tavelo in his blue robes again. His father was also present with bags under his eyes from lack of sleep.

The client, his assistant and four servants waited on the platform across from them. He was none too happy with the chain of events but glad to get his product.

"This will not do. I have no idea what your sapling emperor wishes to accomplish but I do not want to be a part of it."

"We understand. I did guarantee delivery."

"Yes, you did. And I thank you." He turned to the Endagas. "Especially you."

They loaded the goods onto their transport and sped out of the city. Within moments of them leaving, six royal guards came marching down the boardwalk towards the Endaga dock. From the way the leader carried the tablet in his hand, they knew it had to be a new warrant. The leader stopped dead in his tracks as his gaze fell upon the empty locker.

"Where is the shipment?"

He had a hard time containing his rage by the red pools of his eyes.

"Delivered to the client as promised."

Lord Jaubro smiled at him.

"Distribution is to be handled by the courts. What you have done is treason."

"No. The goods were for the client's region and he

was the rightful recipient."

"What the emperor decrees is law!"

"And what does he decree now?"

The leader returned the smile.

"All merchants must divulge their client list and said clients must go through the courts for routing privileges."

"That is not feasible and you know this," Lord Endaga said.

"You will obey!"

"Or what? Bring trade to a screeching halt?"

"You will see. The emperor's reign is absolute."

With that, the entourage turned as one and marched back from whence they came.

Bold Retreat

One thing Tavelo knew going forward was that the emperor would not rest until every merchant bended knee to his reign. And because they surely wouldn't, there was a chance of being pushed into poverty, or worse, slavery. Every merchant kept vigil over the docks to minimize damage whenever the royal officers came around with illegal warrants. They had learned from the incident with his family and carried sweeping documents to encompass every locker on the slips. The only saving grace was even the emperor couldn't afford to have trade cease and the head of commerce was the one making sure it continued to run.

Clients were on the verge of rebelling as well due to their products being held without explanation or rerouted without their consent. The palace was in dire need of supplies after the bloody take over, the emperor not realizing that depleting his own abode would put a strain on its operations. Siphoning from the rest of the citizens was not the correct option. He didn't seem to care if the planet went into an economic crash by his own hands. Out on the distance Tavelo saw a blip in the air and knew what was coming. That would be the best test to see how insane the emperor really was.

A high-pitched klaxon sounded and every person on the docks and beyond looked up towards the sky at the massive transport ship preparing for landing. Its body blocked out the dull sunlight, throwing the area into temporary darkness. Sighs of elation and anticipation echoed along the docks. Then, there was a brief panic as workers scoured the platforms for royal officers. There would be no confiscating that cargo even if defending it meant their death.

The shipment was one that came twice in a three-year cycle. A large order of raw kill preserved in its freshness and ready for consumption. Most people kept some out for only a few days and the rest was stored frozen for a later date. As a race of carnivores, they didn't get much fresh kill since the decline of their wildlife population. Blood was genetically modified to increase volume. Scientists could take an ounce of blood and make it into gallon at eighty five percent purity. Thus, the arrival of the fresh meat was a luxury.

Clients lined up at their merchants docks ready to take possession for their region once unloaded. Everyone had huge grins on their faces. At the barricade, the commander took three of his subordinates and made way to the royal docks. He kept his distance from the workers and merchants, feeling their animosity and readiness to fight. There would be no bloodshed today. The entire planet was waiting for their portion and the emperor had no desire to cause a planetary war.

The containers were revealed as the transport opened its ramp doors. Crystal clear and the size of a bedchamber, each one was stacked top to bottom, side by side, filling the compartments to the gills. Red chunks were packed tight in blood to the point where they barely sloshed inside. They were sealed to eliminate smell and keep out outside pathogens. That didn't stop the people from salivating at the mere sight of them. One by one, the containers were moved out and positioned for merchant carriers.

As the last delivery transaction completed, the local businesses broke out their best fare and readied themselves for the rush. When citizens were happy, it made for great profit. Some threw community parties to indulge together. The meat could be eaten as is and the blood that seeped from it drained into tubes for process at the blood bank.

The Jaubro and Endaga family decided to dine together that evening and there was a moment of silence as everyone sitting at the long dining table in the Jaubro home placed a chunk of meat into their mouths, gently pulling the meat off the fork. They all closed their eyes and savored the raw taste. Lady Jaubro let out a deep sigh and opened her eyes. The rest did the same and then laughter spread across the room. They needed a reason for rejoicing after the past year.

"It is always so amazing. I wish we could bring back our own livestock," she said.

"Only royal scientists can manipulate the archived DNA and create new ones, but they cited it being against their code of ethics," Master Jaubro added.

"Well, they all fled before the fall of the emperor so that point is moot," Lord Endaga said.

"Enough with the gloom," Eterenia snapped as she took another bite of meat and again closed her eyes in ecstasy.

Tavelo watched her eat and curbed his impulse to cover her mouth with his own and eat some of the meat from her. He happened to look away and found her mother eyeing him knowingly. Embarassed, he squeezed his eyes shut and paid attention to his own plate. Eterenia seemed to sense his desire and her eyes narrowed.

Lord Jaubro raised a glass of grain alcohol in the air.

"To fresh meat!"

They all raised their drinks.

"To fresh meat!" They sang out.

They laughed as the rest of the food was passed around.

Only a year after, the emperor pushed his agenda on the citizens of the planet and with more ferocity than before. Clients were threatened and beaten, workers had been murdered and merchants feared for their lives. Lord Jaubro was calling a meeting every moon cycle to make sure all were accounted for. To his sadness, a few merchants had disappeared.

A handful were found, their bodies mutilated along with their entire family while others were just gone. Their houses had been stripped of anything valuable and stored in the palace because no one would buy them after learning where the items came from. A hostile environment arose against the emperor.

Jaubro and his family were taking a stroll around their neighborhood to ease the tension after a grueling altercation with some royal officers that resulted in a stalemate. The other neighbors were doing the same. Everyone was looking worse for wear since a self-imposed curfew was in place. The emperor was not happy about that and authorized homes to be broken in if necessary. Unfortunately, the officers who tried were either killed or unable to get in. Many of the workers had reinforced their citizens home entries free of charge.

A royal transport sped into the middle of the walkway and stopped in front of the Jaubro family. An officer came out and they recognized him as the commander from the barricade. He stood a few feet from them and scrutinized the women. He tsked.

"The emperor wants your wife for mating over the next two years and in return, your family will not be subjected to the new laws."

The three of then reared back in horror, Lord Jaubro pushing his wife and daughter behind him.

"That is unacceptable! I refuse to let something like that monster touch my wife."

"You will obey your emperor," the commander seethed.

The other neighbors, surrounded the royal officers, fangs and talons ready. He looked around, finding his men and himself in a very bad predicament. A high-class merchant came close to him.

"That is not our emperor. He murdered the true ruler. And if you think he can just come into the city and take any woman he chooses, he is mistaken. You snatched one of my associates' wife after murdering him and we will not forgive or forget."

Lord Jaubro went pale at that revelation. He had heard rumors, but it sounded too far fetched to believe. He also bared his fangs and talons, ready to tear the commander apart if he tried to advance. A glimpse at the tablet in his hand showed a list with some of the names marked as completed.

Another citizen snuck around and peeked inside the transport. Her eyes went wide as she let out a shriek. The others turned towards her as the officer in the back came at her, slicing three lines into her face. The commander tried to get through to secure the transport and was attacked by five other citizens. The rest of the neighbors went to the back of the transport and found four women beaten and bound in a pile on top of each other like trash.

With brute force, the neighbors battered the officers to submission and pulled the women out. They were rushed into whichever house was nearest while Lord Jaubro kept the commander busy until it was time to retreat. As everyone got to their entries, the commander and his men gathered themselves up. He gave a blood red scowl at them one by one.

"You will regret this. The emperor's decree is absolute!"

"Yes, you say that every time," another merchant said.

The commander smiled as he spat blood onto the pavement.

"You will know pain. You will all suffer for taking what is his and undermining his rule."

With that, they climbed into the transport and took off.

Lord Jaubro retracted his claws and a deep sadness along with rage took over. All he could think of was that list and he knew the commander was going to finish his collection of women for the emperor. By the look on his wife's face, she concluded the same. His daughter was in the doorway of their home bent over in tears.

What must we do?

The Endaga family heard about the incident via messenger from the Jaubro family and Lord Endaga immediately began bolting the outer doors. He had seen the commander observing his wife on the docks many times, never knowing why. Now, he feared for her. He ushered his wife and son into the lounging room.

"You are not to work the docks at night any longer," he ordered her.

Her face flushed with anger.

"I am just as capable of defending myself as any other," she said angrily.

"Not when there are hordes of royal officers waiting to take you away by force!"

"I will protect her," Tavelo said.

"That's not good enough!" He turned on him. "What do you think would have happened if Jaubro's neighbors hadn't intervened?"

His wife and son became quiet as they took in the truth. Times were harder than they ever imagined. Merchant families had been murdered and no one was safe. The rumors about the abductions also included the fact that none had taken the emperor on his offer. Young and powerful he may be, but his personality was unattractive to everyone.

"If it comes down to it," his father said, "I will make sure we all go together and give him no chance to determine our fate."

Tavelo tried to hide the tears that welled up.

He didn't want to die, let alone his parents. For the first time, he wished the emperor death.

A systematic ambush of merchants began within months and a rebellion had formed. Workers and clients took side with the merchants while citizens tried to avoid scrutiny. Already, the heads of two families were murdered outright. One in the square as he walked with his sister. Both were torn apart and their remains put on display at the palace. The other was eaten by a Volshin set upon him on the docks by a royal commander. A worker and his son were killed due to it thrashing about as it ate, destroying their part of the docks.

The curfew solved nothing since the emperor declared all non-compliant merchants the enemy of the planet. Clients came up with clever ways to circumvent the new laws and keep trade going. The ones who obeyed saw themselves becoming less profitable. Their ability to sustain basic living expenses dwindled. A new poverty had struck the lands.

For their supposed crimes against the sovereignty, the Endaga family was a main target. On three separate occasions, the royal officers had tried to ambush them in the streets, on the docks and near their home. Each time, they were defeated by the family with the help of neighbors and other merchant families nearby. So, they weren't surprised when after arriving home from a meeting, two other families in tow, a small army was seen marching towards them. It wasn't the usual ten or twelve this time.

"Have they gone mad?" Lady Jaubro cried out.

"What madness!" Callesi added.

Neighbors ran out and formed a circle around the street's perimeter. Even with them, they were outnumbered. Lord Endga nodded to his associates and they positioned themselves within the circle. Tavelo squashed his fears and braced himself for the onslaught. To his right, Eterenia prepared for a fight as well.

Twenty royal officers advanced suddenly, flash stepping their way against the barrier of neighbors. Some held the circle while others were cut down giving the officers a straight path to the families. It was rare to see their parents fight, so their children tried not to be awestruck by their sheer power as they were also targeted.

"Leave no one alive!" The commander ordered. His bloodlust was palpable.

The three merchants' wives were back to back in a defensive stance keeping the enemy at bay. Their talons cut through the flesh of every soldier that came within striking distance. In the moment of that fray, they didn't see the one soldier leap over his counterparts and jump down between them, breaking up the triumvirate. Lady Jaubro fell to her knees as Lady Endaga was pushed out. He landed on Lady Callesi and she slit his throat before throwing him off. Four soldiers descend on Lady Endaga.

She was a deadly fighter yet no match for the royal officers trained to kill. Regardless, she was not going to die without dignity. Her talons ripped into the one nearest and used him as a shield. When the other three saw his body as a hinderance, they tore him from her grip and attempted to impale her.

"No!"

Her husband turned his focus away from his assailant and saw she was in trouble.

Eterenia dispatched the soldier before her and went to Lady Endaga's aid. She managed to pull one of the them off, breaking his talons as they exited the woman's flesh. Snapping his neck, she proceeded to the other whose eyes never left Lady Endaga's as he dug deeper. He wouldn't budge. Lady Endaga got an arm loose and stabbed her talons into the face of the other atop her. As he fell backwards, the last one punched Eterenia down to the ground and sliced off Lady Endaga's arm. Wasting no time, he punched his talons in her neck. She halted the strike with her one arm, their eyes locked. Not far away, Tavelo screamed with rage.

"You should have obeyed," he seethed.

Putting all his weight down, his talons severed her head.

And his head went flying as Tavelo swooped beneath him and struck. Eterenia cried out, and he knew why. But there was no time to tell her she was not responsible. Out of the corner of his vision, he saw his father stop in defeat as he looked down at his slain wife. A soldier took advantage of the opening and hit him in the chest. He regained his stance and continued to fight. Tavelo had no time to prepare as four other soldiers came at him, tackling him to the ground to perhaps do the same as they did his mother.

Eterenia, still on the ground, crawled with great speed to Lady Callesi and together the two women were able to take down the three she was dealing with. Tavelo dodged most of the talons coming down on him and somehow got his fangs into one of the soldiers. The rush of blood gave him more strength and he held on despite the soldier trying to gouge out his arm at the socket.

This pain is nothing.

"Endaga!" A neighbor went running towards his father in vain.

Tavelo watched as if time had slowed. A soldier came up behind his father, still engaged in battle with two before him, and punched his talons through his back. A sharp crackling emitted followed by the sound of something wet and sticky pulling apart. From his father's back came a section of his spine which the soldier snapped in half before tossing on the ground.

There was a split second of silence as everyone watched the demise of Lord Endaga. The commander looked victorious and smug until he looked around. Blood red eyes with more malice than he had ever encountered zeroed in on him and his men. He knew in that moment that his time was up. If he escaped what was to come, it would be fate. As the mob went about killing every soldier in sight, a decree he had made for them earlier, he realized that was not to be. Even so, he would take down as many as possible.

Five sped towards him. Their rage oozing from their souls.

"For the emperor's ideals!"

He yelled this as he cut down the first to reach him. He felt talons cut through his back and spun around, dropping to a kneeling position. His talons cut through the man's thighs and he fell back. The ones on the other side, pierced him all at once. Angered by their lack of honor, he used his own to snap off the ones that were near vital organs and pivoted his waist. His legs knocked them all back away from him.

Screeching from the sky filled the air and everyone raised their heads to see a group of Volshins circling the area. An airship moved into view behind them.

"Get to safety!" Lord Jaubro ordered.

Two neighbors grabbed Tavelo who struggled trying to reach his mother and father. Eterenia helped Lady Callesi up and her husband came to assist. Leaving their homes and a street of carnage, neighbors and merchants fled the scene.

The commander collapsed on the ground to his knees and assessed the damage. Out of twenty officers, only eight remained, himself included. He knew the emperor's decree was absolute but losing so many men seemed excessive. Never one to question his duty, the commander thought about maybe requesting an audience with the emperor to address it.

A transport ship emerged from the airship and landed a few yards from him. Only those soldiers still alive were carried off into it. The Endaga remains were also picked up for public display like the rest who didn't obey. He did find that particularly gruesome. He was all about a deterrent, letting the masses see the consequences of an action. What the emperor was doing bordered on derangement. The soldier in charge of the transport walked towards him.

"Can you stand, commander?"

The way the soldier looked down on him in disgust made him want to rip the man's throat out. Deciding to make a show of strength, he forced his body to rise. The soldier frowned at his attempt.

"Follow me then." He turned away and when the commander didn't, he looked back. "No?" He signaled two other soldiers and they carried the commander by his underarms to the transport.

I'll have you gutted for this, the commander promised him.

Lady Jaubro rounded the corner of the deserted neighborhood and leapt up to the top of a housing. From her vantage point she could see the ships on the space dock. Two ships in particular caught her eye and she smiled in approval. A trusted worker had negotiated the price for them. Over the course of a few days all the merchant families had combined their wealth and paid. They were huge ships with one having the capacity to hold at least a thousand. The two could dock with each other and interlock to form a bigger ship.

The hard part would be getting the occupants aboard. Some of the merchant families thought they could weather the storm and not abandon their home planet. She found them weak. After seeing the brutal murder of Lord Endaga and his wife, she decided on a new duty. Their son was still traumatized, healing from his injuries at a hideout. None of them could go home now.

Below on the street, another merchant kept watch for royal officers. They were being hunted like animals by the commander and his minions. The emperor gave him full reign to annihilate any merchants who did not comply. She climbed down and met the man on the street.

"We have to move soon. If the commander gets wind of this, there will be little time to get the ships off the planet."

"Agreed. How do you want to start?"

She thought for moment, her eyes glowing with intensity.

"Converging on the docks would raise suspicion. Have the children and guardians meet in intervals and make way to the first ship."

"And how do you suppose they get through the barricade?"

"Why," she smiled sweetly, "by force. They need to eliminate every officer on the dock."

The other merchant smiled. He liked that idea.

At the hideout, Lady Jaubro went into one of the back rooms to check on Tavelo. He was looking better. Pain still etched his face. She ran her fingers through his long, dark hair, feeling how dry it had become as the days went by. His arm was no longer bound in a sling and the open wound on his shoulder was mostly closed. Without a steady supply of blood, everyone's healing abilities had stalled.

"My sweet boy, I need you to lead for me."

He turned a dull stare at her and she saw the dried bloody tear stains.

"Lead?"

"We are leaving this planet." His eyes widened. She let out a small laugh. "It is no longer a viable option to stay."

He licked his lips with a dry tongue and winced. She handed him a glass of water from the nearby table and waited until he finished drinking.

"When?" he asked. His voice was a tad raspy.

She leaned down and whispered her plan in his ear so no one else would hear. When she sat upright, he had a different expression. One of resolve. Her husband came to the doorway in a huff.

"Come! We must hurry."

"What's going on?" Tavelo asked.

"We need to get the rest of the supplies for the main ship." She caressed his cheek before getting up to follow her husband.

Tavelo struggled to get his outer robes on until Eterenia came to help him. Her face was scrunched up in a frown and dark circles had formed under her eyes. She had cried for hours after seeing his mother butchered.

"Be still, or it will hurt worse than it already does," she huffed.

"It's because you are being rough."

She stopped arranging the last robe around his bad shoulder.

"Do you want help or not?"

He sighed and relented.

"You came and volunteered," he muttered.

"What did you say?"

"Not a thing."

He looked around the room and out into the corridor where other families waited in rooms beyond it. The plan would be set in motion as soon as he was done getting dressed. The quicker, the better. Homesickness never crossed his mind. This world was no longer a place to call home.

The barricade had been reinforced over the past year with a command center in the middle. Nearly twenty officers strolled in and out of it, keeping watch over the docks. They didn't patrol the boardwalk anymore due to the detriment of their lives by the hands of the workers. As much as they touted the emperor's decrees, they still valued their own lives.

Tavelo understood why Lady Jaubro wanted a staggered mob but he decided that hitting them hard and fast would be best. His group outnumbered them three to one. It would be a blood bath and his fangs protruded in anticipation. The first round consisted of offspring, personal body guards and accountants. Each wave would be large and there would be no hiding the fact they were abandoning their home. He scanned the sky for Volshins and saw two circling farther out away from the docks.

Good. Stay over there.

He gestured for the body guards to come forward and pointed to the back end of the barricade. A group of older children surround the younger ones and the merchant families present followed him towards the checkpoint.

An officer noticed the group advancing and held out a hand.

"Halt! What business do you have on the docks? There are no shipments today."

A few more officers came around to assist him. Tavelo smirked.

"We don't need permission to go to our slips."

"Oh, but you do," the officer sneered. "Once you release the lock codes," he tapped on the tablet in his hand, "you can pass. Of course, we would have no more use for you."

A different officer came to his side and whispered in his ear. The officer frowned.

"There has been a change of plans. All merchant families not in compliance," he paused while smiling, "are to be executed."

The officers' eyes turned red as their fangs and claws grew out. From the back end, came shouting and screams which distracted the ones before Tavelo. Taking advantage, he signaled the attack. While they engaged, the children and trusted family servants ran down the boardwalk towards the bigger ship. Workers moved out of their way, helping anyone who stumbled.

All twenty officers were down with three left alive in case they were needed as decoys. It would take the palace three hours to find out what happened at the checkpoint and that gave Tavelo plenty of time to get all eight hundred plus through. When the last ones crossed the docks, he and Eterenia took the remainder of their families after them. The body guards still left killed the three officers and did the same.

The outside of the ship didn't compare to inside. There were living quarters and enough supplies to last decades. Tavelo had no clue where they were going but concluded it must be far. The navigator headed for the helm to get the ship off the ground. From the viewports, he could see the elders closing the other ships hatch.

Each ship let out a loud boom as the propulsion systems activated, lifting them from the dock. Workers diligently released clamps and opened the waterway ramps to give them move room. At a safe altitude, the ships prepared to dock with each other. The smaller ship clamped on giving the bigger a short jolt. The inner hatch opened and Lady Jaubro came aboard.

"Was I not clear about the plan?" She asked Tavelo.

"It was quicker this way."

She let out a sigh as Eterenia fell into her arms. Her father shook his head.

"They will come after us soon," Lady Jaubro said.

"I know."

A loud screeching from higher above made the passengers of both look around for where it came from. It wasn't the sound of Volshins. These were combat ships. Rapid rounds bombarded the ships, some of them penetrating the outer hull. The ship rocked and some of the children began to cry. Then came an explosion that knocked the ship off course.

Alarms went off on both ships and the artificial intelligence spewed out damage reports. The life support warning flashed on the smaller ship and a hole blew into the side of it. Lady Jaubro looked back at the elders behind her.

"What do we want to do?" She asked them.

A silence fell and Tavelo immediately knew what she meant. Before he could try to dissuade them, Lady Jaubro pushed Eterenia from her and backed into the smaller ship. He grabbed Eterenia who started to scream, trying to run after her.

"Take care of my child," Lady Jaubro said to him.

Lord Jaubro stood behind her as she sealed the hatch. Eterenia reached out, her talons clawing at the viewport, eyes blood red. Her fangs grew long and dripped with saliva. The screaming was more than Tavelo could bear so he clamped one hand over her eyes and holding her tight to him, sunk his fangs into the crook of her neck. His gaze fell on Lady Jaubro. She smiled, placing one hand against the dock door.

A fireball hit the smaller ship as it detached, engulfing it in flames. He watched it make a slow descent back down into the docks where many of the workers were doomed to be crushed by its impact.

Eterenia's screams began to subside as the blood drained from her, flowing down his throat. When she finally passed out, he carried her down the main corridor to the nearest living chamber. Another hit pushed the ship and more alarms went off. He hit the comm button for the navigator.

"What are you doing?" Tavelo yelled.

"Can't you evade their attacks?" He added.

"The system's been hit! I'm going to hit the overdrive. Tell everyone to hold on." The navigator said.

He switched to the allcom.

"Brace for a jump!"

He could feel the vibrations as the drive engaged. The huge ship bucked then took off like a shot. They entered space quickly but not before large canon fire found them, clipping the side as it went through a vortex. The view panel closed, and the navigator watched in horror as the coordinates went haywire. The crew was barely able to connect their harnesses as intravenous tubes slithered into their skin to adminster jump medicine before the stars folded in front of them.

The ship entered various dark space, decelerated in a new solar system only to rev up and make another jump. The system was on auto pilot and would not stop until it reached the designated coordinates. On the final jump, the ship came to a halt.

Slowly, the crew came out of their deep sleep and began to assess where they were. A check of the life support systems showed green and the medical doctor released the passengers from hold. From the count, he found no casualties. Even the young children somehow withstood the travel.

The navigator called Tavelo up to the helm. He seemed worried as he approached the main console.

"Where are we?" He asked.

"No idea." The navigator pointed to the fried console that set the coordinates.

"Oh, no." Tavelo's chest tightened. "We're lost."

Ahead of them were seven planets. The closest one

on their path was blue, white and green with a small moon. The gas giant scorching the ship with its light he figured must be its sun.

"Raise the dampening shields."

He had to squint in order to see out the viewing window. The navigator raised an arm across his face. They had never seen such bright light and it was indeed painful. At that moment the engines sputtered. Overhead lights flickered while the AI started up with new warnings. The energy fuel was all but depleted. There was no way of going back without replenishing it.

"No, no, no!" The navigator yelled. "You will last until we land."

Tavelo happened to look down on the time gauge. Twenty two years. For their race, it was nothing but put in context of their journey.

That was a long jump.

Adapting to Earth

In the dead of night, no one noticed the shimmering object falling from the sky. Onboard the ship, the navigator checked the status of the cloaking shields. He had no records of the planet so couldn't take the chance of the inhabitants being hostile or friendly. His passengers were either strapped in or in cryochambers which took a burden off him. Below was an empty plain and on three sides of it were grids of bright lights. Cities along a vast body of water.

He cut the jets and let the craft coast down, landing as gently as possible. The ground rumbled a bit creating a ripple across the terrain but not reaching the cities.

It began to sink.

At first he panicked then thought it may be for the best if the ship went underground. As it went further, he made sure there were areas to vent so they could get out. The translator switched on to capture any communication from all the surroundings and the navigator turned to the rest of his crew.

"Time to get some rest before our next adventure."

"We don't know if our weapons will be effective." One of the crew stated.

"From the compounds collected at entry, I'd say we won't have a problem."

"Well, let's hope we don't end up in a fight."

They left, headed for an empty living chamber while the ship finished its analysis of their newfound home.

Darean Callesi led a group out of the ship onto the crumbly ground above. It was dusk so their eyes were able to adjust to the limited light. After four weeks of hiding inside, it seemed none of the cities' inhabitants noticed anything out of the ordinary on their outskirts. That was ideal on the merchants' side of things. They were not many but over time that would change. He was grateful to the Endaga and Jaubro family except he did not see them as true leaders. That is why he and Pridric, eldest son of the Strana family, struck out to scout the area while the other merchant families were still trying to figure out a plan.

"What do you think? Should we try to the left, right or the middle first?" He asked Pridric.

The tall blonde squinted, surveying the distance between their ship and the cities.

"The one on the left seems to be closer." He looked down at their attire. "We should be able to blend as peasants at least."

The images taken from the scan showed different scales of elaborate clothing that appeared to depend on class. It was the same for the other cities as well.

"It would be best if we all took a city to investigate."

"Yes," Tavelo snapped as he emerged from the underground ramp. "It would." He glared at them both. "Why are you sneaking out in the dead of night?"

"Because," Darean sighed. "I don't think we should draw any attention to ourselves unless absolutely necessary."

"Granted," Eterenia said as she too came up. "But still, you should have told us."

"There are seven great houses. We can cover more ground with everyone."

"This vicinity," Darean started.

"Is a small piece compared to the whole," another merchant kid came out. He was bigger than them with huge muscles, a trait of the Dakien family. "The ship did a three-hundred-and-sixty-degree scan. There are so many other bodies of land. This patch we are on has some atmosphere that doesn't affect us. Though, it is deadly to the inhabitants."

"A dead zone," Pridric added.

"So, that's why no one has come across this land," Darean said. "Fine, we will wait for the others and divide and conquer."

"Conquer?" Tavelo asked.

"You know what I meant," Darean snapped.

They looked up at the sky turning dark and the moon glowing silver, giving off a soft light.

"Beautiful," Eterenia whispered.

With so many areas to explore, Eterenia figured it may take a few years to really understand the planet and its people. Her group snuck into the first city via a harbor and stole some clothes from a nearby shop that was closed for business. She noticed a lot of buildings were dark except for the main taverns. Some of the people gave them peculiar looks and Eterenia thought maybe something was wrong. Then she saw other people dressed similar but of a different style getting the same stares. A couple walked past and scrunched up their faces.

"Foreigners. Why must they always venture here on their holidays?" The man asked.

"Really, darling," the woman on his arm drolled. "They are here to spend money. Is that not a good thing?"

"I suppose. But, they could at least speak the language."

Eterenia realized that the foreigners did speak in a different tongue. She thanked the ship's translator for getting it right so her people wouldn't stand out too much. They walked around for a while observing and she was able to decipher the currency. From there, she instructed her group to emulate the pick pockets in town to gather enough to pay for food and shelter.

At a tavern, her group sat at a table in the far corner. The barmaid gave them a raised eyebrow as she scrutinized their attire.

"Foreigners, huh?"

She shifted her weight to one leg and leaned an arm on the table. Her bosom nearly burst out of the frilly top of a shirt that was cinched tight by a bodice sitting just below them. One of her cousins, made a small sound and Eterenia turned to see his eyes bulging. The barmaid noticed and standing straight, moved her shoulders side to side so that her breasts bounced around.

"Like those, don'tcha?"

Eterenia cleared her throat and gave the woman a mean stare. She huffed and came back to the table.

"What'll you have?"

"Ale, all around," Eterenia replied.

"Any food?"

"How's the bread?"

The barmaid scoffed, then snorted.

"Bread is bread. I'll getcha some."

As she walked off, Eterenia let out a breath of relief. She wasn't sure how their bodies would take the edible fare. Those two things seemed a safe bet.

Their barmaid came back with a giant tray full of round barrel glasses sloshing dark liquid. She got close to her male cousin and leaned further than necessary to set his drink before him. The other men in her group followed with their stares. The only other female in the group, another cousin, took her stein of ale and said nothing. But her expression was one of disgust.

"Thank you," Eterenia said.

The barmaid gave her a wink as she set the loaf of bread on table along with a large knife. Watching the other patrons handle the bead, her female cousin began cutting off equal pieces for everyone. Eterenia took a bite and tried to identify any flavors while she chewed. It was terribly dry. She gulped down some of the ale. That made it a little better.

One of the men came stumbling towards their table and leered at her and her cousin.

Eterenia knew that look all too well.

"Where do you hail from, young ones?" he slurred. His face was flushed pink and his eyes were glassed over. Each step he took was wobbled and she couldn't figure out how he was still standing.

"From across the water," she replied deadpan.

"Oh?"

He fell onto the table, jostling their ales. Pushing himself up, he went to grab hold of Eterenia. Her female cousin stopped him with one hand.

"Do not touch our lady."

The man wrenched his arm from her grasp and turned red.

"Women should know their place! How dare you assault me!"

The tavern got quiet and Eterenia pursed her lips in frustration. The last thing she wanted was a confrontation. The men in her group were about to rise and she held up a hand to stop them. The barmaid let out a loud sigh and came over.

"No harassing the customers. I just fixed this place up from the last brawl."

She took hold of the man and steered him back to his table where his associates snickered. For the third time, Eterenia had to take a deep breath and exhale slowly. With chaos avoided, she gestured for her group to finish the bread and ale so they could leave.

Outside of the tavern, they roamed the streets a bit before finding an Inn with vacancies. Her male cousin found one only a few blocks away and negotiated with the owner. He wanted one room for all six of them, citing low on funds (*which was partly true*), but the keep wouldn't allow it. They had to get two. Eterenia was too tired to argue as were the rest of the group. Getting the keys, they headed for their rooms. The building had eight floors and theirs was on the fourth. The stairs were like a spiral winding up into infinity. Each step they took echoed with the creak of the wood.

The rooms were adjacent and not very lively. Dark wood was everywhere with heavy drapes on the windows and gaudy carpet. All the furniture was a different wood yet equally as dark. She didn't care. There were two beds in the room. She took one while the other two; her female cousin and another male, took the other. She fell face down on the hard bedding and drifted off into sleep.

Garish sunlight beamed through the windows, startling the occupants of both rooms to the point of cries echoing the halls. Eterenia's female cousin jumped out of bed and whipped the heavy curtains across the windows, blocking out the cursed rays. Panting with fear, Eterenia sat up clutching her chest. There was no way she could get used to something so appalling. The inn keeper came banging on the doors.

"What's going on? Why was there screaming?"

Eterenia regained her composure and walked over to the door. Right as she opened it, the keeper's hand nearly hit her in the neck.

"My apologies," Eterenia said. "We were surprised by the sunlight as the curtains were not drawn closed last night."

"Oh," the inn keeper replied. "Well, that is understandable. You are higher up and get the full sun on clear days like this."

His expression was somewhat dubious and Eterenia didn't blame him.

"What brings you here, again," he asked.

"Holiday."

"You foreigners sure like to come around these parts this time of year."

He smiled as her cousin crossed his view wearing only knickers. The dress had probably been shucked off long ago.

"Yes, well. Thank you for checking up on us."

Before she could shut the door, he put a hand on it to stop its swing.

"You're late for breakfast but I can have the servants make you something."

"Oh?"

"It comes with boarding."

"Thank you, we will be down shortly."

At that, she shut the door, him reluctant to let it go smoothly; his eyes glued to her cousin.

Is every male species like this?

Breakfast consisted of cured ham, poached eggs, bread and jam. The fare was quite good in Eterenia's opinion though what she really wanted flowed in the slightly raised vein of the servant girl's neck. For some reason she could almost smell the life blood pulsing. A quick glance at her group and she knew they felt the same. It had been a long time since they had anything remotely fresh. The supplies on the ship would sustain them for decades but it wasn't enjoyable.

"Excuse me, my lady," the timid servant girl said. Eterenia tried her best not to get too close as she turned to her. "The master said you were not too keen on the sun so I brought your troupe these." She leaned a set of parasols against the table. When Eterenia gave a perplexed look, the girl took one and opened it up. The rest of the group let out "aahs" in unison. She closed it back and put it with the others.

"Ingenious. Thank you."

Eterenia grabbed the less frilly one and smirked at her cousin who would get the other.

"Enjoy your holiday." The servant girl curtsied and left the dining room.

"I guess we should take a stroll across town," Eterenia announced, dabbing the corners of her mouth a napkin.

"Yes, we need more currency," her male cousin said.

"And more clothes," one of the other men added. "I believe our keeper and his staff looked at us rather peculiar because we are wearing the same as before."

"That couldn't be helped. Let us take leave."

Eterenia stood up and headed for the door, her parasol tucked under one arm.

They walked for hours pick pocketing and stealing until lunch time. Everyone participated, even Eterenia and felt she had the hang of it. Men didn't seem to mind her accidentally bumping into them. A sly smile formed on her face. The group passed by a restaurant and decided to eat there. The maître d was snooty, wrinkling his nose at them. He set them down near the kitchen and poured glasses of water. When the menus were distributed, he walked away.

A loud uproar made the group look up from their perusing to see a trio of gentlemen enter the establishment. They were dressed impeccably and many of the patrons' eyes gleamed with admiration. The waiter from the next table over was making his way across the room when Eterenia stopped him.

"I beg your pardon, but who are those men?"

He turned with an indignant expression that turned to indifference.

"Oh, you're foreigners." His gaze soured. "Those are the richest merchants in the five burroughs. The De Luce Holding Company is a network of companies and the keystone of our trade industry."

He walked off to greet the men, all smiles and grace. Eterenia wanted to tear him apart. Then her focus landed on the merchants. She nodded to her group and they continued looking at the menus. After lunch, they would follow the merchants and see how they operated. She figured it couldn't be much different than what her family had done for a millennium.

The three men were boisterous and mean, belittling the servants who didn't make one complaint about the abuse. From what they ordered, it was all the most expensive items on the menu. Champagne was delivered to their table compliments of the owner.

Eterenia didn't care for that kind of behavior. Her family was one of the top merchants, but she would argue they were not the type to rub anyone's nose in that fact. One of the men caught her stare and he winked at her. The act made her nauseous and she turned away.

There was a long bang and everyone in the restaurant stopped what they were doing to see why. His face had gone bright pink and he shook with fury as he looked over at her.

"You dare flirt with me, woman?"

The patrons turned their attention to Eterenia and she blanched. Her female cousin half stood up, ready to fight if it came down to that. The owner came into the fray and pleaded with the man.

"I beg your forgiveness. They are foreigners here

on holiday. I have not explained your status."

"Hmph!" The other merchant glared at them. "Foreigners should learn the ways of the land before setting foot on our shores." He turned to his associate. "Really, calm down. She's a twat not worth having." The third snickered at that.

The merchant calmed down and tossed his napkin on the plate before him.

"How will you accommodate me regarding this travesty?" He asked the owner.

To which the owner snapped his fingers twice. Servers came to Eterenia's table and prepared what remained of their lunch to go. It was all wrapped up neatly along with the bill. At the merchants table, fancy looking dessert was set before them.

"If you would be so kind," Eterenia's waiter said to her group.

A path was made for them towards the exit and they gladly obliged. Outside, she bottled up her rage and headed for the park farther down the way. The group sat on the benches and waited for her to say something.

"We will follow them when they leave. Make sure to gather as much information as you can," Eterenia ordered as she opened her take out and took a bite of the meat.

"Are we splitting up?" One of her men asked.

"I want every inch of their workplace investigated."

"What if they don't go there?" The other asked.

Eterenia smiled.

"What merchant do you know has ever turned down a day to make profit?

⁂

Watching the three men work the docks was an eye opener for Eterenia. They were like different people, doing hard negotiations yet making sure the workers were well compensated before having the goods released. She was in awe and it also angered her. Treating the clients was all well and good. Being a beast among society was unacceptable.

There was a tiny office nearby that they owned to keep business flowing. Her male cousin was tackling that, getting images of any records they kept inside. They could decipher them on the ship when they returned. Only one of the men in her group accompanied her. The others were collecting information from dock workers and other merchants.

In her distraction, she didn't notice one of the three men had walked away. A presence came up behind her.

"Are you a tease?" The man hissed in her ear. His tone dripped with venom.

"I assure you, I am merely interested in the trade of this place."

"What does a woman need to know about trade negotiations?"

"My family are merchants. I wanted to see if you ran your business differently."

His hand reached up to her neck then she sensed the man stiffen. She turned around and saw her male companion's talons touching the skin of the man's throat. They barely grazed the surface and would only take the slightest move to let them sink in. The thought of fresh blood nearly made her lose composure.

Her man licked his lips in anticipation.

"You would be wise to not touch our lady," her man said to him.

"A crime family, then?"

The merchant cautiously stepped away and clasped a hand around his own neck, checking for wounds. Her companion retracted his claws before the man noticed. Disappointment set in and she agreed. Shedding blood in broad daylight on foreign land was a bad idea. She quelled her hunger.

"Why would you assume that?" She asked.

"We know about your kind," he spat. "You wouldn't be the first to try and get your hooks in our city. All of them who tried were run out or met an untimely demise." He smirked.

Eterenia motioned for her companion to follow her.

"Come. There is nothing more to see here."

As they left the docks, she could feel the merchant's gaze on them. A glance back found one of the other merchant associates doing the same, except there was something in his eyes that seemed familiar; and deadly.

By nightfall, the group had enough currency to last another few days and a couple of changes of outfits. One of her male companions watched diligently at a clothier shop to see how to put it all on correctly. After that, he knew why they got a few stares. They weren't necessarily wrong, just not well executed. He would test his skills in the morning before daybreak.

They made it back to their inn in time for supper and stowed their acquisitions in the rooms before headed down to the dining hall. As they entered, a few of the guests avoided eye contact while others scooted their chairs away a little bit. The inn keeper frowned and made his way to them.

"Will we be dining in our rooms this evening for some unforeseen reason?" She asked.

When he stopped near her, he went pale and the other guests looked down in embarrassment.

"Word around town is that you had an altercation with our renown merchants."

"There was no such thing. He assumed I was interested in his person. I was not."

Some of the men snorted at that.

"Women shouldn't be so head strong these days." One man said.

"Any of those men are a catch." A woman added. "It's daft not to be interested."

The inn keeper cleared his throat.

"Here, at this inn, you are treated as family. I would suggest you refrain from causing any scandals during your stay."

"That has always been the goal, good sir," her male cousin replied. "We do not want to anger anyone."

"Excellent."

He gestured for the servant to start the meal and they converged on the table.

Once dinner was over, the group sat in Eterenia's room lounging. She was stuffed from all the food and drink and had to admit, it was all to her liking. It had enticing flavors she never knew could make her feel satiated the way she did.

"That was amazing," one of her men exclaimed. "They do eat well on this planet."

"I guess that is its saving grace," another piped in.

"Are we going for a stroll later?"

Her female cousin asked suddenly.

"Yes, let's wait until everyone is asleep. I was granted permission from the night guard. He will stay up to let us in." Eterenia answered.

"Good. I want to get the feel for the night here. It is quite different from our world."

Eterenia stood up and walked to the window. Thin clouds drifted across the dark navy sky. The moon was getting brighter, its light reflecting in her irises.

They passed the time going through the clothes to pick out who would wear what then moved on to the images collected. By ten o clock, they were ready to venture out into the dark. Street lamps flickered on the corners and they were surprised to not be the only ones out. Couples walked arm in arm and entourages of men laughed and stumbled down the walkways, obviously coming from a tavern.

"It's more lively than expected. Almost like home," her male cousin said.

Eterenia nodded and let the scenery sink in. They walked for some time and noticed they had gone far enough that no other soul was around them anymore. Yet, she felt eyes on her and the group went into a defense formation around her.

Loud hissing surrounded them, and a man leapt down in front of them, mere inches away. His eyes were blood red and fangs protruded from his mouth. Pale skin and long fingernails added to his appearance. He went into a stance and his mouth opened wide to reveal the full set as he let out a hiss.

"The master sends his regards," he spoke in a strange wispy tone.

"And who is your master?"

Eterenia was still taken aback by the red eyes and fangs but they were not like her race. She could detect much blood flow and the smell was off. Eight others like him surrounded the group ready to fight. A man came out of the shadows wearing a full-length cape and as he emerged, she saw it was the other merchant who stared at them on the docks.

"My associate lets me take care of unwanted patrons in the city and askes no questions as to how. This is my forte. We don't take kindly to your criminal ways."

"As I have said before, that is not the case."

"Regardless, you are a nuisance. And a danger." He smiled, showing his fangs. "Did you not think I knew your minions were scouting our office?"

"Master," the one in front said. "Why are they not frightened?"

The merchant's face contorted, and his demeanor changed.

"Who are you?" He demanded.

"Indeed, who are we?"

Eterenia's eyes turned red and her talons extended as did her group.

"Kill them!" The merchant ordered.

Eterenia let out a laugh.

This was going to be fun after all.

When every enemy was on the ground, Eterenia went to the merchant and raised him up by his neck.

"What are you?" The merchant asked.

"I would ask the same of you." Blood dripped from her fangs onto the front of his torn shirt. "You are like us only far inferior. What do they call your kind here?"

"Vampires."

Eterenia let the term mull over in her head a bit.

"I like it. Are there many of you?"

"Not really. We are rare beings, not quite human."

"Human? What are those?"

He looked at her with confusion then his eyes went wide.

"Every person on this world is of the human race."

She dropped him and stood to her full height. A thought crept in her mind and when she looked down on him, he scuttled backwards. Taking over the merchant business would be easy. There needed to be more. If vampires were indeed rare then that meant they moved under the cloak of society.

"Are you the master of the vampires?" She finally asked.

"No, we have covens. Mine is ruled by our Queen."

Her male cousin stood from feeding off his prey and spat out the last bit.

"Tastes old and not fresh."

"We have to recycle our blood. Wherever it can be gotten is what we drink to sustain us."

"And feeding off humans,"' her female cousin said as she too tossed her prey to the side.

"I want to meet your Queen." Eterenia wiped her mouth with two fingers, licking the residue. Fear fell over the merchants features. His minions, half alive crawled away from the group. "You will tell no one about this?"

"Who would I tell?" He snapped. "What are you going to do now?"

"We," she smiled down at him, "are going to have a morning chat in two days. Then we set up a meeting with your Queen." She waved him away, knowing he already had the address of where they were staying.

When the streets were deserted except for her group, one of her men came to her side.

"What now?"

"We will head back to the ship tomorrow and hear

what the others have to report." Eterenia picked up her satchel purse and patted down her dress. "Vampires."

"It does have a ring to it," her male cousin said.

To be the ones bearing extraordinary news was dashed as the other merchants converged on the ship gasping about Vampires. Eterenia pouted in disappointment and then her expression turned to anger. The human merchant said Vampires were rare. Darean quelled her thoughts.

"Though these vampires are not in large population, they do hold a significant hold on vast regions. The ones I encountered in the place called Italy were extremely hostile."

"Yes, the ones where we ended up, in a place called Germany, were just as bad," the young Dakien said.

"We did not encounter such strife in France. They were very hospitable," the other older merchant boy from the Bryhel family added.

"It seems, the ones in fair England are just paranoid, my dear Eterenia," Darean added.

Tavelo was quiet and they all turned to him. His mood was solemn but his eyes told a different story. When he realized everyone had stopped talking and focused on him, he sat up straight.

"My apologies. I did hear you all."

"And? What was your experience like?"

"It wasn't so much my encounter but conclusion. You know where I am headed on this, Darean."

"Oh, yes!" Darean cried out jubilantly. "Eterenia had it correct. We will take over reign of these vampires and blend in."

"And if they resist?" Tavelo asked.

The other merchants gave him stern stares.

"Is that what happened?" Dakien replied. "Will the vampires rebel?"

"We annihilate them, of course," Callesi answered.

"Let's not get too hasty. We need their cooperation and status. We should keep a certain percentage of them at least," Pridric said.

"Agreed," Eterenia added.

Darean was not happy with the decision. He did see reason.

"You will have a meeting with England's vampire Queen soon?" Tavelo asked Eterenia. She nodded. "Make sure you convey our strength and that there will be no mercy for those who decline our proposal."

"I know that! If I must, the Queen will die by my hands."

"Now, this is a strange turn of events." Bryhel laughed heartily.

Within a year, all the merchants had taken over the vampire covens around the world. They returned to the ship to get a report on its condition. The navigator and mechanic shook their heads.

"There is no way to get this ship back up until we can find the right resources."

"So, we are stuck here for a while." Darean said.

"At least we have established some status and new identities," Eterenia added.

"And what should we call you now?" Darean asked.

"Erena De Luce," she answered, waving her hand.

"Oh?" Darean turned to Tavelo. "How about you?"

"Valentin Durante."

Eterenia made a face. He shrugged.

"Darean?" Tavelo asked.

"Andrea Sapienti. These merchants have such

fancy names." Darean turned to Bryhel beside him.

"Go on," he urged.

"Theodore Marchand. The French surname actually means merchant, if you can believe it."

"How convenient!" Darean laughed. "Pridric?"

"Pierce Ambrook."

"So," Tavelo said, "aristocratic sounding."

"More like a gigolo," Bryhel snorted. He turned to the other female in the group. "Madam Chalayl, what say your name?"

She smiled sheepishly.

"Celeste Guillarmo. I love the way it sounds."

They turned to the last in the group, Dakien.

"Grieger," he said. "I did not ask what it means. Germany is..." he didn't finish.

Tavelo walked out onto the open ramp and stared at the horizon. The night lights came to life across the cities.

"A new era with new family names," he said softly.

All the passengers vacated the ship by the end of the year with more taking on vampire covens and claiming new names. They stood in a semicircle around the ship as the navigator used the remote console to seal it. The ground engulfed it as it sank from having no power. A giant hunk of dead weight committed to the Earth.

CHAPTER TWO

HEATED DISCUSSIONS

Count Ambrook paced the floor of his library, deep in thought over his son's declaration a year earlier to take their home world back from the clutches of a deranged emperor. Let alone the fact that a fleet of royal soldiers had tracked them down on Earth and waged two attacks. The American government, where many of the coven homes now resided on its outskirts, was still reeling from the damage of the last one and making demands of the covens. He didn't blame them. If they had known centuries ago that the emperor would cross the galaxy to hunt them like animals, a different plan of action would have been implemented.

His advisor, Chancellor Rayne, came into the room and stopped short of the threshold, seeing him deep in thought.

"My lord, you really mustn't let this get at you so much."

Ambrook paused and looked up at him.

"Am I to gloss over the madness that came from my son's lips?"

"Yes, well, he is head strong, like his mother."

"Even she finds it outrageous." Ambrook lowered his arms. "Our parents died to send us off. To go back would dishonor their wishes."

"Would it?" The chancellor sat down on the chaise. "I think they would have wanted the emperor eliminated. The planet returned to its former glory."

"We have no idea what kind of environment the planet is now."

"And, we won't unless someone goes to find out."

"Not my son!"

"Then who, father?"

Chase Ambrook leaned against the doorframe with a smug look on his face.

"If anyone, it should be us elders. That being said, I wish for no one to go."

"Do you not care what happened to your own kind?"

With a flash step, Count Ambrook was across the room and his hand around Chase's neck.

"Don't you ever say that to me again."

His eyes glowed, malice evident.

"Sorry," Chase managed to utter.

He let him go and went back to his place in the center of the room. He didn't think his son incapable or unable to defend himself. The reason he and the other counts discouraged it was that on their home world the only elite fighters were part of the imperial forces. By sheer luck, the merchants were able to hold off being wiped out of existence. Their children had no idea what they would be setting foot into.

"Young master, a little more education is required before you can confidently say it can be done."

The advisor reached over and grabbed a carafe of wine from the nearby stand.

Chase suddenly became still and looked behind him. His guardian, Baltise, sauntered towards him and seeing the count, bowed slightly.

That thing has no love for me, Count Ambrook said to himself.

Baltise was one of the few shifters within their kind and a Volshin. He had no regrets forcing them to fight in the last battle. That's what the ancient creatures were for. The push for independence would have to wait in his opinion. In that barely whisper of a voice, Baltise spoke.

"We have to go. Sapienti is waiting to meet with you."

Chase nodded to his father and followed Baltise out. From the corridor, Count Ambrook could hear that tiny voice say the one thing that made him shudder.

"Hungry."

⬥

Sapienti Coven

Falson checked himself in the mirror to make sure his suit wasn't wrinkled, and his hair well situated. He ran his fingers through to untangle it then stood straight.

"You primp worse than any woman I know," his guardian and lover said.

Demitri was lounging on the chaise reading a book held up high above his head. Falson, flushed with anger, went over to him and knocked the book out of his hand.

"Get up! We're late!"

Demitri swung his legs around and stood so they were face to face. Falson struggled with his impulse to kiss him. If he did, that would be the end of making the meeting on time. That deadpan expression exuded sex somehow and he could never resist it. He reached for his guardian's hair and his hand was slapped away.

"Let's go." He walked towards the door, leaving Falson to stand with clenched fists.

"Don't walk away from me."

"As you said, we are running late."

Falson slammed into his back and wrapped his arms around him.

"I want you," he breathed in his guardian's ear. His lips caressed the crook of his neck.

"You always do. We must hurry."

Demitri gently removed his arms from him and proceeded down the hall. Falson squelched his upset and followed. The meeting was indeed important since it regarded the plan to take back their race's home world. He couldn't lie and say learning they were not human or vampires was not shocking. It shed a whole new light on the conflicts they endured over the centuries.

Of course, he thought Chase was off his rocker when he blurted out his plan after the last war.

In the grand hall sat Chase, his guardian, Baltise, Princess Adelia and her guardian Lariod. They had already been served drinks and made themselves comfortable. The Princess was wearing her usual Lolita goth attire, her long blonde hair fashioned in two pig tails.

"How good of you to join us," she said, sipping her drink.

Lariod was sitting across from her with his arms folded. His sword next to him leaned against the sofa. Baltise was close enough to Chase for him to regain physical contact if needed.

"I'm not late," Falson retorted.

"Shouldn't there be elders here for this meeting?" Lariod asked without opening his eyes.

"All they do is shut us down and not listen to any of our ideas," Chase answred.

"Then who is going to tell us about that planet?"

Falson sat down in the large chair at the edge of the sofa while his guardian sat next to the Princess. She made a face at him and continued sipping her drink. The servants swiftly came over to serve them.

"Chase, in his infinite wisdom, is going by the archives they brought with them."

"Yet those still tell us nothing about what it is like now."

"Baltise," Lariod called out. The little thing raised his head and turned to him. "If a small group of us were to go up against a horde of Volshin, who would win?"

"Why would you ask that?" Chase yelled.

"What are you getting at?" The Princess interjected.

"Volshin."

Both were silenced by Baltise's answer.

"You see, Ambrook," Falson said. "We are going up against our own kind. They are the enemy, yes. But make no mistake about who we are fighting."

Count Sapienti walked into the meeting with a grim expression. Dark circles set under his eyes and his skin looked jaundiced. He had not been sleeping well since the battle ended. That it didn't turn into a full blown war was a miracle.

"All the more reason! As much as I admire your ambition, the two of you are clueless on this matter." He stared down at the Princess and Chase. "Lariod is correct in his research."

"Father."

Falson got halfway out of his seat and bowed. The count gave him an empty stare. His guardian also got up and bowed, receiving the same.

Will he not forgive me?

He had brothers, some older and younger. To be so fixated on him not willing to produce offspring for him and instead taking a male mate, seemed unreasonable. Falson never asked to ascend to the top of the coven.

"And that ship is a piece of junk. No matter how savvy the Marchand and Grieger covens are, it would take a major overhaul and possibly decades to do so," Count Sapienti continued.

"You all demand that we take the initiative but then thwart our efforts. Which one is it?"

Chase's tone was unacceptable and Falson moved out of the way as his father went for him. Baltise threw himself between them and the count halted mere inches from him.

"Please," Baltise begged.

Chase had climbed up the back of the sofa ready to dodge. At his height on the ledge, he saw the rest of them turn their heads away in embarrassment. He fumed, not because of that, but at his own stupidity.

Count Sapienti backed off, wanting no part of the Volshin. Falson inwardly agreed with that decision. He too kept a distance from Baltise after seeing what he was.

"We will discuss the matter soon enough."

Once he was gone, Chase slid back down onto the sofa. Princess exhaled loudly and reached for her cup of tea. She took a sip, her eyes slanted upwards at him. Falson was well aware that her mother had told her plenty regarding what happened on their home world. He also knew she wasn't telling everything.

The way their parents acted around each other signaled a deep bond that they couldn't sever even if they tried. The back stabbing and competitions to see who was better smacked of sibling rivalry.

Were we all related somehow?

That would explain so much. Most of them had no idea who one of their parents were. The Princess couldn't tell you who her father was and he had never met his mother. The same could be said of his guardian. The exception was Lariod and Chase. Their fathers appeared to have only had one mate.

"Now that the drama is over," he said. "Let's go over some logistics."

Lariod leaned forward to be more engaged in the conversation and Chase settled in for comfort with Baltise back at his side. Just as he was about to start the meeting, the rest of the coven offspring arrived. He turned to the horde spilling into the room.

"You are late. If it's not that important to you, leave."

Some stopped in their tracks while others gave him sour faces.

"Stop," Chase said, raising a hand up. To the new arrivals, he gestured towards the seating area. "Join us, there's tea."

The Marchand twins glanced at each as they sat.

"Oh, tea is good," Odette said.

"But bourbon would make it so much better."

Olivier smirked as he finished her sentence.

"Especially with this mood," another coven off-spring continued.

Count Marchand and Queen Erena arrived at the Governor's home around the same time. She had hoped to get there before him, still angry about the last time they were in the same vicinity. As usual, he was falsely charming to the servants while his entourage of killers stayed at bay behind him.

Erena's advisor instinctively moved behind her, an expression of terror and hatred mixed on her face. The Queen's female enforcers were with her today instead of the normal royal soldiers. He seemed to notice. His gaze drifted from greeting the head of the estate to them and a slight smirk appeared before dissolving back into the wide grin.

"Oh, where are my manners," Count Marchand exclaimed. "Ladies first."

He bowed before her and let her pass to also greet the head of the estate. She gave him a stern look and he winked.

"Queen Erena De Luce," the head of the estate said. "So good of you to come. There is much the Governor would like to discuss with you and the count."

Count Marchand sent her a telepathic message.

"Oh, I bet he does, the charlatan."

"This was partly your fault!" She snapped at him.

"Tsk! Hardly."

"Try to be gracious."

They were escorted through the home and led into a sitting room off the main office. The Governor was at his desk getting documents together. Erena had an idea as to what they entailed. From Count Marchand's face, so did he.

With everything he needed, the Governor joined them. He sat in the large leather chair positioned directly in the middle of the sofa's line of sight. Front and center. The head of the estate was in a vintage plushed seat off to the side.

"It is common courtesy to thank you for coming but I feel this was a non-negotiable visit. We have work to do."

He summoned the servants laying in wait to bring in the drinks and finger food, his stare never leaving them. Erena figured he was still quite angry regarding her daughter using his son as a plaything.

"Oh, we didn't have to come at all, Governor," Count Marchand replied. Erena leaned towards him and softly hissed at him for additional effect. "We are not an endless pit of funds for your city's reconstruction."

"This travesty is because of you being here. Your enemy, whoever they are, were after your kind, not our citizens. I think it only fair that you take responsibility." He tapped the stack of documents. "These are the estimates for repair and a timeline for completion. There is also..."

Count Marchand raised a hand to stop him. Erena cleared her throat, anticipating what the count wanted to convey.

"You are not listening, Governor. We will take that only so far. You cannot milk us for everything we have for your benefit."

The head of state interjected.

"We realize you are not made of money, but your

covens have a mass resource. This has been the demand for many of our own wars over the centuries. The country at fault pays when the smoke clears."

"You mean, the country that lost," Count Marchand retorted. "Let's not play games. The millions given so far have not been used for their purpose. Explain this."

The Governor became flush and adjusted himself in the chair.

"There will always be overhead to set up these projects and must be paid before the work can start."

"What are you implying?" The head of the estate asked angrily.

Count Marchand's eyes glowed as he leaned forward.

"You think I don't know what your government is doing?"

"We are no longer afraid of your kind," the Governor balked. "Vampires are an irrelevant species in this new era."

"You've said that before," Erena stated. "What are you basing this new-found bravado on?"

The Governor and the head of the estate grinned.

"We have had vampire hunters for centuries. You think yourselves invincible?"

Erena and the Marchand turned to each other in astonishment then burst out laughing. This made the two men uncomfortable and they sat further back in their seats.

"Oh!" Queen Erena finally let out as she caught her breath. "You think...we are ..."

"Those vampires?" Count Marchand blurted, his emphasis on the first word.

"What?" The Governor asked in fear.

The count and Queen wiped the tears from their eyes and looked up at them.

Their glowing eyes reflected in the two men's.

"You are mistaken," Erena hissed.

"You are nothing but food," Marchand added.

The Governor's fingers gripped the armrests until his knuckles went white. His face began to quiver as he saw his own death in their eyes. He was no stranger to vampires, having encountered them on occasion when a hunter was in pursuit of one. But all of them were old world types who exuded superiority and disgust for regular humans.

For the first time he saw something completely different. These vampires before him had eyes like nothing he had ever seen. The pure red of them, like blood swimming in glass orbs, made him cringe. And the malice that oozed from their presence. This was not disgust or hatred. It was what animals at the top of the food chain had; Indifference for their prey's demise.

"Well, that went smoothly," Queen Erena said with sarcasm.

Her group was the first to get up and leave while the Governor sat frozen in terror. The head of the estate tried in vain to have the man snap out of it. Count Marchand did not help matters when he let one talon extend and flicked the man on the nose. She let out a small laugh. The whole episode was priceless. Arctic air swept through the courtyard and she leaned back with her eyes closed to savor the chill. Count Marchand came up behind her and swatted her ass, disrupting her solace. She glared at him.

"Nice performance, Queen." He said her title like it belonged to a child.

Her head enforcer drew her sword.

"Do not touch our lady," she demanded.

Count Marchand rolled his eyes and continued to his vehicle.

"Why is your horde always so," he circled his hand in the air, appearing to try and grasp something from above, "austere?"

"Because I constantly run into fiends like you."

"That hurts," he gave her one last look. "Erena."

The way he said her name dripped with disdain.

His entourage loaded up in the seven passenger SUV and moments later sped off into the distance. Queen Erena pulled her coat closed and nodded at her enforcer to sheath her weapon. The Count and her may have thwarted the Governor on this hurdle for now. There were more obstacles to come. Namely, the fact that their enemy was still on Earth some-where and could attack again at any time.

Five hours of travel into the dead zone led the elders and their offspring to the disabled ship buried in the barren wasteland. Twelve vehicles filled to the brim with vampires surrounded it and the passengers filed out. Count Ambrook pulled a tablet fob from his coat pocket and swiped his hand across it. A rumble erupted from the ground, shaking it, and the hard-packed soil began to crumble. Beneath, the dirt seemed to funnel down while air pockets spit out more. Adding to the sounds was a whirring followed by a ramp opening to the deep darkness inside the ship below.

"When was the last time any of you inspected this thing?" Chase asked.

He took a few steps towards the hole in the ground and peeked in.

"Decades?" His father answered.

"Oh, come now!" Count Grieger replied. "It's been longer than that!"

Count Marchand forced his way to the front with his technicians in tow. They were all wearing full body Hazmat suits and carried large metal cases.

"Before any of you go, my team will sweep the entire ship and make sure it is safe."

"What could possibly be unsafe about it?" Sapienti scoffed. "It's been sealed for so long."

"Yes," Marchand said. "Who knows what may have gotten into it from the last time. Have you ever seen a giant mutant rat?" Sapienti went pale. "It's fascinating."

"Hurry up and get it over with, then!" Count Grieger commanded.

Chase went to stand by Falson. Their guardians were not far away in case of danger though he doubted anything would turn up out there.

"Not impressed yet?"

Falson gave him a side ways glance.

"Why are you? This thing is enormous. It could hold nearly a thousand occupants and sustain them."

"Exactly. It can be modified."

"You're too smart for your own good. The French would love nothing more than to do just that. Modify it how?"

"Oh, weapons and stuff."

His father, hearing that, looked over at him in exasperation.

"Let's get things set up while we wait, shall we?"

The Marchand twins went back to their vehicle

and pulled out two huge metal cases that resembled mini refrigerators. When they popped them open, it was clear they were indeed that.

Queen Erena motioned for her group to do the same and they came back with four boxes. How all those provisions fit in the vehicles while filled with passengers was a mystery. Each coven had brought enough to last a few hours.

"How long do you think this will take?" Princess Adelia asked, incredulous at the amount of stuff. "If there's anything down there, we kill it and clean the place out. What more is there?"

Lariod sighed loudly and hauled her off to the resting area being erected a few hundred yards away. Queen Erena stared at her daughter in bewilderment.

A loud screeching echoed from the hole, making everyone topside cringe.

"Guess he found his giant rat," Grieger muttered.

Count Marchand came out of the hole covered in a strange fluid that oozed slowly down his suit. He slipped it off and tossed it on a nearby tarp. After taking a few deep breaths, he went over to his coven's canopy and sat in a chair. One of his servants brought a plate of food to him along with a glass of wine. He ate in silence then drained the glass.

"That was an adventure," he finally spoke. "You should have seen it. I admired its tenacity."

"Aside from that. Is it safe to go in and start an inspection?" Count Ambrook asked.

"Of course." Another glass of wine was poured.

Chase Ambrook abandoned his meal and stood up.

"Then let's get this underway."

The elders turned to him with disapproving stares.

"How about after the Count and his technicians have a break first," Falson's guardian said.

Chase looked around and found himself the only one not rushing. He glanced over at the tired looking Marchand coven members and felt a pang of humility. Lately, it seemed like he was slipping back into his old way of thinking and that would not do. It also explained why the other offspring had stopped looking at him as their leader.

Gotta' bring it back in, Chase!

He chastised himself silently.

When an hour had passed, servants packed up the food and the coven leaders, along with their offspring, made their way down the ramp into the dark, inoperable spaceship. The first area they went through was the docking bay. Its sleek metal dulled from time and the floor grates creaked loudly with every step they took. The corridors had gouges along the walls. A memento from whatever creature had been residing within for the past few decades which was the last time it was opened.

Portable lamps had been placed in each area due to the power not working. A smell permeated the group's noses and some of them gagged. At the command center, the coven leaders stopped in their tracks, not going in any further. Confused, their offspring went past them to see why and found nothing scary.

Lariod looked back at the elders and knew the reason. He couldn't imagine being inside a behemoth for so long without any knowledge due to damage of the navigation system. Their lives would have been much different if the ship had gone to its original destination.

The fact that their children didn't understand was part of the problem. He observed the way the others took in the space while the guardians held back. In his opinion, the trip was too daunting. To travel nearly two decades meant so much could happen on Earth and there would be nothing they could do about any of it. Granted, twenty odd years meant nothing to their race. Still, he didn't like it.

"May I state the obvious?"

One of the other guardians broke the silence.

"And that would be?" Chase asked.

"As ambitious and righteous this venture may be, there is one small caveat." He looked over at the elders. "None of the offspring here has traveled in space. We were all born here on Earth."

"What's your point?" The Princess snapped. "Even humans go into space. Why would we be any different? Our parents did so it's inherent in our genes."

The Marchand twins guffawed at that, making the Princess glare at them.

"Oh, my!" Odette snickered. "That's not how that works. You would need to train for such a thing."

"Some of us can actually fly," Princess retorted.

"Zero gravity is completely different. Were you even paying attention in science class?"

Frowns formed among the other offspring as they remembered their stint at the boarding school. It was to their benefit. How it came about was still a sore subject.

"Not particularly," she muttered under her breath.

"Lucky for all of you," Count Marchand interjected. "Our covens have unlimited resources and can fund your camp fees."

"Camp fees?" Falson asked.

"There are space camps, you know," another offspring said.

That's when it hit them. They were going to be forced into another kind of school at the behest of the elders, again.

"Did you think this was a done deal?" Count Ambrook folded his arms. "If this mission is really what you want then you will prepare accordingly. We will not sanction it until those conditions are met."

While Chase fumed, Falson merely nodded. He had a feeling something was up when they gladly brought them to the ship so quickly.

"Sounds reasonable. We agree to your terms." He saw Chase's eyes widen in defiance, but he paid the coven leader in training no mind. "When do we begin?"

INDISCRETIONS

Durante Castle was bustling with activity late into the night as the servants and upper-class occupants prepared for a feast. Count Durante had been tapped to do it after the current rotation was completed. Every month now, they would host a large coven mixer to familiarize themselves with each culture. There was never much need before but better late than not at all. He steered clear of servants carrying mass amounts of flowers and food through the corridors. As a fruit platter happened to pass by, he plucked a piece from the end.

His master at arms came to walk beside him. They continued in silence for a duration until reaching the main hall where they entered his study.

"What brings you to my side this late?" He asked.

"It is about your youngest son, Tamar, my lord."

Durante stiffened at his desk as a twinge of rage came and went. He relaxed and sat back in his chair.

"What about him?"

"I know you have declared him to be sealed along with his guardian, but I have a proposal."

"Oh?"

"Send him on the mission."

Durante sat up abruptly, making the chair ping with resistance.

"And why would I do such a thing?" He yelled.

"Will you hear me out, my lord?" The master at arms raised his hands in defeat.

"Fine. Speak."

"He is volatile, immature and overly ambitious. But, it is based on coven reign. Since that is no longer the case, he may be of use to defend."

"He would be the first to betray them all and take sides with the emperor."

"Surely, you jest, my lord!"

"Look how he launched his assault on his own coven. Don't tell me I am not correct!"

"Begging your pardon, my lord, I think my suggestion is sound. At the least, he would be out of the coven for a short time. If you take round trip and however long a battle may last, fifty years is a good amount of time to change his views."

Durante felt his fingers go numb and realized he had his hands balled tight into fists on his desk. He released his grip and wiggled his fingers a bit to get the feeling back. There was no question he loved his son, just not his actions, or personality for that matter. The child was more like his mother. A power hungry vampire who was on the verge of being Queen until he came and took over her horde.

Over the past two centuries she had behaved, doing as told. He took interest in her only recently. She had resisted his advances at first then staged a coup after giving birth to Tamar. He sent her to the dungeons below. There she remained, having no desire to see her child or him for that matter.

"If I agree, he would have to stay captive until it is time for the others departure to the camp site. I don't want to give him any time for ideas that would jeopardize this."

"Of course, my lord."

The master at arms bowed and turned towards the door.

"Why have you cared so much?" Durante asked.

He stopped at the entrance.

"I believe if he had a higher purpose it may trigger something in him."

With that, his master at arms left the room.

Durante sat back again and contemplated his words. It was true, the boy had no real compass for leadership even though he thought of himself as such. The coup he planned left a nagging feeling in his gut. He said his son would take the emperor's side out of malice. It rang true for now. And would mean the death of his child because there would be no understanding the actions of that monster.

Guests started to arrive a half hour after the time, miffed at being the first since the plan was to be late and have a grand announcement. Much to their bruised egos, Durante didn't instruct the entry servants do so. They were escorted in without any flare. The mix of old and modern throughout the castle made many of them wiggle their nose.

He didn't care about their feelings on his aesthetics. It was something ingrained in him somehow. His family home on their world was similar and made the place feel cozy. Maybe not so much in his sprawling castle that held ten times more occupants.

From his raised platform above the main hall, he could see them all flooding in, mingling with his coven members. The curtains were drawn open for a new arrival and Queen Erena emerged with her entourage. She wore red. The satin dress grazed the floor and a shiny boot peeked from beneath. The overcoat cinched at the waist had an intricate design. Her hair was done in big curls that cascaded around her shoulders. She looked years younger. The Princess, coming up behind her appeared more like an older sister.

Thankfully, the daughter was wearing something modest. He caught a glimpse of his werewolf eyeing her from across the room. Durante sighed with surrender. He had tried to keep them apart. There was no denying how perfectly they matched each other. There were other half breeds within the covens which was a rare event. Queen Erena made a face as she too followed her daughter's gaze.

Durante headed down the staircase to the main level to greet his guests. The last of the food and drink was being placed and he knew that would be the first thing they gravitated to. He also needed a drink. Queen Erena had stirred his loins.

"Please, everyone, gather around," his advisor called out. "Your host has arrived."

Durante walked through the crowd and reached his seat in the middle of the hall. He stood on the raised platform and scanned the room. The amount of colors from the elaborate attire nearly hurt his eyes.

"Greetings my friends. I have prepared a night of enjoyment to be had by all. Do get to know each other." His eyes glowed silver. "And please refrain from any disputes that would lead to physical harm, or damage of my property."

Small laughs were heard but everyone seemed to understand his veiled threat if such things occurred. He bowed slightly and gestured to the displays of fare on each side of the room.

"Indulge to your heart's content!"

Like a hungry mob, the guests descended on the servants to demand drinks of their choice while the food was grazed. Queen Erena and Queen Celeste held back and watched with disdain. Sapienti shook his head and gave Durante a look of pity. His castle was about to be turned into something resembling a frat house.

"You should have gone on the cheap, my friend," Sapienti whispered in his ear.

"Then I would be judged for not being hospitable enough."

"Pfft!" Queen Celeste flicked open her fan and waved it. "For things like this, no one would notice. And I, for one, would've understood."

"Is that so?" Durante seemed dubious.

"Did you really think I spent gobs of money on the mixer at my coven home?" Queen Celeste let out a laugh as she continued to fan herself.

"We wouldn't have thought otherwise," Sapienti said under his breath.

Durante began laughing himself. To have such riches yet throw parties on a budget was comical, even for them.

Queen Erena strolled around the castle, making small talk and inwardly admonished the décor. She had talked to him about it on several occasions, yet he staunchly refused to change it. A kind of sadness leaked into his stubborn answers and she felt bad.

There was a landing at the bottom of a staircase that led to a balcony. The night sky was clear with the stars shining bright. She breathed in the cool air, closing her eyes.

Arms wrapped around her and startled, she tried to move away. The arms held a stronger grip and warm breath wafted in her ear. Knowing who it was, she relaxed and sighed heavily.

"What are you doing?" She demanded.

"Shh." Durante's head rested against her shoulder. His eyes were closed, and he seemed to be breathing in her scent. "Just let me stay here a moment."

She had kept herself away from him for this reason. Even after so many centuries, he would not let her go. All the elders had created new families, interbreeding with Earth vampires and even humans. Her coven's bloodline was mostly a secret since she didn't feel the need to air out the parents of the children in her care.

"You still wish to take me?" She asked softly.

"Always."

Rustling from behind made them disengage and turn around. Count Marchand was leaning against the frame with a grin on his face. He swirled the glass of whiskey in his hand and took a sip. Without a word, he left, raising his glass in a toast. Queen Erena's lips pursed into a thin line. She could tell by the way Durante's expression changed that he was agitated. That did not spell anything good for her. Before he could grab her again, she walked past him. He took hold of her hand but let go when she stopped. As she left the balcony and headed up the stairs, her body shook. Being that close to him did that to her every time.

Time went by faster than expected. When Durante realized the party had gone on through morning and into the next evening, he called an assembly to declare it over. There were rumbles of disappointment. Slowly, the guests got their entourages in order. Belongings were collected, and the servants escorted them to their vehicles. His coven began to settle down into normal routines and he felt a pang of remorse for the servants who had to clean up the mess left behind.

Princess Adelia emerged from the werewolf's bed chamber looking worse for wear. Durante smirked and concealed his amusement at her condition. Stories of her previous conquests were quite famous among the covens so to see her submissive and unbalanced after who knows how long of a session with the werewolf, made some of the coven members' day. Her mother gave her a look that bordered on shame.

The last guest drove off and Durante flopped down on his cushioned throne, exhausted. His advisor came up to him with a strong brewed tea that was known to revitalize. He needed it, deciding to savor each sip. The hot liquid coursed through his body and he settled in with eyes closed. He suddenly opened them as a slight tang lingered on his taste buds.

Blood. His advisor chuckled.

"I figured you may be a little low on circulation with so much partying. Just an added quick pick me up."

Durante leaned back and sighed.

"Thank you. I do not wish to be on the roster for another any time soon."

"I think next time we should take Queen Celeste's approach."

He gave his advisor a warning stare.

"That is not an option."

"I figured with our history, frugality would be a must."

"We are not struggling as our family did on our home world. You know that."

His advisor stepped down and sat on the sofa across from him.

"Still. I don't think you should cater so much to any of them." He stared up at Durante. "Their familys had no love for ours even though we were in the same class as citizens."

Durante took another sip of the blood laced tea and pondered that sentiment. It was true. He wanted to rise above such pettiness. Although, the other covens didn't share the same resolve. On a different planet, with no real rivals, they continued to rank each other by who had what and their accomplishments.

Old habits die hard, as a human saying went.

When he first established the new coven, his cousin was an integral part of it. To reward him, Durante made him his senior advisor, reporting to none but him. The other cousins went off to form their own coven only to have the emperor's command fleet come down and destroy it.

"Are we not better than that?" Durante asked.

"You're too nice. Erena should have been yours and no one else's. She is your Queen by her mother's decree."

Durante halted his sipping, the cup suspended halfway to his lips. He shifted his gaze to his advisor and saw anger in the man's expression. He lowered the cup and set it down.

"Uh uh," his advisor pointed to it. "Finish that. We have work to do."

Frowning, Durante did as requested. His whole body seemed to radiate with energy. All cylinders fired within and he felt ten times better. The previous conversation was apparently discarded by his advisor. Nothing more was said about it. He did want to address that last part. Queen Erena was indeed supposed to be with him. Getting up from his seat, he followed his advisor to his study.

I can always remedy that. He thought.

Princess Adelia scrutinized the birthing records from sixty plus years ago searching for clues of her paternity. Usually, she cared nothing for such things, like her mother. With her relationship intensifying with the werewolf, she began to think about having offspring. She decided that keeping knowledge of where their child came from was not an option. Unlike the elders, many of their children opted for a single mate. She knew her mother had birthed other children before her, yet she had never met any of them. Or, if she had, never knew.

As she perused the pages, taking into account her blondeness, she shuddered to think an Ambrook was her father. Being related to Chase made her queasy. The other options weren't so good either. Of course, it could be some random vampire or one from their direct bloodline. Human history saw many royal families breeding with each other to keep purity. Surely, the same thing happened on their home world.

Footsteps made her look up from her research in a panic. No one should know she was down in the archives. She tensed up, ready to attack anyone who entered that may be a threat. Tiny beads of sweat formed on her brow as she strained to see into the darkness. Her vision was impeccable in the dark and she could read the documents just fine, but the place was like a tomb and devoid of light. Lariod stepped into the room and stopped at the threshold. He didn't move for a long time before his head swiveled towards her. His eyes glowed as he stared at the giant book in front of her.

"What could you possibly be researching? Studious is not a term I would associate with you, Princess."

"Well, that's erroneous on your part, isn't it?" She snapped, shutting the book.

He arched an eyebrow.

"That's a big word for you."

She leapt at him, clearing the width of the table and he dodged in time to see her land where he once stood.

"Umm, you really should stop that. I am well aware of your attacks."

She came up on him, surprising him with her forcefulness and deadly grip as her fingers clawed the front of his shirt.

"You will tell no one I was here," she seethed. "Are we clear?"

Lariod's eyes grew wide and for the first time in decades, she saw real fear. She let him go and went out into the corridor. He began to follow momentarily. She cursed herself halfway up the staircase. She forgot to put the book back on the shelf.

Later in the night, she was able to retrieve the book along with two others and brought them to her room. She sat on her bed cross legged with one of the tomes cradled between her thighs. Something strange caught her eye as she flipped through the pages in each one. There were entries of births recorded but the child was not put in the coven registry.

There were, however, children christened days later then disappearing at the age of ten. The mother was not cited although it was clearly the same woman and then she landed on her own birth year. She sucked in a breath as the entry seemed to expand across her vision.

The same woman as the others was listed and she knew this had to be her mother. The total births ranged in the teens and the number made Adelia's head swoon. Nearly twenty children over the course of centuries was a drop in the hat, but for her species, it seemed excessive. Only four of them were her direct siblings. The others were the missing ones. She sat for a while, chewing on her bottom lip as the information sunk in.

In her reverie, she almost forgot what she as originally looking for and was disappointed when she found no name associated with the father. There was a marker signifying DNA. She began to nod to herself. The only option was to find the samples from every coven and match them up. Her chamber door opened. She paid no mind until a shadow loomed over her. Lariod was perusing one of the books left on the bed and he had a frown on his face.

"If the head advisor or that amazon enforcer found you with these," he stated.

"Which is why you are going to put them back for me. I will look through them again when I have enough information to compare things."

His face went pale.

"Why? Why you trying to find out such things now?"

She shrugged. He appeared to hint at the answer.

"No one is demanding you stay away from him if by some miracle he impregnates you."

"What do you mean, miracle?"

That made her angry, yet he laughed it off.

"Princess, even I know you are not ready to be anyone's mother."

She reached behind her and taking one of the pillows, whacked him in the face.

"I would make a spectacular mother!"

As she said it, her mind rebelled in disagreement. No, she wasn't ready yet, but she would be if the time came.

The meeting of the offspsring was being held again at the Sapienti coven. One of the meeting halls had been designated for them and there were all kinds of research materials along the shelves. A servant came in with tea service and they all took a break to lounge with a hot beverage. Winter was extremely brutal that year and the forecast said it would linger for an extra month. While everyone savored their drinks, Princess Adelia sat deep in thought, watching them. She took in all their features and couldn't pinpoint one that resembled hers.

"Have you ever wondered who your mothers are?" She blurted out.

The room went silent. A good portion of them were indeed motherless, the counts always present. With only two Queens, it was inevitable. To her amazement, Sapienti set down his cup and leaned forward.

"I have thought about as of late. Is she still alive? And, if so, why can I not see her?"

The Marchand twins' expression conveyed nuisance.

"What difference does it make now? Your mother isn't exactly loving, is she?"

Odette projected the question towards the Princess.

"My mother loves me!" Princess Adelia spilled some of her tea as she sat up. "I just haven't been behaving in a way that makes her proud, is all!"

A deafening silence spread throughout the room Some were visibly awestruck at her honest admission. Seeing that and realizing what she said, Princess Adelia moved to get up. She felt the tears burning her eyes, ready to unleash. Sapienti stood in front of her and stopped her.

"I'm glad you finally acknowledged that. There's no need to run. We all know the kind of person you are." He sat down next to her after she eased back into her seat. "As for the question, I am wondering why you asked."

She looked around, trying to decide if they were trustworthy. Lariod placed a hand on the hilt of his sword. Sapienti must have noticed.

"We are all on the same side. The elders do not rule these halls right now. Tell us."

"I was going through the birthing records in the archives chamber." There were some gasped. "They never say it is forbidden."

"Just not something they look kindly upon," the Grieger kid said.

"There are some strange entries and," she struggled to say it. "I believe one of the counts may be my father." Again, that damnable silence. "I have been trying to piece it all together, but the only way for us to know is to find out which markers come from what coven."

"Is that why you've been staring at everyone in

the room since tea began?" Olivier asked.

"Well, with that blonde hair," another kid said.

"Don't say it!" Chase Ambrook shot from his seat, eyes glowing with malice.

"I feel the same!" Princess snapped.

Laughter broke out and the atmosphere became lighter. When it died down and everyone resumed sipping their now lukewarm tea. Odette looked over at her.

"Explain these markers."

"Each entry had a citation for a coven, but they didn't have names, only symbols directed towards a DNA match."

"Hmm. There has to be a document in one of the archives then, that lists every coven's DNA chart."

"That's what I think too. But, where is it?"

One of Celeste's sons tapped his lips then set down his cup.

"I may have an idea. It would be hidden. But in a way where it cannot be readily accessed."

"In plain sight, you mean?" Odette mused.

The possibilities of getting something over the elders and learning more about their lineage built in momentum.

A plan began brewing.

The sun was on its way down, dipping behind the horizon to paint the sky a light bluish grey. The French doors of Queen Erena's bed chamber balcony swayed open as a breeze picked up. Winter had faded with the air was still chilly. She lay in her massive bed with multiple comforters and pillows around her. She hated that her body had acclimated to Earth weather to the point where the cold bothered her on occasion. Her hair sprawled beneath her, making it hard for her to get up if she wanted to. She didn't and that was fine.

Movement on the balcony made her look over to see Count Durante standing there brushing off his robes. He walked right through the doors and shut them. She mentally thanked him for it since she was too lazy to do it herself after wrapping in the covers. Although, she was a little angry.

"What do you think you're doing?"

He sat on the side of the bed and stared at her.

"Paying my Queen a visit."

"Sneaking into my coven can get you killed. If my enforcer caught you..."

"I would dispatch her swiftly and you would be saddened."

She sighed and met his stare.

"What is it?"

"I've come to claim you. I won't take no for an answer."

"The elders have not agreed to such a thing. You should go."

She turned her head away only to feel the bed shimmy. Durante slid up onto the bed, pulling the covers from her until he straddled her.

"All those decades of trying to convince your

mother and father that I was worthy yet being dismissed by you." He opened the flimsy robe she wore to expose her breasts and abdomen. "Your father let everyone have a taste and, in the end, I was granted permission." His hand ran between her breasts then stopped at her navel.

She felt her blood get hot and anger built up. She knew there was something wrong about the way other merchant sons looked at her and the weird memories came up blurry. But she never questioned it because what her father wanted, he got. She fought back tears of rage as she looked up at Durante.

"I do not need their blessing and I will not be denied." He removed his robes, his eyes glowing with hunger. "Eterenia."

Hearing her true name made the tears spill out and he took advantage by bringing her legs up. He spread them around his waist as he entered her. She let out an involuntary cry while her body tried to arch upward, restricted from her hair caught under. Durante leaned forward and met her gaze. Placing his hands beside her, he let his fangs extend, and sunk them deep into her neck.

She gasped loudly as memory flooded in her. The same sensation she felt when he nearly drained her to stop her hysteria as the second ship carrying their parents detached. That sensation of familiarity and the image of the Durante crest swinging before her as long dark hair tickled her skin.

A near scream broke from her lips and her talons dug into his back as she cried in emotional agony. The pain of knowing how much he wanted her and why she held him at bay for so long was unbearable. Every time he touched her, she felt it and concluded she wasn't worthy of him, not the other way around.

He sensed it and held her tighter as he thrust into her slow and steady. Like the first time he had her. She always knew he would never harm her, but did break her heart. He withdrew his fangs and cupping her face in his hands made her look him in the eyes. She moved one of her hands and let her talons tangle into his hair.

"Don't leave me," she cried telepathically.

He kissed her, tasting her essence.

"I never did." He replied.

They made love through the night, making the other spent more than once. Queen Erena submitted to him in every way and had never felt such ecstasy.

This is what I have been missing? Love?

They came together, her cries echoing in the room. He placed a hand over her mouth and laughed softly, gesturing to the door. She smacked his hand away and sat up, colliding her lips into his.

"Not caring is one thing," he said breathlessly. "But I still don't want to deal with Brunhilde."

She gave him a shocked look.

"That is quite rude. And insulting. She is far more superior than that silly legend."

"Mmm."

Rolling around in the covers made them sweat more than normal and Durante was using an already damp section of sheet to wipe off his chest and genitals. She giggled. Then something inside went wide like a fury and she fell back, writhing.

"Ahhh!" Her scream filled the chamber.

Durante held her down, not releasing his gaze from hers. The room began to fade. She tried to reach out and touch his face. Her vision was poor from tears swallowing it whole. The door to her chamber slammed open and she recognized the blurry shape of her enforcer, sword drawn. A sense of euphoria hit her before falling into darkness.

"What have you done?" The enforcer demanded.

Durante gave her a sideways glance as he eased off Erena. He found his robes and put them back on, the enforcer doing her best not to see while keeping an eye on her Queen.

"She's incubating. Do not disturb her."

The enforcer's eyes widened.

"How could you? This is not the time for such a thing. The council."

Durante step towards her until they were inches apart.

"I don't give a damn about what the council wants." He made sure she understood his rage. When she backed off, he did the same. "You know what to do."

He went back to the bed and kissed Erena softly on the lips. As he left, the enforcer was still standing at the top of the small steps, her sword pointed down touching the floor. Her expression was one of shock.

Keeping quiet about her Queen's condition was becoming a hard task. Over the past few weeks, the enforcer made sure her head advisor was the only other person in the loop. The two of them were responsible for getting her dressed to hide any signs of weight gain whenever a visitor came.

All appointments requiring her to leave the coven were being rescheduled. The only one they could not avoid was with Count Marchand and the government agencies.

She walked into Queen Erena's bedchamber to find her sitting on the side of the bed. Her robe had slipped off one shoulder and there were bags under her eyes. A sign that she had slept badly.

"My Queen, there is no reason for you to be up. You need rest."

"Is there not a guest arriving within the hour?"

"I was going to turn them away."

"That is not an option and you know why."

Queen Erena went to stand and slid onto the floor. The enforcer was able to catch her before her head hit.

"Please, I can make them understand."

Her Queen waved her off then relented.

"I need to get ready. If you're not going to help, then leave."

"I will not leave you."

She set her queen back on the bed and went to the closet for an outfit. After perusing it for longer than planned, she found a dress that would not feel too restricting for her. Queen Erena turned to her and made a face at it.

"Is that the only one?"

"We are going to have to send someone to the shops and get you more clothes. You're starting to show more pronounced."

The Queen placed a hand on her belly. A sadness fell over her. Durante was right, of course. The council should have no place in who she mates with. That unspoken rule bothered her. She walked over and began dressing her queen. The head advisor came in and rushed to assist.

"Who's coming, again." Queen Erena asked.

"Count Grieger. He has some reports on a new device for the ship," her head advisor replied.

"Oh yes, the mission our silly children have decided to undertake." Finally dressed, she stood up without help and headed for the door. "Let's get this over with."

Count Grieger sat across from her in the library and he looked conflicted as to why they were there instead of the throne room. He also kept eyeing Queen Erena, perplexed by her state of tiredness. He held a tablet that showed images of the new device and stopped showing them when the queen's eyes closed for a split second.

"Are you alright, Queen Erena?" He asked.

"I apologize. My schedule had become too much, and I needed to rest. I guess my body isn't ready for a comeback yet."

"You should not let Marchand drive you like a slave. He can handle most of those negotiations himself."

Queen Erena frowned.

"I don't trust him anymore."

Count Grieger tossed his tablet on the stand next to him and leaned forward. His face contorted in exasperation.

"Holding a grudge over something so trivial is counterproductive. Stop being childish and let this go."

Her talons extended, and the count snorted. The enforcer stepped forward, hand on her sword. Her queen raised a hand to stop her.

"I take betrayal quite seriously."

"Really? Then, you should have confronted your father on occasion."

He picked up his tablet and stood.

"I will send the full details to your head advisor's account."

Two guards escorted him out and the enforcer watched her queen's demeanor crumble.

Count Durante came to visit later in the evening and was not happy about Erena's state. He laid beside her in bed while she slept and caressed her head. There was a meeting with Count Marchand in a few days and he knew she would force herself to go. Durante was sure Theodore would immediately notice her condition. Her enforcer kept watch by the door.

"I would like to commission you for an extension on your duties," he said to her.

"And what would that be?"

"If Count Marchand decides to bring down some punishment on your Queen, I want you to defend her by any means necessary."

Her enforcer nodded. She was still upset about the visit that ended with the head advisor in the count's clutches and Queen Erena in a life or death situation. Durante had talked to her about it then and from that day forward, she was with the Queen at all times.

"I will not let him or anyone else on the council harm her in any way."

"This is a stressful time unlike others. Please take care of her until I can figure out a remedy."

He stared out through the French doors at the night sky. Out there the enemy was waiting; lurking. They would not wait another century to attack. The covens had to be ready. Even though this was not the best time for her to be pregnant, it was now or never.

"You do realize, she will go back to our home world on the mission?"

"And I will go with her."

"Then you need to know how to fight Katalings and Volshins."

The enforcer went pale and took a deep breath. For a moment, he felt sorry for her but then remembered how deadly she could be. With the right training, she would rival some of his best fighters.

"What about you? Are you also planning to go?"

Durante sat slowly, making sure not to disturb Erena.

"I have a need to see it through."

"Revenge?"

"More than that. Reciprocation and to keep a promise to the dock workers."

She gave him a confused look. None of the elders had told the story of their lives before Earth and they had no intention to do so. The way things were heading, they would have no choice. They couldn't send their little darlings out without them knowing what they were really up against.

"You say I should cut down anyone who tried to harm her. That would include yourself."

"I would never do that, but if by some strange occurrence such a thing happened, you would be outmatched."

"You are not proficient in swordplay. It would be over in minutes," she laughed.

"Oh?" Durante turned to her with glowing eyes. "Who told you such a lie?"

"I have never seen you fight with anything fang and talons."

"If you think so," his eyes narrowed. "Try me."

The enforcer hesitated to speak. She appeared to be thinking if there was some miscalculation on her part. Durante smirked and leaned against the door frame. That was why he found vampires so fascinating.

Their arrogance ran deep.

Queen Erena's vehicle pulled up next to Count Marchand's in front of the congressman's home and he waited patiently for her to come out. He had heard from Count Grieger about her outburst on not trusting him and wanted to confront her. That would have to wait until after the meeting. He needed her to be just as cold and focused as usual. So, he was taken aback when she stepped out looking half dead.

She had on a pastel lavender full length coat. Her shoes were neutral colored, and her hair was in an updo. She pulled the coat closed and cinched it with the matching belt. The way she moved was familiar. He couldn't fathom that being the case. Her enforcer and head advisor followed behind and both gave him a sinister glare. He let out a laugh.

"Queen Erena!" He came towards her for a hug and was intercepted by the enforcer.

"Please stay clear, Count."

"I don't understand the conflict. We are always this friendly."

"She is not feeling well."

"So I've heard." He smiled wide and saw Erena's expression change.

"Whatever Count Grieger said, it was out of exhaustion. It should be forgotten," Erena said.

"I think not, my Queen." He turned to walk towards the front doors. "Trust is a very important issue. We'll take later."

The meeting went as planned, with the congress-man pointing fingers only to be put in his place like the Governor. Queen Erena seemed more tired afterwards, the arguing back and forth taking a toll on her. As they left, Marchand pushed for tea at his own home and in her exhaustion, she agreed. Her two minions were not so accommodating. In the end, he won. They now sat in his lounging area eating pastries with strong tea.

His eyes roamed every inch of Erena while they ate and his eyes glimmered.

"So, my dear Erena." That made her two minions perk up. "About our trust issue."

"I told you, it was nothing."

They engaged in talking over each other.

"I tend to differ. Did I not apologize?" He asked.

"This is not the conversation I want to entertain."

"Answer my questions, Erena."

"I need to go," she said as she set her cup down.

Her hands shook, rattling it on the saucer.

"How far along are you?"

She stopped halfway from the table, the rattling filling up the room amongst the silence. Her hands stilled, and she set it down.

"I heard Count Durante has been visiting you quite often. This is irresponsible of you."

"It's none of your concern. I can do as I please."

"We have an agreement to consult the council regarding these issues."

"No!" She slammed her fist on the table. "All of you have an agreement. I never agreed to it. My mother made her choice but you all ignored it for your own personal greed!"

Marchand leaned back at her verbal assault. It was true, they had not asked her and yes, her mother had given Tavelo her blessing. With so few of them on a new planet, the men felt broadening their bloodline to increase population was necessary. Queen Celeste at some point had openly refused to birth anymore merchant offspring.

"Queen Erena!"

The head advisor rushed to her side and the enforcer moved in front of them as a human barrier. Her sword was coming out of its sheath, her eyes scanning every one of his body guards. Marchand looked at Erena and saw her in distress. He flash stepped to the enforcer, slamming her sword back in its sheath and pushed her out of the way. Her head advisor spun around and he did the same with her.

Queen Erena's eyes opened and fear seemed to grip her. His guards surrounded them and he touched her forehead to check for a fever.

"Don't," she cried out hoarsely. "Don't kill my child."

Marchand stared at her horrified.

"Is that what you think of me? That I would do something so monstrous? That any of us..."

He took a glance at the enforcer and realized she did indeed think the council would murder her unborn offspring. Disgusted that it had come to something like this, he picked her up from the sofa and carried her into the nearest guest room.

"Bring some ice water and a robe." His servants moved fast to obey his order.

Checking back in the lounge room he found her enforcer and advisor getting up from the floor ready for combat. Seeing themselves outnumbered, they thought twice.

"If you harm our Queen, I will hunt you to the

ends of the Earth," the enforcer called out.

"Calm down! I'm trying to help her, you imbeciles."

"Durante gave me a directive and I will see it through."

Him too?

Of course, Tavelo would feel that way considering how the council operated. He had a sick feeling overcome him. He pushed it back as the servants came with the bucket of ice and water.

"Let's get her comfortable and cooled down. She's not going anywhere soon."

What bad timing for a pregnancy.

"She's what?" Princess Adelia yelled.

The servants ran in and out of her mother's room with wet rags and more blankets. Count Marchand had arrived with her in his arms demanding assistance. He brought her into the bedroom and waited until the servants had her comfortable before leaving.

When Princess Adelia asked what was going on, the head advisor blurted out the truth. She pushed her way towards the bed and zeroed in on the small mound protruded from her mother's stomach. She stepped back.

"Who did this?"

"Do you think she became pregnant without consent?" Her advisor snapped at her. "Stop being naïve!"

"I meant," Princess Adelia said through gritted teeth, "who is the father?"

"Count Durante, of course."

Of course? What did that mean?

"Why would you say that? How could she let him impregnate her?"

"This is not the first time." The enforcer said. Princess felt her own eyes bulge in disbelief. "They were to be mated from the beginning as the Queen explained it. The council didn't like the idea so made sure that didn't happen."

Princess Adelia became angered by that. The council shouldn't have a say in who someone could be mated to. It was not their jurisdiction. A thought clicked into place. All this time, her mother could have had a life of true love. On the other hand, she may have not been born. If she were, then Durante would be her father.

She turned away and left the room, heading to the archives chamber for the birthing reports. It was time to match up some markers and find out the truth about all of them.

The offspring met at the Ambrook castle and laid out all the information they had gathered. For hours, they meticulous formed the list that would expose everything. One of the pieces of clues found in the old library made them aware how unprepared they were for it.

"The De Luce family let the sons of the others have their way with their daughter for mating selection?" The Grieger kid declared with a look of disgust on his face.

"Not just for mating. They wanted to combine their wealth, so it was really based on which family was more profitable." Olivier said.

Princess Adelia clamped a hand over her mouth to stop herself from vomiting. The thought of the elders climbing on top of her mother like animals and glee-fully doing it at the behest of her father was revolting.

The others in the room fell silent as it sunk in.

After a few moments of no one saying a word, Falson slammed one of the tomes on the table.

"Let's finish this!"

Stunned out of their shock, they continued to put the rest of the clues together.

Within another hour, they had the list and were stunned again. For the Princess, she was happy to know she was not an Ambrook. The flipside of that was who her father was. They all looked around staring at each other.

It made more sense now.

Enemy Encounter

Satellites maneuvered in space to get a better look at the large object that appeared in Earthspace. On the ground, every government scrambled to get the latest info about its trajectory. The ship was massive and when it broke the atmosphere towards its target in the Americas, a large shadow cast over the entire area. Military personnel rushed to the scene, much to the disdain of the local government. They knew that within hours their cities would be flooded with world leaders and scientists.

The last time something that size made contact with Eath occurred when the meteor crash laid waste to an entire region, creating a dead zone no human could step in. Back then, there was no knowledge or technology to do any real research. Over the centuries, inhabited areas were moved farther outwards to create a safe distance away from it.

Now, in the twenty first century, with hazmat suits not impervious in certain sections, that course was abandoned. Of course, there was an antidote that lasted a few hours allowing for entrance into the outer region of the zone.

The governor of the first city stood in his office watching the monitors his assistants had set up against the wall. For a ship of that size to show up without warning was more than a coincidence. He tapped on one of the screens to zoom in on the marker and let out a loud hiss. They had the same insignia as the vampire's enemy airships. One more thing to make them take responsibility for.

In his castle, standing on the balcony of his study Durante stared up at the sky in shock and horror. From its mass, he determined it was a royal armada ship which did not bode well for anyone.

His servants needed no instructions as they rushed around assembling correspondence for the abodes in the outer regions. He snatched the smart phone from his desk and selected Ambrook's number.

"What are we going to do now?" he asked when it connected.

Ambrook was silent for a moment and Durante assumed he too was staring at the ship.

"I think we're in trouble. Wait, there's a call from Theo."

"Just connect us all!" Durante snapped.

"Is this better?" Count Marchand's voice came through.

On another line was Erena.

"I knew they would send for reinforcements, but this is overkill," she said.

"That's precisely the point, my dear," Marchand replied.

"I have a call now," Erena said.

She sucked in her breath.

"Who is it?" Ambrook demanded.

"The Governor."

They all went silent. That was the last person they wanted to deal with.

"Tell him we're on our way," Ambrook instructed.

"We will take as few vehicles as possible. Let's go before that thing starts spewing airships."

Marchand disconnected them from the joint call.

The Governor and Congressman gathered an emergency meeting and cursed themselves for letting it get to such an unfathomable scenario.

"God damn it all to hell," the Governor yelled.

"This is what I had feared all along." The Congressman stood at the edge of the estate watching the ship hover a short distance away. "Have we reached those fake vampires yet?"

One of his assistants came up to him holding a phone in his hand.

"They are on their way, sir."

A line of military vehicles was spotted speeding down the roadway. Following them were four combat tanks fitted with large cannons. The Governor's assistant raised a pair of binoculars and zoomed in on the first car. Every soldier inside had a stern expression.

"They look angry, sir."

"As they should be."

Above them, the ship's hull opened from the bottom and a smaller ship descended. The two men recognized its design when it got closer. By the time it landed in the courtyard, the military line and four vehicles full of vampires had converged on the scene.

The commander in charge of the military detail charged up to the Governor and Congressman, his face contorted in a fit of rage. Five more high ranked soldiers came out of the vehicle locked and loaded.

"You better explain this shit!" The commander demanded. "We let it slide when you had that civil outbreak that you assured us you could contain."

"And we did," the Congressman replied angrily.

"Then explain why this alien ship came straight for this area and plopped down on your front lawn!" The elders had cautiously emerged from their cars and the commander's gaze shifted to them like a laser on target. "Who are these people?"

"That's a little harder to say." The Governor's eyes turned to slits as his hands clenched.

"Spit it out!"

"Vampires."

The commander's expression changed and one of his eyes twitched. His men shifted from one leg to the next, their stance becoming awkward. They all looked around at each other.

"The hell you say?"

"They're vampires. Well, something like vampires. That ship is their enemy's."

"And you know this how?" The commander's face had turned a deep shade of pink.

"That civil unrest was the result of their enemy who infiltrated Earth in smaller vessels attacking the town." The Governor replied. "I had to contact the Congressman when things got out of hands in order to dispatch our military units."

"So, this is the fault of these...things."

The other soldiers aimed their weapons at the elders.

"That will not do."

The male voice came from up ahead and within seconds, a large group of uniformed alien beings stood before all parties. The one who spoke was leading the pack and his demeanor screamed malice. His eyes glowed silver and the men behind him drew swords. Half of the commander's men swung their weapons towards them.

"You better stow that shit! Bullets are faster than those sticks you're waving," the commander said.

"I doubt that," the leader said.

"Please!" the Governor shouted. "There is no need for bloodshed."

The alien leader turned his gaze on him and he cowered in fear. Count Sapienti srepped forward.

"Why have you come with such a large fleet? This planet has nothing to do with our fight."

"Exactly. I have come to take you back and bend to our emperor's will as the slaves you were destined to be. For the sake of our planet."

A shift in the mood made the leader frown. They all felt it and the commander, who was hunched over while berating the politicians, stood up straight and turned to the leader. To the Governor, he asked.

"How long have these vampires been on Earth?"

"I couldn't say exactly, but at least two centuries?"

"Two and a half, more or less," Sapienti added.

"Well, now we're in a pickle, aren't we?"

"I will not be ignored!" The alien leader yelled.

He reached the commander in a split second. His eyes went wide as he got his hand on the gun before being struck. The commander went flying backwards and his men opened fire. The tanks positioned themselves so that they aimed at the large ship hovering in the sky. To the military units' horror, the bullets were either sliced in half or deflected with ease by the alien squad. As they advanced, the elders moved to defend them.

The melee lasts less than a few minutes and was halted when the blade of a sword sat on the alien leader's neck. He looked up, glaring at the wielder. Count Ambrook stared back with glowing red eyes. All the Earth soldiers were down, and the enemy had stopped their assault midway in response to their leader's situation.

"What is the meaning of this?" the alien leader demanded. "I would spare this place if you submit."

"Don't believe any of that," Count Marchand said. "They would raze this region without a thought, knowing you wouldn't be able to chase after them."

The alien leader smirked, and Durante had a flash of memory.

"You are the son of the royal head commander."

He pushed Ambrook out of the way and his unit regrouped, as did the humans.

"Ah, yes. Your family was personally dispatched by my father. His glory was short lived since the rest of you managed to escape."

"An emperor with no loyalty, yet you offer yours to him," Sapienti spat.

"You know nothing!"

"No, you are just a child. You are the one who has no clue."

"We will retreat for now," the alien leader said. "But I will be back to negotiate with the humans. You will obey the emperor's decree."

The alien unit turned in unison and marched back to the convoy ship. As it ascended into the main ship, the humans attempted to get their composure back. Ambrook stood and sheathed his sword. He went over to help up the commander. The man reared back from him, still categorizing them as combatants.

"We are not the enemy, commander. We only want to live here and be ourselves. As you heard, we fled our home world because of what the emperor is doing to it."

"So, you want asylum?" He patted the seat of pants to get rid of the dirt. "What makes you think the governments of this planet is going to allow that?"

"I will vouch for them," the Congressman said.

"The shit you are! Did you not say they were goddamn vampires?"

"Oh, we got rid of most of those on Earth. We just liked the way they were organized and took over." Sapienti gave a wide smile.

"Huh?"

While the commander stood confused, the elders huddled for an impromptu meeting. The Governor and Congressman also went off for a discussion. The tanks didn't move and neither did the cannons.

The estate was put on lock down and a communications room was set up inside. The Commander got in touch with the President of the United States and relayed the message that the rest of the world was not in danger as of yet. That the situation was a domestic matter.

This was not the first time an alien ship had appeared on Earth, but it would have been nice to have a warning. Preparation for such things was necessary to keep some resemblance of peace. He demanded the elders be detained. When his soldiers tried to do so, the elders made it clear they were not to be underestimated.

A military convoy was assigned to follow them home but as the first few elders were dropped off, they turned back. The dead zone was in the middle of three continents and the covens were peppered around its perimeter. They were not prepared, fuel wise, to make such a journey or prepared to die. In the third car, Durante laughed.

"What are they thinking?"

"It was quite entertaining," Marchand said.

Erena sat quietly, her eyes half closing and opening frequently. Durante put an arm around her and let her head fall on his chest. She went to asleep instantly.

"This was way too much for her," Ambrook said.

"The timing of everything is just bad," Sapienti added.

"At least we know the United States is on our side."

"Now, we just have to convince the others and we can breathe easier."

The De Luce Castle loomed ahead, and it was decided they would make a stop there for awhile.

Once Durante had Erena comfortably in her bed chamber, he went back down to the main hall next to the throne room where Count Sapienti, Ambrook and Marchand sat lounging. They had already tapped the servants to bring drinks and were sipping on spirits. From outside they heard a helicopter and knew it was a military chopper. They all looked up in weariness and continued to drink. Sapienti set his aside and adjusted himself on the sofa.

"Suggestions? Gameplans?"

"The emperor is desperate. Something must have happened with the planet's trade industry," Ambrook said.

"I had a feeling it would collapse without the co-operation of the clients and workers."

Durante sat on the edge of his seat, leaned forward with a flute of champagne dangling in one hand. He stared at the other side of the room thinking about the alien commander and how similar he was to his father.

"He's angry because of something that didn't satisfy him. My guess is he murdered every one of our parents to prove a point and it back fired."

The others halted their drinking. It was no secret that is probably what happened. The moment their ship went down, they knew it was a sacrifice to keep them safe.

"I want to behead that commander like he did your parents," Sapienti stated.

"You would have to get past me first." Durante's eyes flashed silver.

"Shall we address the second question?" Marchand asked.

"We must figure out a way to keep that ship here on Earth and keep the negotiations in flux while our mission gets under way," Ambrook suggested.

"A lot can happen in fifty years on Earth," Sapienti said.

"Fifty years? Where did you get that timeframe from?" Marchand cried out.

"It took us over twenty to get here," Durante shot back.

"That's because the navigation system was knocked out of whack. Thirty tops to get there take out time to get vengeance and head back."

"That's still a long time for humans to deal with that pissant commander."

Another helicopter was heard above but this time it got closer.

"You must be joking?" Sapienti yelled.

They all got up and headed to the staircase that led to a balcony above the great hall. Sure enough, a military chopper was landing on the castle lawn. Four men in suits came out followed by six soldiers in full gear. Marchand rolled his eyes. The men hiked up to the giant double doors and looked around for a way to signal someone to it. They stepped back in surprise and the soldiers raised their weapons as the door swung open to reveal a crew of servants.

The first man's voice carried upwards as he spoke.

"We are here to discuss business with the head of this," he turned to his counterpart and the other man whispered in his ear. "Coven."

"Why are you yelling, sir?" The head servant asked.

He took a breath and stopped before he spoke. His face went flush, and he finally looked ahead of him at the servants.

"My apologies. Is the master of this castle available?"

"Our Queen is resting," the female servant said tersely.

All four men in suits were now pink with embarrassment for assuming a male owned the castle.

"I meant no disrespect."

"Of course you did. There are men with guns pointed at us." One of the men turned around and fervently waved the soldiers to lower their weapons. "You will be leaving those at the foyer."

"We are not coming in there unarmed," one of the men said.

"Then I am afraid you may not enter. Goodnight."

The servants on either side of the doors started to push them closed.

"Wait!" The first man yelled. The doors halted. "We will comply. Is there someone in the Queen's trust we can discuss these matters with?"

"There is. This way."

She motioned for them to follow, the other servants taking their weapons as the doors were slammed shut.

Count Ambrook let out a heavy sigh.

"Should we wake her?"

"Not on your life," Marchand cried out. "Get her advisor. We will facilitate."

Durante signaled for a servant and whispered the request in her ear. She immediately ran to fetch the advisor. Within minutes, the military entourage was entering the main hall. By the looks on their faces, they were trying not to be impressed. All of their eyes had a hint of green in the whites, a sign of the antidote coursing through their veins. They would not be visiting long.

"What brings a U.S. envoy to our Queen's castle so late in the night?" Sapienti asked.

Servants funneled the men to the sofas and offered them drinks. The first man held up a hand.

"We are here on business. No alcohol allowed."

"That's when it's necessary," Marchand muttered as he took a sip of his.

"Is it usual for more than one leader to be at another's home?" The man asked.

"When we have mixers, yes. This was a special occasion." Durante answered.

Queen Erena's head advisor came into the room with tablet and stylus in hand. She moved to stand in front of the men and looked down on them as if they were rats in a sewer.

"How dare you nearly disturb our Queen!" Before the men could reply she stepped back and sat on the sofa across from them. Durante and Marchand flanked her. "I am the Queen's head advisor. You will tell me what business you have with her and I will relay it in detail."

Realizing she was quite serious and not in the mood for fluff, the first man cleared his throat and sat forward a bit.

"We need to establish if asylum is an option given your species' nature."

"And what nature are you referring?" She asked.

Her eyes flashed and one of the other men sat back further in the sofa.

"You have identified your kind as vampires. Those creatures," the elders gave him a stare. "That particular species is detrimental to humans."

"How so? Are there not other predators on this planet that do far worse than drink blood?"

"Of course. But your kind hunt humans for food."

"That is incorrect."

The man leaned back a little and stared at her in disbelief.

"I beg your pardon?"

"Earth vampires do such things. We are not like them. As was stated before, we wiped out most of them but kept enough for nostalgia. Our goal was never to erase any of your kind, even if some of them were blood thirsty animals."

"Then what you're telling me is that traditional

vampires of folklore are nearly extinct?"

Her lips curled upwards in a sinister smile.

"Correct."

As promised, the alien commander returned to the congressman's estate. His staff watched the convoy ship land on the lawn again, scorching the grass beneath the frost. The ramp opened, and the commander strolled down with a comical expression. His long robes were open and cinched at the waist, making the fabrics flow in the breeze. A full length body suit resembling pleated leather was exposed beneath them.

His eyes had a playful sheen to it and the Congressman was suddenly aware of his helplessness without the elders to protect him. Regardless if there was no malice coming from the alien.

"We didn't get to have introductions last we met," the alien commander said.

"Yes, well, you attacked us for no reason."

"My sincere apologies. I get anxious when my prey is in reach. I am Commander Gallic of the Emperial Fleet."

His robes swished across the ground as he came closer. The rest of his soldiers stayed back in triangular formation near the craft. When he was only a few feet from the congressman, he stopped and glared down at him. The congressman had not realized how tall the alien was before. Slender, all muscle and a brute.

He thinks nothing of killing.

"You wish to negotiate with the leaders of our world but you must know, you have no jurisdiction here. This is not your world, or your solar system, for that matter."

The alien commander's eyes narrowed.

"We shall see."

The Congressman motioned for him to follow and they entered the new hub for communications with the other countries. Each room they passed had been reconfigured into mini command centers. At the end of the hall was the main area, filled to the brim with soldiers and government personnel flown in on a moment's notice. The head military commander was barking out orders, sending soldiers scrambling. Wearing fatigues with weapons strapped on the thighs and waist, he was ready for combat. He happened to see the two men and his face scrunched up in disgust as his gaze landed on the alien.

"What is he doing here?" The military commander asked rudely, turning his full attention to them.

"I came to negotiate, as I said before," Commander Gallic replied.

"Oh yeah? What kind of negotiation?"

"You hand over my planet's criminals and I don't destroy your entire region."

"And, the other option?" The congressman asked.

"There is no other option."

"That's not a negotiation." The voice came from one of the vidscreens and the Secretary of Defense for Great Britain was present. "They have been here before some of our countries were barely established, which makes them more citizens of Earth than every living human."

"They fled their home world out of defiance and they must pay the price."

Commander Gallic was having a hard time containing his rage.

"Then they are refugees and since they seek

asylum, though it should have been done so long ago, we will go through our due processes."

Gallic's eyes glowed and he looked upward as his head tilted down.

"And how long will this take?"

The Congressman looked to the Secretary and the military commander, his lower lip receding into his mouth.

"Five years, give or take."

The Secretary said it with a poker face.

Commander Gallic's demeanor changed. He raised his head and a creepy smile formed.

"Is that all? Then I would like to see this process in full."

"I beg your pardon?" The congressman said.

"I am now fascinated with how you deal with off worlders. It would be a learning experience."

A servant came in with a tray of snacks and beverages. Commander Gallic eyed it with interest.

"Human food looks quite similar to ours." He grabbed some of the small hors d'hourves without asking and shoved them in his mouth. As he chewed, his eyes glanced up as if contemplating the flavor or if he liked it. "Not all that appealing but satisfying." He turned to the servant. "Send some to my soldiers."

"Now hold on just a minute!"

The military commander yelled.

"Is there a problem?"

"Yeah, there's a problem! How many soldiers you have on that ship?"

"Oh, ten thousand," he replied nonchalantly.

The congressman shut down his emotions so the alien wouldn't see his reaction. The military commander and Secretary appeared to do the same. One ship with such a massive force was not what they imagined.

"We don't have the capability to make food of that large quantity," he said.

A look of disappointment crossed the alien's face.

"We can get it. It will just take some time," the military commander finally said.

"Are you certain?"

"Pop up mess halls is a staple of the military."

The Congressman and Secretary gave him a stern look. When the alien wandered off to the other side of the room, the military commander gestured the congressman closer to the vidscreen.

"You want to piss off ten thousand of those creatures? I say give them some tasty human food and keep them happy."

"You're right." The Secretary nodded. "See to it. I will make sure the other countries pitch in after I explain the situation."

"Umm." A soldier came up to them and they turned to see what he wanted. "I'm not trying to be insubordinate, but aren't they like vampires or something?"

The four men turned to see the alien commander leaning closer than normal towards a female servant's neck. His eyes glowed, turning from silver to a dark pink. His mouth opened exposing fangs dripping with saliva.

"You will refrain from that!" The congressman yelled as he crossed the room to rescue the woman. "No feeding on humans."

"Surely, you jest," Commander Gallic spoke, as he turned away and stood. "What is the protocol for the so-called elders?"

The room went still as all eyes landed on the Congressman. He swallowed hard and adjusted his suit jacket.

"We have a registry," he began, "of volunteers. It's very discreet." He cleared his throat.

"So that's why they flocked here," the military commander said softly while nodding.

"We don't have enough volunteers to satisfy a horde!"

"Blood bank?" The other soldier suggested.

Commander Gallic's devious glare made the Congressman shiver.

Monster.

The Congressman went into his private study, the only place not occupied by machines and soldiers. He sat down at his desk and pinched the bridge of his nose with eyes closed. He knew the covens had their own supply of blood that they somehow managed to make larger without acquiring more. But they also knew where to get it in an emergency. He touched the screen on his desk phone and hit the auto dial for Count Ambrook.

"Congressman," the count answered. "What's happened?"

"You can tell, hmm?"

There was a pause before the count spoke again.

"Tell me."

"Your world's commander requests blood. He has ten thousand soldiers. What am I supposed to do?"

"So, you want us to open our banks, possibly draining them for the sake of the human race."

"No!" The congressman clenched his hands into fists. "I know you can get it from one of your private vendors and multiply the quantity."

"Of course. I am relieved. We can have it by end of the week."

"And what should I tell him until then?"

"Tell him what you told us when the volunteer program was being implemented. He must wait."

Another pause.

"I will contact you when it is complete."

"Thank you, Count Ambrook."

The call disconnected and the congressman sat back in his chair. He now had to figure out how to explain that to a blood thirsty alien army.

Preparing for Departure

Erena gave birth to a son with everyone in her inner circle present. Durante stayed by her side through the entire ordeal while her daughter stood farther away looking green like she was on the verge to vomit. Known for being a creature of bloodlust, the messiness of birthing was too much for her. Erena managed a smirk before her body gave out from exhaustion.

The little one's cries echoed all around the stone birthing chamber. Her royal advisors erupted into congratulatory claps and coos. One of the midwives carried the bundle over to her and she wrapped him in her arms. He calmed down and his face smoothed out, becoming less flushed with pink. Count Durante sat next to her and got a good look at his newest son. Erena glanced up at her daughter.

"Will you not come and welcome your brother?"

Princess Adelia gulped, holding her fingers against her lips as her cheeks puffed. She seemed to get herself together and walked over to them. She scrutinized the newborn for quite some time before saying.

"He's cute. Can I eat him?" Her eyes glowed red.

Durante leaned over to her and they met eye to eye.

"If you try to harm my son, I will tear you apart. Princess."

Her daughter glared at him and stood.

"I was joking!" She spat. Her gaze fell on the others in the chamber and they didn't find it funny either. "Why would you take something like that so seriously?"

She turned away quickly to leave but Erena saw the hurt on her face.

"Come back here, Adelia," she called out.

"What for? It's obvious I am not wanted here."

"I said," Erena sat up on the dais. "Come back here."

She didn't raise her voice and there was no need. Princess Adelia turned back around, desperately trying to wipe tears from her face. Durante looked embarrassed.

"You made my daughter cry!"

"I'm sorry."

"Tell her that!"

Princess Adelia returned to her side. Erena pulled her close, resting her head on her bosom.

"You are a mess and disobedient, but you are still my precious daughter." She caressed the top of her head.

"I am sorry for offending you," Count Durante said.

He moved a lock of hair from her face and she slapped it away. That made everyone laugh. She frowned in humiliation.

"Big baby," Durante sent to her telepathically

Her eyes narrowed. She did not reply.

Boots striking the main corridor of the castle caused occupants within it to turn and identify the source.

They were met with the sight of an elite combat unit marching forth. The leader had piercing blue eyes and a demeanor of purpose. His jet-black hair hung just past his shoulders and bounced along with each stride he took. Well-shaped pink lips were pursed tight.

Under one arm, he held his helmet and in the other hand was a small box wrapped in decorative paper. The four soldiers behind him kept in perfect sync and their eyes forward. The people moved quickly out of the way, some even pushing others aside before the group passed.

The leader headed straight for the throne room and entered without announcing himself. Erena looked up from her newborn laying in a raised bassinette beside the throne. She took in a sharp breath, her hand moving to her chest. Princess Adelia stared at him trying to determine if he was friend or foe. He may be of the coven but that didn't mean he was loyal to the Queen. Something about him seemed to catch her eye.

He stopped at the bottom of the throne and made a small bow.

"My Queen, my congratulations on your newest spawn." He held out the small box.

Her head advisor came over and took it from him then handed it to Erena.

"How dare you come unannounced and address your Queen with such insolence?" The enforcer already had a hand on her swords.

He gave her a look of distaste, which angered her more. Princess Adelia stepped forward to defend her mother if necessary. His cloak moved, revealing the insignia of his army. The enforcer hissed before stepping back. Princess Adelia was confused and looked between the two.

"Has my father been here this night?" He asked.

Erena let her hand fall into her lap. She took hold of the box and looked down at him.

"He will probably be here shortly. What have you given me?"

"Not you, woman," he replied. The council gasped. "For the little beast."

"Mother!" Princess Adelia said with intensity. "Who is this mongrel?"

With a flash he was on her, his short blade poised under her chin, one of her arms pinned behind her ready to snap. They locked eyes and he grinned at her attempt to not show pain or fear.

"Stop it!" Erena commanded.

He was back standing before her in a flash, his weapon back in the sheath attached to his back. The princess was visibly shaken while the enforcer hung back on the opposite side of the room.

"I was only teasing. Though, she really is worthless." His eyes glowed as he stared at Adelia. He went back to the previous conversation. "Did he send a messenger with the time?"

"Count Durante will be here at his leisure."

Erena slowly removed the wrapper from the present.

"Hmm? So, he has free range of movement within these walls?" He asked.

"Is that problematic for you?"

"Not particularly. I rarely see the man."

Princess Adelia regained her composure and jumped down to stand before him.

"Why do you not wish to know your father? Are you not curious as to the kind of man he is?"

"What relevance does that have in my life?"

"He's your sire, why not..." she abandoned her speech, seeing his bored expression.

The tearing of paper interrupted the silence in the room and everyone watched Queen Erena open the box. She lifted a silver chain with the family crest emblazed on a silver disc.

"The council would have given him that in due time," an advisor scoffed.

The medallion turned, and the advisor's mouth clamped shut as the others admired the piece. Shown on the back in precise detail was an image of Queen Erena holding her newborn in her arms.

"When did you see this? How?" Erena wiped a tear from her left eye.

He frowned and let his eyes form into slits.

"Are you shedding tears for that?"

A scuffling in the halls made them all turn to see Count Durante enter the room. At first, he seemed to walk in normally until he was mere inches from his oldest son, mothered by Erena.

"Do not disrespect your Queen, Tervan."

His voice was low, the intent noted.

"I wasn't. It was a gesture of concern. One in power with an audience should not show weakness for such things."

Exasperated, Durante walked away from him and climbed up to the throne steps to see his new son. He lifted him out of the bassinette and walking back down, handed him Tervan.

"If I must," he sighed. He looked at the boy for a long time as if waiting for something. When the baby opened his eyes, he grinned. "There you are."

Durante, noticing the insignia, turned his head to Erena, giving her a quizzical stare. She frowned and shook her head. Tervan, now done placating their whim, handed the baby back to his father.

"The other reason I have come to you is for an audience later in the week."

"Is that so?" Erena leaned forward.

"It would be beneficial if Count Durante were present as well."

Princess Adelia glared at him for addressing his own father that way. But seeing Count Durante think nothing of it made her face crumble with sadness. Tervan rolled his eyes in a sideways glance away from her.

"So be it." She motioned for her head advisor. "Make sure to set time aside for the General."

Lariod had a strange look on his face as he watched General Tervan that the princess couldn't decipher.

"I thank you, my Queen." He bowed again before turning and walking towards the corridor. He met Lariod's stare as he passed him. A smirk crossed his lips. Princess Adelia was now curious as to why that interaction bothered her.

The General's meeting was held in the Queen's chamber corridor that looked out over the horizon. The sky was a pale blue as the dawn faded into full morning. He had removed his cloak and was now in sparse battle gear with his longsword at his hip. While strolling along, enjoying the air, he kept an eye on his mother's movements.

Why are you so exhausted?

His father stood sentry instead of her enforcer and Tervan thanked whoever was responsible for that. He never liked the amazon regardless of her professed loyalty after her mother killed the vampire's queen.

Not yet born, his thoughts on how the situation went down was a keep your enemies closer sort of deal.

"I heard you are preparing to go back to your home world," he said.

"You don't approve," she said.

"I will accompany her," his father added.

He stopped in front of the archway of the balcony. His eyes glowed as he turned to them.

"It is a suicide mission and I will not allow it."

"'Not allow...'" His mother became angry. "I am Queen! I do as I please."

"Last I checked the records, you fled because you could not win."

His father, standing with arms folded, let his arms drop as he too appeared ready for a fight.

"Even I have no idea how to take down a Volshin nor Kataling. What are you planning to do when you get there? Beg the emperor to see reason?" He saw them both struggle with an answer. This is what he was afraid of. With all the proposed planning to get the ship up and running, they were missing a crucial detail. "How many warriors are slotted to travel with you?"

"Eight hundred."

"And that is how you all lose and get killed."

He walked into the chamber and stood before them.

"If you're going to at least think about surviving, my army is at your disposal."

Within the dead zone was a new scattering of activity from the horde of technicians doing testing and repairs on the alien ship. Marchand had left them to their own devices, confident they would continue to work diligently around the clock. Two years later, the final diagnostics tests were complete. The ship was raised from under the sandy earth to sit above ground after being buried for centuries. Its hull was dulled with age and creatures had made homes in the crevices. Extermination of those and sanitization measures cured most of that. The ship was starting to look reliable.

Marchand drove up to the site in one of his many high-end sedans. In the passenger seat was Count Grieger with a permanent frown. He stopped the car at the nearest tent and got out. Count Grieger looked around then reluctantly did the same. Both men were wearing expensive suits, having just left a business meeting with military and government personnel regarding their status.

The first technician left his portable work station and greeted the two men.

"Good to see you again, my lord."

"How is progress?" Marchand asked.

"We are nearly done. The Germans have repaired the navigation system."

"Of course we did," Count Grieger huffed. "My techies are just as good as yours."

"This isn't a contest," Marchand said to him while glancing sideways. "Can it fly?"

The technician went back to his work station and tapped on the touchscreen.

"The thrusters are at optimal levels. I don't see why not."

"Are you going to pilot that thing?" Grieger asked Marchand laughingly.

"Or course not. I'm not going back."

Grieger turned to him in shock.

"But your children are set to go! Are you going to let them go without you?"

"Who said I was letting them go?" Marchand's face went flush and his eyes glowed angrily.

"I guess I will have to do it then."

This time, Marchand was surprised.

"You? And what, you are taking the oldest two?"

"Someone has to keep watch over those brats."

"Tavelo and Eterenia will be on board."

"Exactly. Those are the brats I am referring to."

Marchand let out a loud guffaw.

It was true Erena and Durante were some of the youngest among the elders. Sapienti was the oldest with Ambrook and himself not far behind. His demeanor became serious as he thought about the journey and what they would probably face on their home world. No. he wouldn't change his mind. Anyone in his coven willing to volunteer he could sanction. Except his twins.

Hunger pains assaulted Commander Gallic and he reached for the bowl of fresh bloody meat, killed only a few hours ago. It didn't have the same taste as humans, but it did the job in a pinch. Nearly three years on Earth found him observing the species in jaw dropping disgust. He determined them to be weak and illogical, not worth the handful of bloody meat in his hands. Shoving a fist full in his mouth, he chewed slowly, blood dripping down his chin.

On the screen in front of him played a television show. He didn't understand the fascination of sitting all day mesmerized by the images. It appeared to exist in almost every culture he had been exposed to. One of his men walked into the ship quarters and leaned down towards him.

"Commander, we are picking up energy waves within the outer regions."

"What kind are they?" he asked, yawning.

"Like our ships, commander."

The Commander sat upright and turned to his soldier.

"I want footage. Track it down and tell me what and where it is."

"Of course, commander." The soldier backed out of the room.

Commander Gallic leaned forward and rested his arms on his thighs.

What are you playing at, you fugitives?

The first fleet had come to Earth and had not succeeded in their mission as he later explained to the emperor. The fugitives had breeded Volshin and Katalings. Since the fleet had none, the battle was lopsided. Still, the casualties were as expected. He sat back and continued eating his snack. A sly smile crept on his face. He had a little secret. And even if the fugitives happened to find it, it would make no difference.

He knew the governments were intentionally dragging out the asylum process to keep him distracted from what the fugitives were up to.

"Not so clever, are you, humans?"

Ambrook spotted the enemy spies from a few miles away. His vision zeroed in and he saw a strange gauging device aimed at the ship. One of the soldiers had a viewer that recorded video and took still images. He rubbed the bottom of his chin trying to figure how to proceed.

"Should I get rid of them?" He said it more to himself. Someone picked up on it.

"That would defeat the purpose, Count," Count Browning of the lower covens said.

"Do you think the commander would follow us back?"

"Not likely. He seems to have a new agenda as of late."

"Which, in itself, is terrifying."

Behind them, the technicians were testing the ship's hovering ability. Sandy dirt swirled around beneath it like a mini tornado, pushing against the industrial strength tents. All of the workers wore goggles to protect their eyes. The whole area looked like a space lab in the middle of a desert. Every other day, a military chopper would fly over taking footage.

When the elders last met with the world leaders via teleconference, they told them their plan. The leaders saw it as an opportunity to nip the issue in the first stages. It was clear the commander was on the verge of attacking, regardless of the governments' decision. Marchand was mostly silent during the interaction and that made Ambrook feel like the count was either hiding something or found something disturbing.

"What is that thing?"

Ambrook pointed at the weird device.

Count Grieger came up behind him and snorted humorously.

"They are using that to figure out what kind of ship it is by its energy output." Ambrook and Browning went pale. Grieger laughed. "Let them. As far as they know, it is only a transport ship. The weapons have not been installed yet."

"I still don't like it," Ambrook snapped.

"Come away. There's no need to shed blood so early in the day. Get out of the sun."

Ambrook looked up at the grey sky that was still too bright even after centuries of living on Earth. He glanced back at the two enemy soldiers huddled under a covering to block it. He understood that action all too well.

Marchand tapped the edge of his desk with a rolled up document one of his servants had acquired days before the meeting. He had gone over it many times and at first, it angered him. A sense of fear gripped him. Then he became leery of what it meant. Now he was trying to figure out a way to use the information for their mission's benefit. A soft knock on the doorframe brought him out of his thoughts.

His daughter, Odette, stood in the doorway looking upset. She was probably there to plead her case, again. He had expressly told her and her brother that under no circumstances would he let them go on the mission. The argument was hostile, and both parties said things they shouldn't have. Still, he stood firm.

Before he could ask her what she wanted, she stepped into the room.

"Why? What reason do you have to deny us this opportunity?" she yelled.

His face contorted in anger and he kept his rage

down by making tight fists, the document crumbling into a thin bowtie shape.

"Because," he finally said. "Neither of you are capable of fighting on that level!"

Her face went slack while her eyes opened wider in shock. He knew it stung, his twins having pride in their fighting skills over the decades. They were in fact deadly, though not enough to go up against an entire planet of their own race.

"You," she said softly. "You don't believe in us."

"That's not what I said!"

He slammed his fist down on the desk as he rose. The look of dejection and hurt on her face made him regret speaking how he truly felt. She turned away, still in a daze.

"Daughter!"

She didn't turn around, walking stiffly as she entered the corridor. From his desk, he could see the tears stream down her face. As she disappeared down the hall, he leaned over and cursed himself.

"God damn it!"

He threw the document across the room and stood in a rage. Defeated, he wiped his face with one hand and sought his mobile device. He sat back down at his desk and hit the auto dial for Queen Celeste. It was time for an intervention regarding the other matter that came to his attention.

A meeting was called for all the coven leaders and their offspring to assemble at the boarding school's auditorium. While everyone else filed in to take their seats, the main coven leaders sat at the table on the stage front and center, absorbing all the hate that would be flung at them by their children.

The lower house coven leaders looked even more nervous, not agreeing with their solution. Tensions ran deep in the large venue. Once all were present, the groundskeeper shut the double doors and brought the long wooden piece down to lock it in place. Some turned out of curiosity, wondering why they were being locked in.

Count Ambrook sat in the center of the table as the head coven leader. To his right sat Count Durante and Queen Erena. On the left was Marchand and Sapienti. The end rounded the panel with Count Grieger and Queen Celeste. He pulled the microphone closer to him.

"Thank you for attending. I know some of you are upset and I understand completely. The doors are sealed for a good reason. We may have to contain the room once this is over."

Looks of concern followed and the atmosphere changed.

"This will only get worse," Sapienti sent to him personally.

"It was brought to our attention some time ago that many of our offspring conspired to find their birth lineages."

He watched all the children involved squirm in their seats. To his surprise, Princess Adelia stood up, her face full of defiance.

"What did you expect? We were to go on living on this planet based on parental relations with their children and not wonder about our own?"

Olivier also stood. He looked run down, his face gaunt. Marchand seemed to diminish in presence when the young man looked up.

"Part of the planet population's mantra is knowing

where you come from and how it defines one's identity. You have essentially taken it from us. We are nothing but cogs in a wheel to preserve your race."

Stunned silence filled the room. Ambrook felt himself heat up with anger along with the other elders.

"Don't you ever say such things!" Queen Celeste yelled. "Not ever! You are our precious children. Not things for us to own." Tears welled up in her eyes. "You are my precious child." She slumped back in her seat. "I never once thought of you as..."

Count Durante placed a hand on her shoulder as she cried. Olivier stood rooted in his spot, processing what Queen Celeste just revealed. His sister sitting beside him, had finally looked up and stared at the woman who was their mother.

"What does that mean?" Another coven child asked.

His voice quivered along with his body, obviously angered. "Are we all related to each other?" He yelled.

"In a way, yes," Falson answered.

The young man turned to his father who sat a few seats over in the row before him.

"You are my son," the lower count said without turning around. "That's all that matters."

"Then who gave birth to me?"

The young man's eyes went dark red and his talons grew. Many others in the room followed suit.

Here it comes, Sapienti warned Ambrook.

He no longer regretted sealing the doors.

The elders sat in the lounge room exhausted and blurry eyed. Celeste was calmer, barely consolable. She sipped her brandy while constantly wiping tears from her face with a handkerchief. They all had a drink in their hands and the bottles were within reach in the center of the room. The servants had been sent away after delivering them. Everyone looked guilty. After they all had a long moment of taking enough spirits to alleviate it, Sapienti set down his glass and leaned back in his seat.

"That went well enough as planned."

"No! It didn't!" Count Grieger countered. "That was a travesty. We had to subdue our own children."

"You can't blame them," Durante said. He took another sip of his whiskey. "I find it reassuring that the children from our covens did not respond when the others attacked."

"Princess Adelia was very non-vocal." Marchand added.

"She knows who sired her. I think she has not come to terms with it," Erena said.

"Hmm, well, he wasn't exactly a choice we would have made. You were in a rebellious stage, if I recall correctly."

"It was not rebellion," she retorted.

"He was reckless and full of blood lust. I could see where you might have found that appealing." Sapienti emphasized the word might.

"Now that that's out of the way," Ambrook said as he set his glass down too. He turned to Marchand. "Are you going to tell us what's eating at you?"

The count sat up and tilted his glass, emptying it down his throat. His eyes flashed silver and the others reared back as a precaution. He twirled the empty glass in his hand.

"I think," he said slowly, "I may have found a wormhole the commander used to get here."

"That's obvious," Sapienti said.

"No, this one is different." He set down the glass and sat back. "How long would it have taken his ship to get here after the last unit, who we fought and defeated, relayed the message for reinforcements?"

Right as some of them were about answer, everyone's expression went from surprise to dark. The fastest the message would have been received, as they now know would take maybe ten years and another ten for the ship to be deployed. Yet, here the alien commander was in only half the time.

"We could be back much quicker," Erena said softly.

"But if we used it, won't he find out?" Celeste asked.

"Doesn't matter," Grieger answered.

"He can contact the palace and have a fleet in Earthspace." Marchand continued.

The thought of the entire planet being engulfed in a new war made Durante sick to his stomach. Erena wasn't too keen on the idea either. As much as they miss their home world, Earth had become one. Sure, they preyed on humans, on occasion. That did not mean they wanted them exterminated.

Movement in the hall, made Celeste shoot out of her seat and head after whoever it was. Curious, they crammed into the doorway like high schoolers and watched her pursuit. She swept up behind the twins and grabbed them together into her iron hug. At first, they struggled then went slack, leaning against her. She kissed them on the cheeks, her tears dripping onto them.

"I would die for you," she whispered. "Don't ever forget that." She stroked their hair.

"We're not babies," Odette protested as she tried

to stop her from messing up her hair. "Even though our father seems to think so."

A hissing sound came from Marchand and the elders saw his face turn pink. Celeste gave him a dirty look and he slinked back a little. She turned her attention back to the twins and made them look at her.

"What they said to you about not being capable of winning is only partly true." They stiffened but she refused to let them go. "We need you to defend this home. Earth. Are you going to trust it in the hands of the lower covens? You are leaders and they need to be led."

The twins expression changed and a new comprehension showed.

"Oh, she's good," Grieger whispered.

"That's what I was trying to say, but they wouldn't listen," Marchand softly seethed.

"Mother's intuition," Erena said. "You needed to say the right words, the right way."

He muttered something under his breath which made Durante start to laugh but was cut off by Grieger clamping a hand over his mouth.

One small victory was had.

Departure was getting close and Erena had little patience for her daughter's hostility when it came to the mission. She was not letting a rogue like her go into space, let alone their home world where she would either be captured or killed. Once again, she had come into the throne room unannounced, ready to state her case.

"I am part of the initial planning with Ambrook and Sapienti. How do you justify excluding me at such an important time? I will not rely on him," she pointed to Tervan, "to protect you when it counts!"

"Stop yelling," Erena said through gritted teeth.

"And secondly," Tervan interrupted. "I am the Queen's blade. Who else would be capable of that?"

Princess Adelia gave him an animal like growl. A side effect of being with a werewolf.

"What would you have me do? Send everyone else off while I stay safely in my coven?"

"Have you forgotten?" Erena raised an eyebrow.

Tervan laughed as the Princess stood mid rage, now confused. "The enemy is still on Earth, dear Princess," he stated.

Erena stepped down from the throne. Her advisors parted to let her by. She placed her hands around the Princess' face and frowned.

"I need you to help lead our forces and keep the enemy at bay until our return. There would be no point to this if he is left to ravage this planet."

Not only did the Princess' eyes go wide, so did the rest of the room.

"You want me to reign in your steed?" The Princess whispered.

"As my most prominent daughter, you would be next in line if something happens to me."

Princess Adelia wrenched herself from her mother's clutches.

"Nothing will happen! You are to return as planned!" She stepped away and straightened her jacket. "I will keep the throne unoccupied until your return. If anyone tries to usurp your reign I will cut them down myself."

Erena smiled, proud of her daughter and also amused by the looks on some of her council members' faces. This would be the best opportunity to take over the coven. She knew they had no taste for what punishment the Princess would dish if they tried. Tervan's expression changed as he too understood what had transpired, although he didn't seem too happy about it.

CHAPTER THREE

HOMEWORLD

Amid the swirling sand of the dead zone, a caravan of vehicles sped towards the alien ship resting in its center. As the large entourage arrived near the ships edge, they surrounded it in a semicircle. The doors opened to let out members of the various covens wearing attire wholly different than their usual flare. Underneath flowing robes, they wore full body suits designed, by Grieger's coven, for combat.

In the four cargo trucks were select soldiers from the top covens. General Tervan stepped down from the back of the first one and surveyed the area. He was not happy with the number of people who were combat ready. When the weapons were installed, Marchand readjusted the capacity for the ship. Originally able to accommodate one thousand, it now dropped to eight hundred and fifty. The only way they would be victorious in their efforts was if the emperor was dead and the planet was in a lawless state. Which they all knew was not the case.

He saw Chase Ambrook adjust his robes, not being used to them. His guardian was beside him, as always, nibbling on a chunk of meat in his hand. Falson Sapienti and his guardian stood solemn, seemingly nervous.

You should be, the General chided him silently.

Queen Erena and Count Durante emerged from their vehicle looking almost regal in colorful robes that represented their family. Count Grieger somehow appeared staunch in his robes. Of the elders, they were the ones in addition to Count Sapienti going. He still was in shock after his mother left the De Luce castle in the hands of Princess Adelia. Images of the walls raining in blood came to mind.

"Are we ready for launch?" Chase Ambrook asked Count Marchand.

Marchand turned away from the diagnostics screen on his tablet and frowned.

"How about getting ready for boarding first?"

Miffed, Chase looked away.

Count Grieger went up to Marchand.

"Have you reconsidered?"

He eyed the twins hovering around their car. They had already prepared for if their father granted their wish by wearing the same attire as the others.

"Celeste would be livid if I told them yes."

"Hmmm?"

Marchand let out a loud sigh. He continued doing the last minute checks and began the sequence to open the hatch. The front section of the hull slid upwards to allow for the ramp to extend down.

"Your chariot awaits," Marchand announced.

Supplies were loaded up first, forcing the anxious passengers to wait nearly two hours before they could board. Next, the crew went in to start up the launch sequences and do another internal check from the command center. Falson's guardian came up to General

Tervan and the two men stood staring at each other for a split second.

"What do you need, guardian?" Tervan asked curtly.

"I am not one to run from a fight these days, but if it looks like it's going to go even a little bit sideways, I will take Falson and my lord and head back to the ship."

Tervan's eyes flashed with intrigue. He found a new liking for the guardian.

"I would be either right behind or already there."

"Good to know."

They stayed in their own space for a few moments before Demitri turned, walking back to his master's side. Count Ambrook lingered away from the rest of the passengers, watching his son's inappropriate enthusiasm. His attention turned to the Tervan and there was a pleading in his eyes. Tervan knew what it meant; keep my son safe. He wasn't sure if he should be insulted. His job was to make sure of everyone's safety. He had no intention of letting anyone die on the mission.

"We're ready for the passengers," a voice boomed from the external communications.

Tervan walked to the front of the trucks.

"First battalion, lead them in. Second will flank the sides. The rest of us will take up the rear." He yelled out his orders as they scrambled from the trucks. "Move out!"

Count Ambrook and his wife went to their son and each caressed his cheeks before hugging him. Chase tried not to look embarrassed as the other offspring taking the journey snickered. They didn't have long before they too were bombarded with affection from their parents. The passengers loaded up from nearest to farthest. As the Durante coven went up the ramp, he saw the twins in a frozen state of despair.

Marchand got into his car and sat inside for a long time as if waiting for them to do the same. When they didn't move, he pushed the button to roll down the windows. He took a quick glance at them and flinched at their demeanor. Tervan stood near the end of the ramp.

"Go." Marchand rolled up the window. Before it fully closed, he said, "Come back to me. And to your mother."

The twins, struck with elation and shock, walked unsteadily towards the ship. They glanced back at their father in the back of the car and Odette blew him a kiss.

"Hurry in!" Tervan yelled.

Startled, they flash stepped to the ramp and headed up. Tervan motioned for the rest of his men to follow and when the last one passed him at the top, he stared down at the coven members who remained. Looks of trepidation and sorrow was what he saw. He brought a clenched fist to his chest and bowed. The hatch closed, and he made his way deep into the ship.

Their navigator, the son of the previous one, brought up the visual screen and set the course for their home world. His father had taught him everything he knew. He saw that Marchand had programmed the coordinates for the wormhole into the system. The rest of the crew concentrated on their tasks, not missing a single thing. He was more nervous about the trip than anything they may encounter on the home world.

"Weapons?" He asked the artillery specialist.

"Charged and ready."

"Engines?"

"All is a go," the engineering head answered.

He touched the icon for the ship communications intercom.

"All passengers, prepare for departure. Those in support roles strap in. Everyone else, get into the holding pods."

In the holding chamber, Durante watched the other coven members climb into the pods and settle themselves. Tiny tubes squiggled towards them and entered the skin as the hatches closed. The technicians in charge of monitoring them went to each one and set the timers. A shadow fell over him and he turned to see a technician waiting for him to get into the pod nearby. Durante climbed in. A quick glance to his side and he found Erena already in a deep sleep, her warms folded across her abdomen. Trepidation crept in and he wondered if this was the right thing to do. He knew it was too late for that.

The hatch closed, and he felt the pinprick of the tubes sink into his flesh. He began to feel the cold as his body went weak. His eyes had trouble staying open and for a moment he panicked.

"Don't fight," the technician said. His voice muffled through the thick casing. "Breath normal and let the drug take effect."

He did as instructed. Slowly, his body relaxed, and darkness took him.

The technician went over to the commlink and tap the icon for the bridge.

"All passengers are in the sleep pods," he announced to the navigator.

"Good. Strap in and get ready."

Commander Gallic watched the fugitives' ship speed towards space and sneered. He expected as much but still did not like the fact that the Marchand's minions had discovered it. He wanted to keep it a secret for as long as he could. Now, he had to kill time pretending to be amused by the humans while waiting for the second fleet to arrive. With the elders gone, he planned to level the fugitives' homes and kill off every offspring. They were born on Earth with no formal training on merchant affairs, therefore useless to the emperor.

His soldiers and he were asked to move to a new location. They now resided in a multilevel apartment building. He had his own place while the others were four and six to a unit. It was more spacious than the living quarters they had at home and that angered him a little. The emperor was a monster. That only meant he was stronger than them.

Why would I not obey his will?

He could at least treat his soldiers better with more acknowledgement of their work.

A sudden dread came over him as he realized what he was thinking. He wondered if it was the effects of being on Earth.

"What would you like to do, commander?" One of his soldiers asked.

That brought him out of his thinking. He turned to him and made a playful gesture.

"Fire some rounds at them for good measure to make it look like we care."

"Of course, commander."

The soldier bowed and left the room.

"Incoming!" The second navigator yelled.

Within seconds, the ship shook from a blast dangerously close to the thrusters. It was already past the clouds and heading into the stratosphere. The pilot had not engaged them since there was no need until the ship entered space. The view screen activated to show the commander's soldiers taking pursuit.

"Speed up," the head navigator ordered. "The faster we get to the wormhole, the less likely they are to follow."

Four enemy ships flanked the sides and their weapons turned on the fleeing ship. Right as they fired, the pilot maneuvered the ship into a straight drop, causing the enemy to hit their own. They went spiraling down to the planet floor while the pilot brought the ship back up and increased speed. More enemy ships were coming up behind them. He saw their weapons glow with anticipation to fire and made a decision.

"Fire the thrusters."

"Now?" The navigator cried out.

"You have a better idea?"

"It would send us through the wormhole ahead of schedule. The shields aren't at one hundred percent yet."

"By the time we reach it, they will be. Do it!"

The navigator let out a sigh and punched the commlink for the engine bay.

"Engage thrusters."

"What? Now?"

"You want to get shot down before we even get off the planet?"

"Engaging thrusters."

The ship lurched hard before it shot forward into the outer ring of Earth space. It kept going at high speed as the crew scrambled to secure themselves. The wormhole loomed closer and its mouth sat gaped open ready to swallow them whole. When the ship reached its edge, the enemy ships backed off, letting them soar through.

Darkness folded over the ship then a multicolor light show played before it. At a steady speed, it coasted along, the crew in a state of limbo. Finally, it ended, and the ship arrived in a new solar system. The thrusters shut down and the ship crawled to a snail pace. On the bridge, the crew came out of their stupor and rushed to set things back on course.

"Where are we?" One of the crew asked.

"First check point," the navigator answered. "From here, we can set a normal rate of travel." He looked up at the viewscreen and surveyed the planets ahead. "Let's used that closest planet's gravitation pull as a sling shot."

"Passenger vitals?" The ship's corman inquired.

"All green. No damage inside the ship. Only a few dings in the hull." The engineer replied.

"Setting course for the first jump." The navigator began working the console.

"I'm not ready," a crewmember said. The others looked over at him in awe. "I mean, I've never been in space before. This is mind numbing to me and now we're talking about jumping." He took a glance around at everyone staring at him. "Okay, let's do it before I flip out."

"Youngsters," the pilot muttered. "Let's head out."

The navigator nodded and initiated the next course. This time, the ship's launch sent them all pinned back in their seats as the G force pushed down on their bodies.

With a wink, the ship became a spec of light and disappeared into the void.

On the last jump, the ship arrived in their home world's solar system. A bright sun loomed near one side, shining bright on three of the planets but barely reaching the other four. The second of the four was their home world. A grey orb of dark clouds and scattered land mass. Even from their distance, the crew could see an array of different ships hovering around it. Most of them displayed the royal insignia, seeming to patrol the area.

It would take another three months to reach the planet so the pilot set the cruise control and touched the ship's communication icon.

"Wake them up. We're here."

Technicians flooded the sleep chambers and activated the wake sequence on each pod. Random beeps filled the air followed by the hiss of exhaust releasing. One by one, the passengers were roused, their movements unstable at first.

Sapienti slowly rolled over and let his feet flop to the floor.

"How long?" His voice was harsh and raspy.

"Only about three years. We're going to take our time now. A few months to go."

Sapienti nodded. He slid out of the pod and used its edge to hold himself up. A loud retching made him look its way and he found his son on hands and knees vomiting on the floor. His guardian was by his side not the least bit nauseous. Chase was not looking too swift either, his skin paler than normal and slightly green. His guardian was not fazed by the journey.

Further down, he spotted Durante helping Erena

out of her pod. They both ran their hands across their own skin to check for any differences and walked over to him.

"Been a long time since we traveled, hasn't it?" Erena smirked.

"It's an adjustment." He nodded upwards. "The children don't seem to be faring so well, though."

Grieger strode up to them, and let out a hearty laugh.

"Come! This was your idea, young ones. Show more spunk!"

"Don't make fun of them," Erena chided. "They're doing better than I hoped."

Another offspring spewed vomit on the floor."

"Or not," Durante said.

The mess flowed towards them and they side-stepped out of its line of trajectory. A technician went over to the boy and stuck a needle in him while he was still hunched over.

"Anti-nausea medicine," he explained.

"Of course." Sapienti got his balance and headed to the living quarters.

Everyone else who was able to do so, followed suit. Sleeping in a bed sounded way more relaxing than deep sleep in a pod.

Durante woke up startled, bolting upright from the plush bedding. His vision was blurry. He waited until it adjusted to the dark before checking the timer. Over ten hours had passed, and he gasped in shock. The last time he had slept so long was after the battle on Earth.

Beside him, Erena stirred awake. Her hair had come undone and splayed across the pillows. He ran his fingers through it, letting the strands wrap around like coils.

"Uhn." Her face scrunched up and she rolled over.

"Time to get up. We need to walk around and get circulation going."

"Warm," she whispered.

Her body moved closer to his until they touched, her backside flush against his hip. He leaned over her and said softly.

"Don't tempt me Erena. I won't stop even if you beg."

She turned to him and they stared at each other for what seemed like minutes. The chamber door slid open and Sapienti stood in the frame.

"Really? Can you not control yourself, Tavelo?"

He reared up, offended.

"I was not the one seducing the other!"

"Is that so?" Sapienti caught the sly look on Erena's face as did he. "A stroll, perhaps?"

"My suggestion as well."

Durante threw the covers off and stepped down onto the floor, stark naked. He didn't notice the shocked, yet leering, stare of Erena or the exasperation on Sapienti' face. With slow ease, he dressed back in his robes and turned to Erena still in bed.

"Why are you still there? Let's not keep Count Sapienti waiting," he emphasized his title.

Erena raised a limp wristed hand to cover her mouth as she slid out, still in her dressing robe. She gave Sapienti a strange look before going over to the storage bin to fetch her robes.

"You always lacked a sense of shame, Tavelo," Sapienti said.

"What am I to be ashamed of, exactly?"

Durante asked, perplexed.

"Not a thing. Nothing at all," Erena sang out in a low voice.

When she too was dressed, Sapienti turned towards the corridor.

"Shall we, then?"

The trio made their way deep into the ship to the atrium. Other passengers were already walking along the pathways that circled tree lined sections. The view panels had been opened so they could see the stars rushing past. Marchand had installed mini ecosystems to mimic a park with small gardens scattered about. If they didn't know any better, they would never have known they were on a space ship. Chatter was kept to a minimum as many of the offspring stared mesmerized by the scenery.

"Who would have thought," Sapienti said with a smile.

His eyebrow raised a bit as he glanced around the large room.

"What?"

Durante asked, almost dreading the answer.

"Vampires in Space."

Erena sputtered and clamp a hand over her mouth. From a few feet away, Grieger let out a roaring laugh, his body bending over from the outburst. Durante's lips pursed into a thin line as he gave Sapienti a disapproving look.

The bridge was alive with every crew member rushing around in preparation for landing. Their home world was right in front of them and anxiety began to set in. Royal patrol units were everywhere.

They had already seen another ship attacked then boarded.

"Approaching the planet," the navigator called out.

The three counts and Queen Erena stood at the center of the bridge, wide eyed in nostalgia at being back home after so many centuries.

"What are we hoping for, here," the pilot asked.

Sapienti shook his head and broke the moment.

"That someone will recognize this ship's call sign and willing to sneak us in under the radar. Or, at the very least, as a client ship." The others averted their eyes.

"And you think the royal soldiers won't intercept?"

"Why would they?" Sapienti frowned.

"I am only stating a possible scenario," the pilot said.

"We're being summoned," the communications officer interrupted. "Sending the call sign now."

They all waited patiently, yet nervous about what the outcome might be. After some time passed, Grieger became irate.

"What's going on? There should be a communicae by now with a slip designation for us to land!"

"Wait!" The communications officer raised a hand, signaling silence. "There is a transmission coming through on a private channel. Encrypted." He concentrated on the message and then hit an open channel. "Receiving. Please go ahead. This channel is now secure."

"Are you really the merchants' children?" The male voice sounded full of relief and fear.

"There are four of us," Sapienti replied. "Endaga, Dakien, Jaubro and myself, Callesi."

"As much as I weep in joy for your return, I also

fear for your lives. It has become much worse than you could imagine. I can get you to the surface in one of the client docks. But, please," his voice quivered. "I beg you to find safety. Even if it means fleeing from this place once more."

"We thank you for your concern. And your assistance. We will take your words to heart."

The communication ended, and the officer turned to them.

"What's the plan now?"

"The same as before," Grieger replied loudly. "We go down there and try to free our people from that monster!"

With that said, the pilot sat down in his seat and gave the order.

"Prepare for landing!"

A beam of light showered the ship and a symbol was blazed across its bow. It guided them down to the designated dock area. The ship broke through the clouds and on the other side was the central hub. Client ships hovered over the dock slips, not landing. Their shipments were being sent down via automated loaders. As they passed one of them, they saw armed guards on the ramps blocking the royal soldiers from coming anywhere near the loading areas.

"Looks like the clients decided to hire their own security units," Grieger said.

He leaned forward against the side viewer and looked down at the docks themselves. They were in shambles. Sections were missing, the tell-tale signs of a deadly battle while other areas seemed intact, almost pristine. From a distance he could see how haggard the workers were. They toiled endlessly under the scrutiny of the royal soldiers pacing back and forth around them. There was the anticipation of waiting for one of them to slip up.

Grieger's anger had risen.

Their ship settled in the locking arms and was clamped down. A large group of workers immediately gravitated to it, blocking the view of the ramp as it opened. Erena stepped down onto the docks and nearly swooned from her first breath of the planet's air. The scent of blood, metal and sea wafted in her nostrils. General Tervan came by her side and caught her before she fell. Durante and the other counts followed directly behind.

A gaunt man with ragged clothes came up to them and bowed at Grieger. In an almost low howl of a voice, he spoke.

"Dear cousin, it is good to see you."

At first, Grieger seemed confused. Then, he looked into the man's eyes so similar to his own and nearly gasped in horror. He drew back. The man's face saddened. Grieger reached for him and they embraced each other tight. Tears of rage and sorrow filled Grieger's eyes and he squeezed them shut, not bearing to let anyone else see.

Durante stepped away, not sure what to do. Tervan came around them and went to talk with some of the other workers. He kept a keen eye on the royal soldiers, assessing their strengths and weaknesses. The workers were glad to help.

Another man came up to them and they assumed him to be another worker, his appearance just as worn down and haggard as the rest. When he spoke, they knew it was the one who sent them the encrypted channel. Sapienti recognized him almost immediately.

"You were one of my family's clients," he said.

"Yes, I was."

The man's expression was one of despair.

"Why are you here working transport for the docks?"

"I am stuck here. The royal council confiscated all my cargo and impounded my ship. All of my crew were either imprisoned or murdered."

"Why? What madness is this?"

"I refused to work with the representatives the royal court sent. They were not going to give me fair trade compensation and implemented restrictions on who and where I could sell."

"I still don't understand," Sapienti said.

"They stripped me of my client status."

All four former merchants went slack jawed. To do such a thing would cause a rift in trade, yet they saw it still in place. They collectively figured out they were missing some key element in all of this. Durante leaned closer to them but only spoke telepathically.

"I think we should tread very carefully."

"That was the plan in the first place," Grieger snapped at him.

"What we need," Tervan interjected, *"Are a few brave souls to get us information."*

Erena rubbed her bottom lip, a scowl on her face, as she thought about something sinister. Her eyes lit up in a shade of ice and she smiled.

"I know how."

They all turned to her, questioning.

Ruling Monster

Erena gave herself praise for remembering how her mother set up secret rendezvous around the city and nearby prefectures. If they were as viable then, chances were good that they still remained in place. It had taken weeks to establish enough trust to get the information they needed. Now it was time to implement their plan. To avoid suspicion, only a small group debarked the ship. She was nervous as they passed by a unit of royal soldiers who gave them a once over before returning to their vulgar jokes about the dock workers. Her blood rushed through her veins in anger and she could feel her body heat up.

Stay calm, she chided herself.

Beside her, Durante appeared to be doing the same. The group made their way silently across the boardwalk amidst the sounds of man and machine working in desperation. When they arrived on the pavement of the district streets, Erena let out a sigh of relief. She turned to Sapienti and Grieger.

"This is where we part ways. You memorized the locations?"

"Who do you take us for?" Grieger huffed.

"Let's hurry," Durante said.

Each elder took five others with them.

Her entourage was two of her coven children, two from the general's unit and one of Celeste's young sons. She eyed the lone young man and felt something off kilter about him. If memory served, she was sure his name was Caden. He turned his gaze on her and she flinched away. Durante had their son, the general, and two of his soldiers along with two from his own coven. They all waited until reaching the end of the town before dispersing in different directions.

Royal soldiers were scattered about everywhere they went except the alleyways. Erena assumed they had learned their lesson from centuries ago. As she thought, the alleyways were being watched over by disgruntled citizens daring them to engage. A band of six descended before them and blocked her groups advance. The band of rogues wore dark cloaks that hid their features.

"What business brings you this way," the apparent leader asked. "No one comes here unless they are fools or seeking refuge." The leader's head moved up and down. "You do not appear to need refuge."

Talons protruded from the sleeves their robes.

Erena removed her own hood and motioned for her group to do the same. Her eyes glowed silver and she stepped closer to the rogues.

"I am Eterenia Jaubro. If you think you can take me," she showed her fangs and hissed. "Then I will oblige your request for combat."

The rogues seemed to hesitate. Their leader stepped back. A man flash jumped his way across the rooftops and landed by the leader. He whispered in his ear. The talons retracted, and the hoods came off.

"What madness! Have you come to seal your fate?" The leader cried out, albeit within earshot. "The emperor is still waiting to severe your heads."

"I came to help and get back our planet," she retorted.

The bandits let out communal gasps.

"A revolution?" The leader asked incredulously.

"Do you plan to live in the shadows of fear for the rest of eternity? So, our people deserve such a life?"

"It's not that simple!"

"Where are the hideouts? I will plead my case with the others then."

The leader clenched his fists. She could tell he was contemplating if he should. He finally lifted his head and gave her a stern stare. Without saying a word, he turned and headed farther down the alleyway. Erena and her entourage followed. His small band of rogues were close by acting as lookouts.

They went deep down into the underbelly of the city via secret passageways built into corners behind buildings. For nearly an hour, they trekked through the wet darkness of tunnels and sewer systems until they came upon a stone door at the end beneath a storage hold. Its doors were pried open by two of the bandits.

On the other side was a long corridor. Light flickered where it ended. As they rounded the corner and into the light, Erena was gifted the sight of merchants hunkered down over a large table arguing about trade. They stopped mid conflict and all eyes landed on Erena's group.

"What is the meaning of this?" The first man asked the bandit leader.

He moved to accost him but was held back by his colleague next to him. Another man standing opposite leaned back and stared in shock at Erena. He was much older than the others and thus knew exactly who she was.

"Eterenia Jaubro!" He said.

Everyone else in the room went still. She scanned their faces and began to recognize a handful of them. The bandit leader moved forward.

"She has come to ask that you meet your doom against the emperor."

The merchants gave him a disapproving glance and he scuttled back behind Erena's entourage.

"Is that true?" The older man asked.

"I wish to set a wrong, right," Erena answered.

"You are going to go up against the emperor with an army of citizens?"

"We outnumber the royal troops by an overwhelming twenty to one."

"Yes, but we are not as combat savvy as the royal soldiers."

"No, but I have brought others who are."

"I only saw maybe twenty of you clumped together in the town square earlier," one of the bandits said.

Erena looked back at him and smirked.

"Did you really think I would unload a crew of nearly one thousand for all to see?"

"You are very much like your mother," the older man said softly.

Erena met his gaze and she saw the sorrow. There was no denying the emperor murdered every merchant on the downed ship. She also knew he probably displayed their heads along the royal road as a reminder to the citizens how much of a monster he truly was.

"How many of you have returned?"

"Only four," Erena replied. "We have established a life on a different planet and the others had to stay and defend it."

"What volatile planet did you end up on? Defend it? From what?" another merchant asked.

"The emperor's royal fleet."

Silence engulfed the chamber.

From the moment Durante and his group headed towards the building that housed merchants in hiding, he felt the tail. His son shook his head slowly as a signal to not engage. They both wanted to see what the spy would do. He hoped Erena did not run into any trouble since it was clear the royal soldiers were indeed suspicious of the group when they left the boardwalk. It had taken nearly two hours to get to the first check point where a couple led them to the hideout. Standing in front of the doors, Durante had misgivings about letting the enemy know their location.

"This way, please," the woman said.

She knocked on the door in a secret code and they opened tentatively. A young man's face peeked out from around the frame. When he saw her and the other man, he motioned them inside. As the last person entered the building, Durante looked up to see the spy leap up and disappear on the other side of a rooftop. He let the servant shut the door behind him and proceeded in with the rest of his group.

Inside the building was a large meeting room located on the lowest level. The stones wept from condensation while dim light reflected off their sheen. A fire pit consumed of roaring flames sat at the edge of the room, making the place humid.

Merchants, workers and servants billowed around in a frenzy getting illegal shipments in order. One woman stood out from the rest. Her tired eyes and thin arms, despite their strength were part of what made her so unique. She looked like his mother.

The woman wiped her brow with the back of her forearm and looked over at his group. Her motion stopped, the arm dropped limp to her side. A flash of electricity passed her eyes and without warning, she ran to him. He had no time to prepare as her body slammed into his. Her thin arms wrapped around his waist and he felt tears soak his shoulder. He returned the gesture by holding her to him. A quick glance at her face let him know how much time had passed.

"You're alive," she cried.

She let him go and pushed herself away to get a good look at him. Wiping her face with the palm of her hand, she nodded in approval.

"For now, yes. By the way you are all moving, you can guess why we have come."

"We? Who else has come with you?"

"Lady Eterenia, young Callesi and Dakien."

His aunt held a fist to her chest and again nodded.

"Is that all?"

His son came forward and placed a hand on his sholder.

"What the woman means is what forces have you brought." He locked eyes with Durante's aunt. A silent battle of will ensued. "There are nearly a thousand of us. Most of them soldiers from my personal army."

"Are they strong?" She asked condescendingly.

"We shall see, won't we?"

"Enough."

Durante looked up and listened.

"We don't have much time. You have a spy and he has left to bring reinforcements."

"Who? Tell us the name!" A merchant yelled.

"I do not know his name." Durante described the man and nearly everyone in the room frowned. "I guess he was not trustworthy to begin with?"

The people began to move faster.

"Get the shipments to the alternate rendezvous points and head to the docks. We'll just be ahead of schedule which should throw them off momentarily." The man in charge turned to Durante. "How many of us do you need?"

"None," Tervan answered. "If anyone is to be caught, it will be us. We want to meet the emperor at some point anyway."

"He'll kill you all first."

"I don't think so. He has a bone to pick before that." Tervan waved the people off. "Go. We will get word to you soon."

Not ten minutes after the room was cleared of everyone except Durante's group did the doors burst open to reveal a unit of royal soldiers. The leader was nearly seven feet tall with a swaggering gait and red eyes full of bloodlust. He stopped his walk as he got to the threshold and stared down at Durante. Saliva dripped from his fangs.

"Fugitives returning on their own. The emperor will be pleased. You will come!"

The leader reached out and wrapped taloned fingers around Durante's neck, lifting him from the floor. A large stone hit the behemoth in the side of the head, forcing him to drop Durante. When the leader turned to the culprit, he was sidewinded by a merchant who had ran in behind him.

To his right, Durante saw some of the workers and merchants had indeed stayed behind to fight. Two men grabbed the spy while he sat on a rooftop watching the show. In rapid cruelty, they tore his limbs from his body, not giving him the option to scream or beg for his life.

This is not what he wanted and began to think of a way to save them without getting himself killed in the process. He watched his son cut down a royal soldier with ease and grace, terrifying him. Another enemy advanced and he maneuvered downward, catching the man under the neck. He extended his claws as they touched skin and stopped shy of his brain.

"Stop!" he yelled. A momentary break in fighting lowered the din. "We will comply. But you will not harm these people."

"You do not make demands!" The leader said while his hand continued to crush a young girl's windpipe.

"Oh? The emperor is fine with you bringing us in as corpses, stripping him of his glory?" Tervan chided with him.

The leader dropped the half dead girl and came to stand over Tervan. His son did not back down an inch. They stood exchanging the same air space until the leader smiled wide and leaned back up.

"You are quite cunning." He walked backwards to the busted doors. "Leave the rodents. Take the emperor's prize." He turned around and his vision came upon a pile of body parts that was once the spy. The leader sneered in anger.

"He was justly rewarded," Tervan said.

The leader roared as he stomped to the transport ship. His soldiers abandoned their opponents and surrounded Durante's group. Before he could say anything, they attacked with such brute force that he didn't have time to defend himself. A blow to the head sent him into a dark place.

Rough shaking roused the prisoners inside the transport. Sapienti used one arm as leverage while he tried to get in a position to sit up. He took account of where he was and grimaced. A sharp pain invaded his head and he placed a hand on the small knot near his temple. From the tiny port window he saw why the transport shook so hard. The operator was a lousy pilot, not able to make smooth turns or stay in a straight line. He caught a glimpse of the guards seated on the benches above them with mouths set thin from clenched jaws.

Next to him was Durante, out cold. Dried blood ran the side of his face stemming from a head wound. His son was sitting quietly, watching over him like a warrior. No one else dared to move. A guard happened to look down and saw Sapienti was up and pushed him back down with a booted leg.

"Trash should never rise above my feet," the guard yelled.

He looked over at Tervan and made a motion to get up. Something in Durante son's eyes deterred him and he settled back on the bench. For the first time, Sapienti was glad to have the general in their midst.

The transport docked, and the hatch opened to let in the grey gloom of morning. Ahead lay the palace in all its splendid glory. Sleek silver metal reached towards the stars, accessorized with bright jewels on each level. None could mistake the riches of the royal houses.

Yet, it all seemed false somehow.

The splendor had faded. All twenty prisoners were shoved out onto the smooth tiled road that led to the entrance. Along the walkway were twenty feet tall spikes caked with centuries of dried blood and brain matter. All of them were empty. Workers had climbed atop them for a good scrubbing in preparation for new trophies. They eyed the prisoners with pity.

Sapienti cursed himself for letting Chase and his son's guardian accompany him. Where Chase was constantly trying to see his surroundings, Demitri was disturbingly quiet, making a mental map of everything around him. He hoped that would come in handy when they manage to escape.

They walked in an orderly fashion down the long road, empty of worshippers for now. He was certain it would be filled with an unwilling crowd of spectators within the coming days. Signs of battle were noticeable around the area and he wondered if it was from a rebellion of citizens or soldiers. Many of the previous emperor's soldiers were kept because if not, the army would be greatly depleted. The palace entrance began to swing open. Its heavy, metal door nearly two hundred feet high whirred in protest at being pried apart against its own weight.

The entire parade of soldiers and prisoners made the nearly one hour long trek through the halls and upwards to the throne room. It was a massive chamber littered with treasures from other planets piled in heaps along the walls. Lush fabric, worn with age, lined the walkway all the way up to the foot of the throne where the emperor sat at ground level. Lights of shimmery gold illuminated him. Which did nothing to soften his aesthetic.

Emperor Manel sat in a relaxed position, one leg crossed over the other, his head resting on the hand of an arm propped up by the elbow. Blood red eyes, absent of white, bore into them. His long lashes fluttered as he seemed to twitch in a personal struggle. Dark blonde hair trimmed short to the nape of his neck had the look of not being washed in a while.

"You have returned for the punishment you deserve."

His voice was calm, almost soothing, apart from the malice that dripped within. The soldiers pushed the prisoners further in. He surveyed them, and his face turned ugly.

"Where are the other merchants?" He demanded.

"On our new home," Sapienti answered.

The emperor's stare moved to him and his expression grew worse.

"You dare address me as some sort of leader for your associates? Only the Jaubro family has that right."

"Then we have come to negotiate."

Erena stepped forward to stand next to Sapienti. Durante and Grieger flanked them as an act of protection. The emperor's gaze fell on her like a blanket of filth and she appeared to force her body not to stagger back.

"Your mother tried suggesting the same thing. You know what I did to her?" His eyes gleamed like fresh red meat at room temperature. "We impaled your father to the ground and made him watch as my soldiers defiled her in the very space where you stand." Erena held fast but her composure was crumbling. "I had her decapitated mid screams. That didn't stop the last few from getting their fill."

Some of the group, already looking green from nervousness and the depictions, finally gave in and spewed hot vomit on the pristine carpet. The emperor smiled in delight.

"I ripped your father's tongue out, so he couldn't even cry out for his beloved."

"Why?" Erena whispered. "Why have you done this?"

"Why?" The emperor yelled as he sat up, gripping the arm rests of his throne. "All she had to do was submit to me and I would have spared her family. But no, she stuck to her irrational sense of pride and loyalty!"

"Which you apparently know nothing about," Chase Ambrook spouted.

The others looked at him as if he had gone mad. His face was contorted in a rage none of them had seen before. The emperor, shocked at first, peered at him more closely and grinned.

"Ah, yes. The Strana merchants. I removed their entrails and hung them to dry. The heads were destroyed since they were useless to me."

Chase moved and Demitri held him back with brute force. The general's fingers moved like he was playing an instrument, his weapon in the hands of one of the soldiers behind them. The emperor rose from his seat and Sapienti felt the soldiers move farther back. He came upon Erena in flash. His fingers lifted her chin up so that they were eye to eye.

"You want to negotiate? Then fulfill your mother's duty to me as your emperor."

"And, what? You let us go?" Chase asked.

The emperor's eyes never left Erena's.

"I will kill all of you except ten of her choosing."

He laid his sight on Durante. "And you will make a great pet for my enjoyment."

Erena wrenched from his grasp and Durante stepped in front of her. Sapienti felt dread. In seconds, the royal soldiers were upon them. General Tervan barreled through the first group as he caught sight of his sword and rammed into the soldier who had it in their possession. He swiftly retrieved it, using it to sever the soldier's arm. As the soldier howled in pain, the general cut the noise short with a swing of his sword across his neck. The head rolled to the side.

Chase punched his talons into the belly of a soldier while he slashed another in the midriff, cutting deep. Demitri had a steady hand as he too got hold of his weapon and ran through two soldiers who came at him. Erena turned to the quiet Caden and her eyes went wide. Sapienti snuck a glance as he tried to break free from a soldier's choke hold and saw it too. Eyes red as the emperor's locked on the ruler and his body began to distort.

"No!" Erena cried out.

The emperor saw as well. With a sweep of his hand, we knocked the first wave of royal soldiers back away from the throne area. The fighting ended abruptly.

"I did not order you to take action!" The soldiers still standing halted in terror. "Take them to the dungeons. You," he pointed to Erena. "Will stay here in the main palace."

General Tervan went into a defense stance next to her. Both men stared at each other, communicating in pure animal code.

"The merchant leaders will accompany her." He turned his attention to the soldiers. A new kind of ugliness covered his face. "Get this filth out of my sight!" His voice boomed like a megaphone as he pointed towards the dead and bleeding soldiers around him. "I will kill anyone left if it is not done in the next half hour."

His red orbs moved rapidly back and forth, making sure to convey his will on all of them.

Sapienti finally had the answer to two things at once and so did the other leaders. Young Caden was a Kataling.

And so was the emperor.

The coven elders, along with Chase, Demitri, Tervan and Celeste's son, were escorted to a bed chamber that could easily hold fifty people. Durante knew it had to be an orgy room. He nearly gagged at the thought of the emperor doing as he pleased to a room full of captives who were undoubtedly drugged to minimize pain and screaming. There were signs of it all around them but only if they looked closely. Erena must have come to the same conclusion as she lingered near a cushioned seat debating if she wanted sit or not.

"It smells like," Chase began to say. He held his tongue instead.

"Exactly what it smells like," Grieger added.

"Why put us in here?"

"Really, Ambrook?" Tervan asked.

Chase went flush, knowing the answer.

"Now what?" Demitri asked.

He sat down on a seemingly clean lounge chaise, keeeping his hands on his thighs.

"We try to reason with that monster," Grieger replied.

"He could have killed everyone in that room," Tervan said bluntly.

They all contemplated that. Durante frowned at its truth. He was not willing to die yet but he was also not going to let Erena or himself become playthings for the emperor. After a while he settled down on the edge of the massive sized bed and thought about their options.

Having never been inside the palace before, he needed to find a way to get a rough layout. The direction the others were ushered towards the dungeons told him there was a secret way because the corridor had no doors. Finding out where was the key.

As if reading his mind, Demitri came up to him and sat down. Tervan did the same on the other side of him.

"I watched from the moment we landed at the palace road," Demitri said.

"And what have you assessed?"

"Not only is it beyond huge in size, it is also sparsely manned. It seems many of the royal soldiers do not wish to be here."

"Hence, the mass groups around the city and docks." Tervan said.

"So, we find a sympathetic ear in one of the soldiers," Chase interjected.

"For what reason?" Sapienti asked.

"To let some of our group go and warn the others. If we can get the upper hand with a surprise attack, that monster may bend enough to hear reason," Chase replied.

Durante was taken aback by Chase's brilliant deduction. So many times, the boy seemed too self-absorbed to do anything meaningful and then pulls off something like that. He saw it in the last battle on Earth. His son gazed upon the Ambrook child with a new light as well.

"Well, there's a nice plan. How do we find one of these lost souls?" Grieger asked.

"I know a few," Demitri answered.

"How?"

He turned to the count and gave a tiny sinister smile.

"I observe."

Durante felt a tug of creepiness from the guardian. He hadn't quite gotten familiar with the young man, but he knew enough of his history to be wary. Not much for being on the offensive, he would defend his own life by any means necessary. He wondered if the guardian was indeed an ally.

Naïve Children

The twins knew something was amiss when they watched the small group of soldiers move around the different parties as they headed into the city. What alarmed Odette was a few of the citizens talking to the soldiers while sneakily gesturing towards them. She decided to go out and stroll the docks to get some information and nip the traitors in the bud. Traitors. Were they really? This was their planet. At the same time, the emperor was in the wrong. What did that say about those continuing their loyalty to a psycho. Her brother arched an eyebrow at her as she thought those things.

"Suggestions, my sister?"

"I'm sure you have a few yourself."

"Oh, I figured out who the rogue workers are snitching out our people."

"Are you going to deal with them?"

"Of course." He smiled wide. "Discreetly."

She turned towards the rest of the coven passengers in the atrium.

"We need to find a way to infiltrate the palace with

a minimum force. Say, two hundred of us. Getting ahead of an execution announcement would be ideal."

"Volunteers?" Olivier asked sweetly.

Nearly twice that many raised their hands and the twins were elated. It was going to go better than they planned. They decided to pick the total by lottery and from there, go out in sections to find the culprits. In the meantime, taking out the soldiers would be a priority. Not kill them, necessarily, but keep them locked away somewhere out of their hair.

"Where can we put them?" One of the coven children asked.

"Can we scan the area for a decent location?" Odette asked the communications officer. "A place close enough to reach but far enough away to not be obvious."

"Hmm. I will see what I can come up with. Meet me on the bridge in a few hours."

He left the atrium and the twins gave each other a nod. They donned their hoods and led a group of fifty out onto the docks to deal with the spies.

A merchant scanning his shipment for processing was interrupted by a group of four who came onto his slip. He turned to greet them and immediately seemed shocked. He got close to them and began to whisper.

"You shouldn't be out and about. There are spies here."

"We know. That's why we have come. To get rid of them."

The merchant looked around without moving and brought his attention back to them.

"They are protected by the emperor. In exchange

for letting him have their mates and only killing off half their families, they get free reign and first choice on the docks."

That disgusted Odette. She had heard some of the stories from the past and would rather die than submit to such a thing.

"And do the mates get returned?"

"If you call it that. Most of them are unreachable mentally, the money made used for their care. The others kill themselves either before or after being released. No one wins."

"That can be remedied," she said.

The merchant gave her a nod towards another merchant and backed away.

"Sorry, my lady, but this shipment is accounted for. Maybe the merchant two slips down has something you can negotiate for."

He went back to his shipment and Odette gestured for her group to follow as she headed that way. She was well aware of the other merchant keeping safe distance behind them. A ball of rage formed in the pit of her stomach and she calmed herself. This was not the right time. He had to be lured with finesse and she knew he had workers doing most of his dirty deeds.

Food came to the large chamber hours later and the elders looked at it then each other to see who would test it first. None of them trusted the emperor to not have it laced with drugs. The soldiers who brought it in saw their expression and themselves became insulted.

"We do not feed prisoners tainted food!" The first of them snapped. "Eat and be energized!"

He motioned for the others to finish up and leave.

"What kind of contradiction is this?" Chase asked. "Either hate us enough to kill or let us go. I don't understand their logic."

"As I said," Demitri added. "They are in the middle of a bad situation. Loyalty to their emperor and a duty to protect the citizens."

"The safety of citizens should come before the emperor!" Grieger said.

"Stop arguing!" Erena sat down at the table where the food was placed and plucked a chunk of meat from it. "I'm starving and have no energy to think clearly right now."

Reluctantly, the others came to sit with her and began to devour the food, not caring if it was tainted or not. When the platters were nearly empty, they slowed down their consumption and settled back in the chairs.

"This meat is somewhat fresh," Sapienti stated.

"When you demand dominion over a shipment, that can happen."

"I wonder how many citizens had access to it."

"Probably close to nil." Tervan shoved a piece of bread in his mouth and chewed before speaking again. "Did you not see how gaunt and under nourished many of the dock workers were?"

"They were insulted," Demitri spoke. The group looked over at him in confusion. "The soldiers. It's better than originally planned."

"Yes," Grieger said. "They were not too pleased with our response."

"Then we make our move when they come and collect?" Chase asked.

Tervan shook his head.

"Too soon."

"What if the emperor decides to make his move before we do?"

"I believe," Tervan said. "He is thinking of how to get what he wants without stirring up more dissent amongst the citizens. You could cut the tension with a blade."

"I agree," Durante added. "We may be here for months." He glanced over at Erena. "He is surely going to try and persuade, if not forcibly take, you."

Erena's face scrunched up in anger and the small fruit in her hand squished out between her fingers as her grip tightened.

"I would never let that happen," Tervan said calmly.

"And how would you stop it?" Durante yelled.

"I would kill her first before he had his way."

Stunned silence followed. The look on his face let them know he was serious.

On the third week of captivity, Erena was informed by an armed group of guards that she had been summoned by the emperor. The others protested, ready to fight. She signaled them to cease. There was no reason for more bloodshed and she felt being alone with the emperor could give her time to sway him into reason. As she entered the throne room and saw the look in his eyes, her confidence wavered. The guards moved back to the far edges of the room.

Emperor Malen sat with one leg crossed over the other, his fingers tapping on his knees.

"Eterenia." He uncrossed his legs and leaned forward, sniffing hard at the air before her. "You are ripe for conception. Just like your mother."

Erena went pale. She moved away from him. He was on her in a flash, pinning her down to the floor. His overly gorged eyes bore into hers. She began to fight with all her being, having no effect as he brought her up more than once and slammed her back to the floor. She managed to turn over on her stomach, kicking and squirming her way from underneath him. To her surprise, he grabbed hold of her ankle and swung her into the nearest wall. She fell in a heap, her head going numb as her vision went. He dragged her to the middle of the room and used one of his talons to rip her robes open in one swipe, exposing her body.

"You will obey me," he seethed in her ear.

She let out a strangled scream, tears streaming down her face. Half morphed, the emperor forced himself into her, causing blood to splatter on her midriff. This time her vocal chords obeyed, and she screamed with every horrifying thrust he delivered. His lips pulled back, showing a row of sharp fangs as drool ran down his chin.

He was enjoying himself.

Covered in blood, the emperor let out a high-pitched shriek and climaxed. His head was thrown back, his eyes fluttering with ecstasy. When he was finished, he looked down on his half-conscious conquest. His oversized member, now limp, slid out and to the side. Not one to let fresh blood go to waste, he began licking it all off her body. His tongue flopped out like a snake and slithered inside her to get the rest.

"You are quite satisfying."

He stood naked, his body streaked with deep scratches from her talons as she fought, and took a few slow breaths. The guards standing in wait at the corners tried to suppress their disgust and horror.

"Take her to my breeding chamber. I will finish her off later."

They reluctantly walked over and picked her up by the arms and legs. As the emperor stayed behind in the throne room, he sat down and began scratching the armrest with his talons. He was not as satisfied as he claimed by any means.

He had scoured the archives about the original species of the planet and knew one of the merchant families held that bloodline. Ancient blood that could be manipulated to create monsters. Since the Jaubros were one of the oldest, he bet on them. A hybrid of Kataling and Volshin had never been accomplished. That was his goal. It would be the ultimate predator and under his control.

He stopped gouging his throne and stood back up to retrieve his tattered clothes. Either way, he would get a birth out of her and depending on what it was, he would decide to keep or eat it. Like the others.

One of the royal scientists came into the room and bowed.

"Are you in need of my services, my lordship?"

"I want you to accelerate the new ones' incubation. No need to draw out the process."

"I thought the Jaubro female was to be yours for special purposes, unlike the other."

"I may change my mind."

"What is the time line you need?"

"Three months."

"That is quite dangerous." The emperor glared at him with hunger. "Of course, that is not an issue. I will get it done."

He bowed as he exited the room in a hurry.

At the first shop on the outskirts of the board-walk, Odette lured the two merchant workers towards the back and waited for them to show up. When they blocked her exit, looming over her with anticipation of entertaining themselves, her group surrounded them. Confused, they turned around and were swiftly beaten unconscious.

The shop owner pulled back a curtain and her workers helped them get the two culprits into a transport they had waiting out in the alleyway. From her view, Odette could see the merchant sitting in his transport at the front of the shop, waiting for his men to come back with a report. She nodded at two of her group and they went around to ambush the man.

They hopped into the pilot seat as he protested. The first closed the hatch and it sped off towards the rendezvous point. Odette followed in theirs. On arrival, both transports were stowed out of sight and their prisoners were hauled unceremoniously into the abandoned building that used to be a thriving busi-ness according to neighbors.

The place had been raided after the family was dragged out and murdered. No one wanted to occu-py it regardless of how much the price was reduced. Eventually, the royal council declared it a ruin.

"You can't do this to me," the merchant cried out. "I am protected."

"We know. And we also know how you became well compensated." Odette leaned over him, her eyes flashing silver. "How did it feel, knowing what you put your wife through for the sake of what? A few shipments you could barter on your own?"

He became angry and writhed around against his captors until he was able to sit up.

"I did what I must to save as many as I could! You have no right to judge me!"

"Oh, but I do. Tell me." She got even closer. "Who do I remind you of?"

He squinted in hate until something caught him off guard. He tried to rear back from her while the two coven men holding him wouldn't budge.

"The moment I saw you, I was reminded of a lower house that always seemed to give the other covens trouble. Not quite loyal but willing to save their own hides at the expense of others." She stood straight. "But even I think they would be ashamed to see what remained of their family like this."

Tears streamed down the man's face as his head flopped down to his chest.

"We can't win. You won't succeed in whatever it is you're trying to do. We have survived almost three centuries this way. He doesn't bother us as much as he used to." He lifted his head up. "You'll ruin everything!" His face contorted in anguish.

Odette looked over at her group members and silently begged for a resolution. Killing him would only bring him salvation from his sins. And there was the problem of his family wanting to retaliate out of some misguided purpose. There were a few of that family's lineage on the ship and she contemplated using them to make a case. One of the merchant's workers had come to and slid a glance over at her.

"You will get us all slaughtered," he said.

"We are here to save this planet and bring back order," she said. "Why do you not want to be free?"

"No one can stop him. He is the worst kind of

monster among monsters."

"He's not invincible. He can still be killed!" Odette retorted.

"How naïve. Child of Bryhel."

He turned his head and settled down on the cold stone floor.

Erena woke screaming after two months of unconsciousness to her body giving premature birth to the emperor's offspring. Blood ran freely, splattering over her and the attendants. Their faces were distraught as they used their hands to retrieve the stubborn creature. A loud shrieking filled the room and Erena felt her entire being start to fade.

"Do not let her die!" One of the attendants yelled.

"Why? The emperor cares not for these females once they give birth. He'll probably eat the child if he doesn't like it."

The first attendant grabbed the other by his shirt while holding on to the crying infant, planting a stain of blood and fluid.

"She is of the Jaubro bloodline. I will not let the emperor destroy our legacy!" The other attendant frowned. "And if you try to stop me, I will strike you down here."

"Fine. As you wish."

He rummaged through a cabinet and pulled out a rolled cloth. Spreading it open, he attached a vile of blue liquid to the injector gun and administered it to Erena. Her body became hot then relaxed, free from pain.

"He's going to kill us all anyway. No use trying to save ourselves anymore," the second attendant muttered. "Are you going to present the child to him?"

"Over my drained corpse!"

"He'll still want it for lunch."

"That's too bad. I won't give him this child."

"You didn't give him the other one either," the attendant muttered.

A week went by before Erena was transported to the giant chamber where the rest of her people were being held. Wrapped tight in her arms was her newborn, sleeping silently. Durante waited until she was set on the round bed in the center and the guards left before going to her.

Laying in a heap on the prisoners' chamber floor was Caden, barely conscious clutching another newborn. In female form, the young one shivered under the heavy covers. The soldiers had brought them in only hours before. No one dared to pry the infant from her clutches. Durante finally caved.

He left Erena's side to get a peek at the child and sat back in shock. Big red eyes gouged with blood, absent of whites stared up at him. Tiny talons tried to rip apart the cloth holding them at bay. There was pain and sadness exuding from him.

His eyes burn in fury.

"That monster. What has he done?"

He stroked the baby's cheek with one finger. It squirmed then gurgled. Bloody spittle oozed from its mouth.

"At least he didn't kill them," Tervan said.

"That's no consolation!"

"What is the purpose of this? Why?" Grieger cried out.

"No idea. One thing is certain," Chase said. "We need to get out of here."

Baltise stared up at the sky listening to the high-pitched call of the Volshins circling the docks. Their cries were hateful and filled with pain. Baltise wanted to avenge them and bring the emperor down for the crimes against his kin. From his distance, he could see they had been in their altered state for weeks, maybe even months. The only way that could happen would be through drugs and torture.

He felt his talons dig into the flesh of his palms and blood drip from the wounds. Hands grabbed hold of his wrists and forced his own open. He looked up at one of the Grieger coven kids and tried to get away from that smiling face.

"Don't hurt yourself. Save that rage for the real fight."

The Grieger kid licked the blood from one hand and Baltise pulled his hand away. He noticed other coven men lusting after him lately whenever Chase was not around. Movement from behind made him turn around and he saw Falson reach over and knock the offender on his ass. His eyes went red. Baltise placed his hands on Falson's chest and pushed him back gently.

"Don't. He's not worth it."

The Grieger kid regained his balance as he got up and gave Falson a nasty glare.

"Chase sharing that one with you now?"

He spit on the ground and backed away.

"Go back to the ship if you can't follow the plan," Falson ordered.

"Whatever."

He walked back to his group already engaged in conversation.

Baltise removed his hands and stood by Falson.

"We might not be able to fix this."

Falson followed his gaze upwards at the Volshins.

"We have to at least try though."

The communicator in their ears beeped and Odette's voice cackled.

"We have a lead on their whereabouts in the palace. It won't be easy."

One of the other coven children leading a group tsked.

"All we have to do is sneak in and get to killing off the guards inside. After that, the emperor is a sitting target." Others resounded in agreement.

"Let's hope you're right." Odette said.

"As long as you don't get in ours or the general's way," one of the general's commanders said.

He adjusted his sword on his hip and marched forward followed by forty-nine of his best fighters.

"I will bring you victory or peace," Batiste declared to the Volshins above.

Mournful screeches were the reply.

Another month inside the palace went by, giving the coven leaders time to figure out a strategy. Extra food was being sent, and everyone took turns forcing Celeste's child to eat. Erena had regained her strength. The rage in her expression as she cradled the infant made Durante steer clear. Her own newborn was not quite healthy but fairing better than the other.

Soldiers came to the chamber entrance.

"The emperor wants you," the first one spat.

"I will not go," Erena replied.

Tervan stepped before her.

"She will not leave this room without me or my father."

"That is not for you to decide."

The soldiers pushed through the room, slamming into Tervan and got hold of Erena. They started to drag her towards the doors and a fight ensued. Within moments, another unit of soldiers came in to break it up.

"What is the meaning of this?" The leader of the second unit demanded.

"They refused to let us take her," one of the soldiers still holding on to Erena's arm said.

"Oh? No matter. The emperor has no qualms about having an audience to his decree."

Scuffed up yet determined to stand their ground, the group let themselves be escorted to the throne room.

The emperor stood at the floor to ceiling windows behind his throne. His red eyes scanned the city below, a disgusted expression on his face. He wore a black robe with gold trim while constantly flicking the tips of his fingers with his thumb as he failed to acknowledge their presence. He happened to see their reflection in the window and turned around to verbally assault them.

"Prosperous! Merchant families turned trash after breeding disloyalty to their emperor should be publicly executed. I am thinking of a banquet during the event. Maybe this time I can feed your remains to the Katalings and Volshins. They get ravenous after I've starved them for weeks on end."

Chase's talons were extending while his eyes went bright red. Tervan pulled him back and whispered something in his ear. Still angry, his eyes not reverting, Chase remained still. Erena's expression crumbled with sadness. The emperor appeared puzzled at their response.

"You feel sorry for them? Beasts only good for battle and cleaning the meat packing cargo holds when emptied."

"You are a Kataling! How could you do that to your own kind?" Erena cried out.

"I," the emperor said through gritted teeth, "am the son of an emperor! I am not one of those things with no thought or ambition!"

Caden, back in male form, was on the verge of rage and the group wasn't sure if they could contain him. The emperor pushed them all out of the way and came to loom over the boy. He picked him up by the neck so their eyes locked.

"So young and stupid. Do you think they accept you as one of them? You are only good for their use as they see fit." He tossed the boy across the room.

And that is when things turned for the worst.

Chase flash stepped towards the emperor as the elders yelled out, "Stop!"

He went flying to the other side of the room, hitting the wall with a loud thud. The soldiers moved to subdue them and were accosted by Sapienti and Grieger turning to engage. Durante went to secure Erena only to be punched in the gut by the emperor. His vision blurred from the intense pain as he felt himself crash to the floor.

The emperor grabbed hold of Erena and slammed her down like a ragdoll. He straddled her, catching her wrists when she went for his neck with her talons. With one hand, he held both her wrist together above her head while the other sliced her robes open to expose her nakedness beneath.

"I told you to submit to me. You will obey."

He slithered one of his talons into her, going deep enough to cause bleeding. Erena screamed. A blur of darkness swept across her vision between them and the emperor hit the base of his throne.

Standing before Erena was the boy Kataling. Not yet fully grown, he was still a mesmerizing sight. Tervan dispatched his opponent and dragged his mother to the doorway. Sapienti picked up Durante and followed suit.

A horrid strangled shriek filled the room, stopping everyone in their tracks. The emperor morphed in seconds and attacked the younger Kataling. Blood flew everywhere as the young one tried in vain to stop the larger from biting into him. Suffering from his wounds, the younger staggered and fell in a heap. The emperor moved in for the finishing blow.

Having seen enough, Grieger scooped up four swords from the downed soldiers nearby and with two in each hand launched them. They struck the emperor squarely in the chest area, knocking him back away from the young Kataling already reverting to human form. He let out another shriek and before he could recover, the group had fled, the bleeding boy tossed over Grieger's shoulder.

They took twists and turns, whoever ended up in the rear making sure to look back in case their pursuers got close. So far, they had avoided killing any of the soldiers. That is not what they came for. As they reached their prison room, seeming to have outran the soldiers, they made a stop to reassess their options. The infants had been left alone with guards who were now missing from their station. Demitri took Caden from Grieger and checked his wounds.

"This is bad. His wounds are deep." He wiped sweat drenched hair from the boy's face. "Fucking monster."

"We need to stop the bleeding, or he'll die." Grieger said.

"Celeste would never forgive us," Sapienti added.

Loud noises echoed from the hall and they tensed up, ready to resume fighting. Count Grieger set the boy behind him and Demitri came to his side. The sound of a hundred boots striking the tiled floor signaled the end for them. At the height of the thunderous noise came the appearance of six coven children out of breath.

"We found you!" The first girl yelled jubilant.

Sapienti's hand failed him and his weapon fell to the floor. Disbelief crossed his face as more coven people crowded in. The birthing attendant pushed forward with a syringe and plunged it deep into Caden's abdomen.

"This should stop him from bleeding out."

"How?" Durante whispered. He was still having a hard time breathing.

"It's a coagulate." He started to explain then saw exasperation on Durante's face.

A young coven boy blushed in embarrassment for the attendant before giving Durante the answer he sought.

"Oh. We had help from some of the soldiers, and this guy." He pointed to the attendant. "I guess they aren't all crazy."

The attendant stepped back from them.

"You have to hurry. His guards will be hunting for you. He has no intentions of letting go of those infants. Whether he keeps them or devours them, he will still claim them as his possessions."

"Devour?" The first coven girl asked in horror.

Erena retrieved her newborn and clutched him tight with shaky arms as her expression paled at the thought.

"What about you?" Grieger asked the attendant.

"I'll probably be dead before the day is done. Not that I won't fight but will surely be outnumbered. It's how they operate. I can at least show you the best escape route."

Tervan glanced over at Demitri. The young warrior had been spot on. Durante took off one of his outer robes and helped the general cover up Erena while Demitri found some fabric lying around to wrap up the boy barely able to hold the infant fter it was place in his arms.

"Let's get out of here," the first girl said. "The soldiers who helped can't keep their comrades at bay for much longer."

The group of twenty formed a tight assembly and moved cautiously through the palace.

Outmatched

Durante and his entourage, along with the birthing attendant, kept watch of their surroundings as they maneuvered around the outer perimeter of the palace. The sky was an angry grey where rain spattered the land. It had already moved away from their area, leaving a misty fog that hovered a few feet from the ground. The air smelled of wet moss, the palace nearly covered in the green mass. It had taken longer than they liked getting out of the palace due to constantly stopping to hide.

With half their numbers unable to fight, engaging the enemy had to be avoided. He had to carry Erena on those occasions when she fell in and out of consciousness. At the stone steps that sprawled down into the outskirts of the city, they all gasped. The emperor had dispatched half his army out into the nearby regions in an attempt to capture his prey. Soldiers swarmed around every corner, harassing passersby and breaking into homes.

"Now what?" Sapienti asked, sounding defeated.

"We keep going," Tervan said.

"The rest of us are waiting at the docks," the coven girl leading the group stated.

"Once you cross the river below, you should be able to move undetected for a while. I wish you good speed," the attendant said.

He attempted to back away. Grieger shoved him forward.

"Get moving. You're coming with us."

"What? I can't..."

"We need more medical personnel. You were going to stay and die? Not on my watch."

The attendant refused to budge. When Tervan, still holding the Kataling boy, pushed him hard enough to send him to his knees, he silently relented. Getting back on his feet, he followed the others down the wet, stone stairs.

At the river, the first to arrive tested its depth. The rain had raised the levels. Not enough to deter them. They all waded through, for some the water coming up to their waists. Tervan raised Caden higher above his chest while letting the boy's feet submerge in the coolness of the water to bring down the fever from his injuries. Only the soft swishing of water was heard in the open field.

Erena handed her infant to Durante and walked on her own. She sighed, feeling the cold water wrap around her and closed her eyes. Thoughts of vengeance ebbed away for a moment. Her body shook but she paid no heed. She knew they would have to fight as soon as they entered the city streets. What they all needed was a blood supply and that was scarce even in the forests of the planet.

"Is there any way for us to replenish?" She asked the attendant walking beside her.

"There is a supply house in the second quandrant."

"What's there?" Durante interjected.

"Containers confiscated from the annual shipment."

The elders stopped, causing the young coven leaders to do so as well.

"Annual shipment of what?" Chase asked.

He watched as the elders' eyes turned red and drool begin to form at the corner of their mouths.

"Twice every three years, we receive a shipment of freshly slaughtered goods from other planets whose blood is compatible to our own. It was distributed evenly among the masses until the emperor decided who would get what and how much," the attendant explained.

"Then that is where we are headed. We need all the strength we can muster," Erena said.

"Yes, well, the second quadrant is still an hour away by foot at a normal pace and the supply house is heavily guarded."

"That's not a problem," Chase said.

Sapienti gave him a strange look and Erena rolled her eyes, understanding the two men's objective. Even Durante had a similar expression creep across his face. She saw the attendant move further away, sensing their murderous intent.

"Lead the way," Chase ordered the attendant.

They entered the second quadrant nearly two hours later, their progression slowed down yet again from lack of energy and the wounded. The supply house sat in the center. A monstrous sized square facility ten stories high spanning half a kilometer on all sides with one way in or out. As the attendant proclaimed, the entrance was surrounded by twenty or more guards.

"Well, we would have been evenly matched," one of the coven boys stated, looking around at their entourage. "I say we're at two to one."

"Which is perfect," Chase added.

Tervan set down Caden and stood before Erena.

"You stay here. When it is all clear, we will signal you. Can you lift him?"

Erena nodded then sat down beside the still sleeping Caden.

"Let's go," Sapienti commanded, pushing the attendant forward. "You said you would fight."

With lightning speed, Tervan converged on the unsuspecting guards near the east side of the cube and cut down three within seconds. Chase got a hold of another right as the guard next to his prey ran to a panel near the entrance and hit it. An alarm echoed all around them and Grieger cursed, knowing it could be heard for miles.

"Make it quick," he yelled. "Reinforcements will be here sooner than we want."

In rapid succession, everyone capable of fighting dispatched the guards outside and proceeded to take out the ones inside. Four guards were already climbing up the sides of the containers.

"Stop them!" Sapienti yelled. "They are locking down the canisters. We won't be able to unlock them in time if they succeed."

"On it!" A group of coven children replied as they leapt up to do his bidding.

The attendant stared up at the first container. There were six of them inside the supply house. Each one was five hundred feet in diameter, laid out two by two. He eyed the one on top. A guard came at him, short blade raised high, ready to puncture his neck. The attendant whirled around and caught him mid swing, snapping his forearm then taking the blade to severe his head. As the guard's body dropped to the floor, he saw Grieger standing on the other side, surprised.

"And here you had us thinking you had no skills in combat."

"I never said that," the attendant replied softly.

He went around to the side of the top container and hit the release button. The dark shield panels unlocked with a clank and they receded to reveal the contents inside. When the top section slid off and folded onto the side, the smell of blood flooded the room. He stared into the sloshing pool of liquid and fleshy chunks.

The last of the guards dealt with, the entourage converged on the container and gazed upon it with awe.

"Oh my god!" The coven girl leader exclaimed.

Chase's eyes nearly bulged out of their sockets. Shuffling sounded behind them. They turned to see Erena coming towards them dragging Caden.

"I said we would signal for you," Tervan said.

The look she gave made him flinch.

"Give him to me," the attendant said.

It took three of them to haul Caden's limp body up. The attendant grabbed hold of his arm then tossed him into the container.

"What are you doing?" One of the coven children cried out.

Before any of the others could say anything, Erena,

Durante, Sapienti, and Grieger jumped in as well.

"Oh," Chase said.

The attendant let out a sigh and followed suit. Within minutes, they were all submerged in the bloody soup.

Erena emerged slowly, her eyes gorged with blood. She let out a soft hiss, exposing her dripping fangs and licked her lips. She swam to the ledge and pulled herself out. The two infants lay docile. She scooped up some of the contents and slowly fed them both. Her infant drank easily, his eyes no longer gorged and now a brilliant blue. The other cried with each dose, his eyes not changing. Erena caressed his head, anger filling her.

The attendant came out and took over the feeding. Next came Durante. She felt a pull of desire seeing him covered in blood, his dark hair plastered against his face, framing it. His blue eyes now red like hers. One by one, the entire entourage climb from the ooze satiated.

Except the Kataling boy.

"Why is he still not out?" Erena asked the attendant. "What's wrong?"

"He probably needs more time."

"We don't have any," one of the coven boys said, pointing to the entrance. On the horizon, they could all see a wave of hover crafts coming their way.

"We are not leaving without him," Erena sneered.

"Is one life worth..." the attendant began, his words stopped short by Tervan wrapping his hand around his neck.

"We are not leaving without him," he reiterated. "What my mother says, goes."

He released him and slid down the side of the container to ground level.

The soldier reinforcements, fifty strong, were about to be met by a group grossly overfed and covered in blood.

On approach of the compound, the imperial commander caught sight of the rebels and sucked air through his teeth. He knew how strong and invincible one felt after feeding from the giant tanks. A closer observation found him calculating the age of his prey. Aside from the merchant offspring, the others were mere children, barely a century old. He snorted, confident in his victory. The hovercrafts landed on the outskirts of the perimeter and his men filed out into formation.

"Split into three groups," he ordered. "Make sure to take out the young ones first."

His soldiers obeyed, converging on the waiting rebels who stood inside the entrance of the supply house.

"Here they come," Sapienti hissed.

His voice came out a drunken slur.

Tervan cocked his head to one side as he watched the soldiers split up. As they grew closer he moved towards the youngsters on the end.

"I see your plan," he chided.

Confused, Chase followed him out of curiosity. He understood moments later.

With loud shrieks and the hard thud of flesh on flesh, both sides collided. Erena's talons grew long as she struck forward with closed fingers. They sliced through the neck of her first assailant, protruding out the other side and into the soldier behind him. She yanked them out, spraying blood up into the air as they retracted. Another soldier came up behind her, his short blade piercing her right shoulder. She saw its tip push out of her chest. Angered, she dropped down to her knees and forced him over her head. When he landed in front of her, she grabbed him by the hair and with a mouth full of fangs, she bit deep into his neck, taking out a large chunk.

The attendant had gathered the two infants and hid in a dark spot of the cube's corner. He could still see the fighting below and prayed none of the soldiers had the inclination to look up. Most of the younger coven children were getting hurt worse than the others due to the number of soldiers engaging them. Chase and Tervan tried their best to shield them while taking out any soldier that got too close.

Durante and Grieger fought side by side against six soldiers who seemed to not falter after receiving near fatal wounds. Seeing the enemy numbers not dwindling as fast they would like and the fresh injuries slowing them down, the coven elders felt a sense of dread. In desperation they fought, nearly out of breath and energy.

Large bubbles erupted from the bloody slosh followed by two giant pincers clanking against the sides of the container. Black sleek skin glinting red emerged with blood gorged eyes peering above. The Kataling crawled out and down the sides, the strike of the pincers echoing. The attendant attempted to make himself and the infants smaller in hopes of not being detected by the Kataling.

Below, the soldiers halted, staring up at the monster. Obviously young, it was still a formidable sight nearly ten feet in length and half that in height.

Its mouth opened.

Erena pushed two of the nearby coven children down to the floor along with her. The others did the same, leaving only the imperial soldiers standing. The ground shook as the Kataling charged forward, mowing through them. Loud crunching and the wet sounds of chewing commenced.

Within minutes, the floor was covered in carnage and the soldiers who managed to avoid the onslaught fled to their hovercrafts. Erena squeezed her eyes shut and tried to block out the sounds. One of the children lifted their head and she pushed him back down. When he looked over at her, he realized why and laid flatter.

With the Kataling on the rampage, anything moving in the vicinity was fair game.

The commander dragged himself up into his ship, gasping for breath. His intel had assured him the Kataling boy was incapacitated and no longer a threat. He cursed himself for not making sure of the thing's location first. Looking around, less than thirty of his men were accounted for.

"Retreat for now. We will regroup and track them."

"Should I send a report?" One of his men asked.

He turned to him, eyes red with rage.

"Absolutely not! We only bring news of victory to our emperor." He pushed the power icon on his dash. "Let's go!"

The imperial soldiers lifted off and disappeared in the horizon.

Almost half an hour went by before the supply house went deafeningly silent. Tervan sat up on hands and knees and surveyed his surroundings. Off to the edge of the entrance was Caden, naked, covered in blood with tears streaming down his face as he took small bites from a nearly clean bone. Slowly, everyone got up from the floor, careful not to slip on the remains. Erena went over to him and caressed his head.

"Are you okay?" She asked. He shook his head. "I know." Erena pulled him close to her. "Come now. We must go. Time to leave this place." He simply nodded, dropping the bone.

Tervan eyed the vat of blood and chunks.

"I think we should replenish and take some of it with us. Just in case."

"Good idea." Grieger brushed himself off. "There should be carrying sacks for filling."

The attendant leapt down with the two infants and let Erena takes hers. He went over to the Kataling boy and place the other in his arms. He watched the boy pull the infant close to him and weep silently. Erena found a wad of fabric tarp and wrapped it around Caden. The coven girl leading the group moved her blood encrusted hair from her face and turned to Durante.

"We must get to the docks even quicker now. No doubt, we'll have to fight our way through again."

"I agree." Durante went to join Grieger and the others to search for the filling sacks. "Let's speed this up. I want to get back to Earth. It seems this is no longer our home."

There was a sadness in his tone and Erena felt the same.

The emperor's red eyes stared out into nothingness as he devised a new plan in the event of his mens' failure. Which should never be an option. Loud bangs and screaming from outside wafted upwards in the air to his ears, making his blood run hot. The mere thought of sinking his teeth into the left-over carnage enticed him.

Smoke billowed near the docks and he rose from his throne. He calculated the time of the prisoners escape and knew there was no way they could have reached it so soon. Meaning, help had been standing in the wings. He nearly bolted out of his seat then slowed as a new thought invaded his mind. A sinister smile crept up on his lips and he leisurely walked to the entryway, his personal guards in tow.

"Ready my ship."

"Of course, my ruler. Where would you like to go?"

"We will stop them from leaving this planet. If that somehow fails, we follow them when they escape."

His head guard stopped.

"We have already dispatched a second fleet at the request of Commander Gallic. Are we going to let these rebels leave after the devastation and disrespect they have caused?"

"I will hunt them to the edge of the universe. They will not get away with my children!"

He wondered if he had a misconceived notion about the Jaubro bloodline being the one he needed. His hands clenched as the inconclusive DNA results from his head scientists last week filled his mind. If not the Jaubro line, then whose?

"This carnage can be cleaned up without me."

"And who are you leaving in your steed?" His advisor asked.

"I will deal with that before departure."

"Very well."

The group continued to the elevator.

The emperor's demeanor shifted to annoyance. He didn't like being challenged by lower beings in his court.

Energized and fully supplied, the group headed towards the docks, maneuvering around the heavily guarded areas. They were still not in any shape for full on brawls. Another hour hike and the docks spread before them as they came to the edge of the hillside. There was more smoke than usual. They all looked closer and saw the other coven members fighting alongside the merchants against imperial soldiers. Above, Volshins circled in disarray, not joining in to assist the soldiers. Chase rushed down searching for his guardian.

"Wait!" Durante commanded. When Chase kept going, he followed. "Don't be a fool!"

He managed to pull him back as a soldier came up from below and barely missed slitting his throat. Durante kicked the soldier in the face, sending him back down. Up ahead sat their ship, ready for boarding. The ramp was down and being defended by a row of coven members.

A strange reverb filled the air and the Volshins contorted and screamed. Durante looked up to his left and saw the emperor standing on the ramp of his imperial ship as it cruised towards the docks. His expression was one of elation. On each side of him stood a glowing column that his hands rested on. The sound came from those. No longer confused, the Volshins changed course and headed down towards the docks.

"Aw, damn it!" One of the coven boys yelled.

"Take cover!" Sapienti commanded.

They all jumped to the platform only to be confronted by a horde of imperial soldiers charging forward.

"Take the infants and head to the ship," Durante said to the attendant. He pointed to the coven children nearest him. "Protect them at all costs." When the Kataling boy refused to move after handing over his infant, Durante stepped close to him. "You too. Your mother will never forgive us as it is. We need you to be safe."

"I won't be a burden. I will fight." His voice was barely audible.

Durante rubbed his forehead and let out a sigh.

"Fine. But, only to defend."

As soon as they were underway, the elders once again readied themselves for a fight. They moved between their assailants like a wave, sending arcs of blood above them. Chase caught sight of Baltise and sped to him. Further ahead were the twins, covered in wounds and enemy blood. Both appeared crazed, having gone mad with rage.

Halfway to the ship, a Volshin crashed down in front of the elders' group, cracking the platform planks. It writhed about, trying to get on its feet and spread its wings. Fully erect, it let out a shriek that sent them to their knees while covering their ears.

"It's not in its right mind." Sapienti said. "It's suffering."

The reverb sounded again and the Volshin attacked, talons raised. Two of the coven children were sliced across the chest and fell back into their comrades. From behind the Volshin came a low growl. To the elders' surprise, Caden in Kataling form was behind it.

Durante's heart sank, knowing it was no match for the giant Volshin. The two monsters wrestled with each other, tearing flesh with fang and talons, the Kataling getting the worst of it. Before it fell to ground badly wounded, a smaller Volshin came to its rescue.

Baltise knocked the disoriented Volshin out of the way, his wings causing a draft. Using his talons, he dragged the Kataling to the ship's ramp. Chase appeared and waved an arm at them.

"Go! We'll make a path for you!"

The entourage fled inside the ship while Tervan and two others took up the rear to ensure their safety. At the landing, Erena stopped and turned around. The twins, Baltise and Chase had not followed. She searched their faces. When they found her gaze they all gave a smile.

"What are you doing?" She snapped. "Hurry!"

"We're staying," Olivier yelled back over the din of noise. "The emperor will try to stop you. We'll hold him off as long as we can."

"There is another ship we can take," Chase added. "We'll catch up."

The smile on his face told her the rest; if they survive.

"Your fathers will never forgive me if I let you do this," Erena cried.

She flashed back to when they had first fled their home world. From behind, Durante pulled her away.

"There's no other way. Look!" Durante pointed at the emperor's ship halting to hover above the docks.

Erena resisted.

"You have to trust them, Eterenia."

"It's not them I don't trust!"

He forcibly led her back in, also taking a glance at the four children fighting an army tenfold their numbers.

The emperor watched the chaos below. He saw the rebels' desperate retreat then decided to try and derail them first. Withdrawing his hands from the tuning columns, he snapped his fingers. One of the commanders came to his side.

"Destroy that ship. If they can't lift off, I win."

"Of course, my master." The commander strode back into the ship. "Ready cannons! Lay the enemy ship to waste!"

One of the rebels down on the docks locked eyes with him. It was the son of Eterenia and the Endaga boy. He sneered in disgust at the mingled bloodline. His gaze did not waver. Then the rebel bolted to the ship, disappearing inside. The emperor had a suspicion as to why. He came to understand one thing about the son; he was far too crafty. A thin dome of shimmer erected around the rebel ship as the cannon fire hit, obliterating the area surrounding it.

He tsked.

The shield fell away and from the sides of the rebel ship, weapons extended then swiveled to aim at his. He stood dumbfounded at first, knowing that model ship was not manufactured equipped with weapons. Anger consumed him.

"Evasive action!" He ordered.

His ship tilted sideways, barely missing the platform where he stood, clipping the outer hull.

He saw the rebel ship's thrusters engage and it rose above the water.

"Commander!" The soldier hurried to him and made a quick bow. "Deploy a tracker."

"My master?"

"I said I would hunt them to the ends of the universe," he seethed, staring into the commander's eyes. "I will not be denied."

"As you command."

One of his captains, came to his side.

"Master, we can use the previous fleets navigation records to find their new world."

The emperor turned to him.

"I will not search that planet's surface for my prey. I want to know the exact location of their homes. Where they live. Where their children are."

The captain stepped back in fear.

"Of course, Master."

When the rebel ship reached the edge of the stratosphere, he watched the tracker strike its hull and embed deep in the frame. He smiled. Turning away from the scene, he headed back to the bridge as the ramp sealed behind him.

Chase saw the fiery trail headed straight for the ship hit and heard Olivier curse. He knew that not long after their ship makes a jump, the emperor would follow and there was no way to stop him.

"We have to push his soldiers back and get those Volshins down," Odette hollered.

"And the Katalings running around the town square?" Olivier asked.

"One thing at a time," Chase said. "Baltise."

His guardian didn't respond.

He saw his wings flapping slowly in a steady rhythm. Something about it filled him with trepidation.

"Baltise?"

The Volshin took off in flight into the mass of Volshins circling in the air for prey. Many of them were twice his size yet he barreled through and knocked three of them down into the water. He made a wide curve back and went for more. Blood rained on the merchants on the docks.

CHAPTER FOUR

Return to Earth

Screams of agony filtered throughout the ship as the wounded were carted off to the medical bay. Once it was full, empty chambers were used. The attendant helped administering sedatives to keep them all from thrashing about. From there, he turned his attention to the naked Kataling boy. The fabric he had been adorned with after the supply house battle had long been shredded by his shifting. His cries were excruciating to the ears, making some of the others cringe into fetal positions. The wounds were deep and still oozing. His infant was in distress, being psychically connected.

He went to the nearest compartment and rummaged around until he found a packet of liquid marked as sealer. He grabbed the application gun, loaded the bag into it and primed the injector.

"I need you to stay still for me," he told the boy. "This is going to sting for a bit."

Working as quickly as possible, he coated every gash. The skin tightened on each one, forcing the liquid further in until it formed a jelly like consistency.

He motioned to one of the medical attendants.

"Help me get him up."

Three others took hold along and they lifted him up into a cryochamber. The boy wailed, still in pain. The attendant picked up the infant and set him atop the boy. While he soothed the infant in preparation for travel, the chamber was initiated. Strong painkillers mixed in with the sedative made the boy go limp. His eyes filled with tears as consciousness slipped away. He managed to touch his infant's leg before going under.

The attendant attached the secondary tubes to the infant and waited until it too was in deep sleep before hitting the closure icon. The digital display showed the two vital signs slow to a crawl.

"Now that's done. Time to check on the elders."

"Do you need any help?" One of the medical team members asked.

"No, I think I can handle it."

He left the medical bay and went to the nearby chamber where Erena, Durante, and Greiger sat looking glum on the bunks. Dried, caked blood had flaked off to exposed bare skin. He looked down at himself and noticed the same.

"Maybe the first thing we should all do is rinse off, so we can assess the damage better."

They stared up at him for a moment before nodding one by one.

Unabashed by each other's nakedness, all four stood in the communal shower under the gentle spray of water. Red and pink swirled around at their feet. Durante had placed his hands on the wall and seemed to be barely holding himself up. Erena felt no different.

They were all exhausted.

The strain of fighting constantly had caught up with them. He began to slide down and Grieger caught him, falling sideways from lack of strength. The attendant relented to his own body and went down.

Tervan appeared in the entrance in time to see them haphazardly on the wet floor with the water still running. Not caring about their situation, he too let the water rinse him off. When the water ran clear, he bent over the attendant and smacked him hard across the thigh. The man jolted from his slumber and backed up against the wall.

"What?" He mumbled.

"Help me get them up. This is a disgrace. We can't let anyone see them like this."

"Oh."

The attendant looked around and grimaced. Grieger half slumped to the side with Durante in his arms and Erena bent forward with her head nearly touching her knees was indeed a sorry sight.

"Understood. Give me a minute."

"You take those two. I got my mother."

The attendant, blurry eyed and exhausted, did his best to treat the coven leaders' wounds. He watched the general patching himself up like a battlefield surgeon. The attendant applied an astringent to a large gash on Durante's arm. Durante jolted upright, gasping for air, and clawed his way towards something. That startled the attendant from his weariness. He wrestled the elder back down and continued with disinfecting the wound.

"What?" Durante started. "Are we?"

He seemed disoriented.

"This is better than letting it heal and administering antibiotics after the fact."

Erena, lying on the table next to Durante, had awoken.

"That makes sense," she said.

"Except in a battle where there's no time for that," Tervan added.

Grieger sat up and scratched his head.

"Could have sworn we were taking a shower." He smelled his skin and perked up at the scent of soap. "Hmm."

Tervan tossed the sealing tool on the tray beside him and stood.

"You were all slumped on the floor like dead rodents. It took both of us a while to get you out here for treatment."

"Why didn't you get help?" Erena asked. She saw his expression and rolled her eyes. "I don't think anyone on board cares about our state right now."

"You're wrong. Tell me," her son said. "How does it look when the leader of your clan is down for the count and unable to communicate the next plan?"

"Do you always think in military terms?" The attendant asked.

Tervan whirled on him.

"Do you always act spineless in the face of loyalty and danger?"

The two men were inches from each other, both their eyes glowing.

"Enough!" Sapienti yelled. He was up and sitting on the table, legs hanging from the side. "We need to establish any damage to the ship and a faster route to get back."

"Maybe some clothes first?"

Durante lifted himself from the table and shivered.

"What?" Erena said laughingly as she struck a pose. "Not into the sheet fashion?"

They all looked at her, not saying a word. Grieger finally started laughing. The others followed, breaking the sour mood. Erena slid off the table.

"Come, my fearless mates."

Clean, refreshed and fully clothed, the coven leaders exited their chamber and headed for the bridge. Tervan followed, a dire expression on his face from visions of the fight in the supply house and Volshins swirling the skies in anguish. He kept his head lowered as he walked along the corridor. A few of his men had also decided to remain on the planet and assist the coven children who, in his eyes, were too naïve to win such a battle.

"You're frowning," his mother spoke.

He looked up and saw her head tilted back towards him. Her blonde hair seemed brighter than normal, making him aware of the drastic contrast to his own dark locks. Beside her walked his father and he felt a twinge of envy.

"I am just contemplating the outcome of the mess we left behind. Those children are smart, devious, even. But, they are greatly outmatched."

"Ambrook is going to be livid," Sapienti said.

The bridge doors open before them and they entered the dimly lit area. Protective shields shimmered on the outer hull as the ship passed through the deep dark of space.

"Where are we?" Tervan asked.

The navigator continued his duties as he responded.

"Second quadrant. We are headed to this solar

system's core so we can make the next jump. ETA, two hours."

Grieger let out a long sigh and stretched his body upwards. He walked over to one of the view panels and stared out at the stars. Tervan went over to the monitor displaying a map with their route charted.

"How long before we get back to Earth?" He inquired.

"About five years, maybe less if we're lucky."

He turned to his mother and gave her a questioning glance. She stared sideways towards the ceiling and pursed her lips in thought. Then she nodded, and her gaze fell on him.

"That should be good enough. I can't imagine the covens not being able to hold down that small force for such a short time."

"I guess we should take account of things," Grieger said, turning away from his view.

"I will check on Celeste's boy," Sapienti added.

"Let us know when we're close to the jump point," Tervan said to the navigator.

"It will be announced over the communication system. You should prepare now, though."

"Noted."

Tervan and the coven leaders left the bridge and headed down to the medical bay. Time to count their losses and admit temporary defeat.

Chase ran over to the general's soldiers forming a barricade along the docks. He was thankful that they had stayed to fight. Although, the situation appeared grim. The merchants were barely holding their own while protecting the goods. After being on the planet for a time, he understood that was their main priority. Even if this fight ended in defeat, they would still need merchandise for trade. He came up to the nearest soldier.

"We need fire power to compete with this new turn of events. Can you somehow acquire one of their battle ships?"

The soldier cut down an imperial soldier who came at them from a blind spot then turned to him. His blood red eyes were like jewels.

"When you say acquire?" His voice was deep, yet soothing. Chase backed away from him.

"I mean, take one down and use it to then cripple the emperor's ship."

"Hmm." The soldier glanced over at his colleagues. "Shall we?"

Four of them broke ranks and followed the first soldier down to the other side of the docks where two of the imperial ships were hovering low, delivering crossfire. The remainder spread out wide to cover more ground. Static crackled in his ear and he realized his commlink was still working.

"Ambrook," a young man's voice called through the transmission. "We are inside the palace. Commencing to take it over."

"There were more of you besides the rescue team?" He asked incredulously.

"Double the fun," the young man laughed.

"The emperor is out here with his fleet laying

waste. They shot a tracker onto our ship."

There was a long pause.

"The ship has left?"

Chase felt a sense of guilt. He should have relayed the situation earlier. As if reading his mind, Odette's voice came through.

"It's too late for regrets. We fight until we can no longer. Take the palace. We will deal with the emperor."

"So be it," the young man said. "For the glory of our houses."

The crackling ceased, and Chase let a small smile creep in.

Talons raked his back, disrupting his moment. He turned around, coming face to face with an imperial soldier who seemed to be deranged. The soldier kept coming at him as he blocked and dodged his assaults. He noticed the over dilated pupils in the blood gorged eyes.

A feeder.

He had heard about them from Count Sapienti. Their main purpose was to drain a body dry, similar to how Volshins feasted, leaving a leathery corpse. The soldier got within mere inches of his face, his mouth opening wider than deemed possible, showing two sets of fangs for optimal feeding.

Chase fumbled along the back of his bodysuit and found the short blade. He swung up it in an arc between their bodies and rammed it straight under the chin. He could see the blade in the feeder's mouth. That didn't stop his advance. With crazed abandon, the feeder leaned in further, chomping his jaws shut and nicking Chase by the neck.

"Get off me!" Chase yelled, using his own weight

to counter. He got enough distance to raise his foot and pushed the feeder back to the ground.

The feeder ripped the blade from his head and got ready to pounce when talons sliced through his neck, severing the head from his body. A last gasp of breath and the feeder was dead. Chase stepped back and exhaled loudly. Standing with one foot on the feeders back, Olivier flicked the blood from his talons.

"Really, Ambrook, be more cunning."

Above them, they saw the imperial fleet being bombarded with firepower from two of their own ships. From the palace came four more ships attacking the emperor's.

"Well, look at that," Olivier said. He smirked at Chase. "And you were thinking we weren't going to win."

With all the attacks going at full force, it was becoming clear that it would take more than that to take down the emperor. Odette leapt down to Chase and her brother then also looked up. Stopping the fleet from leaving was no longer a viable option. On the other side of the docks, the emperor's ship engines fired. It took off into space like a bullet followed by a fleet of twenty ships.

"That's what I was afraid of."

Chase's arms drooped. He stood in despair.

"We tried. Now it's up to our parents to stop him," she said.

On the ground, the imperial soldiers looked up in confusion. It became apparent that the emperor didn't relay his plans to all his soldiers. Chase looked over at the twins. This might turn out to be an advantageous event.

He tapped his commlink.

"Whoever is at the palace, the emperor has left the planet."

Crackling. Then.

"We know. Our enemy has made it clear it makes no difference."

"Oh, but it does," Chase said, smiling. "It does."

The moment the emperor's ship was gone, the Volshins and Katalings became disoriented. No longer controlled by the strange reverb of sound, many of them fell to the ground, exhausted. It made Baltise's job easier. When the last one was down, he floated down to Chase, reverting to human form. Chase caught him and staggered back holding him tight.

"Now," Odette said. "Shall we clean this up?"

The imperial soldiers turned on them in unison, eyes glowing, their attention back to the fight at hand.

Inside the palace, with Tamar taking the lead, the group of coven fighters burst into the main hall and were confronted by rows of imperial soldiers. At their center was the emperor's new head commander arrogant in his stance of authority.

"This is your end, merchant trash," he said. "None of you will leave this palace intact."

"Is that an assurance?" Tamar asked.

"You mock me?" The commander exclaimed.

He nodded his head, signaling the first rows of soldiers to attack.

"Oh," Tamar spoke. He turned to his comrades. "Kill them all."

The coven children gladly acknowledged with extended talons and red eyes. He went straight for the commander, taking him by surprise with his speed.

"I see you have some skill, young one," the commander sneered.

"Shut up and fight me, you ancient sack of bones."

"I will show you what age and experience means."

With reflexes faster than Tamar's, the commander dodged his advance and bent forward. He came up nearly face to face, his talons out. Tamar was able to move back enough so that the talons cut shallow through the front of his bodice and grazed his chin.

Shaken, he refused to show his surprise at the veteran's move. Instead, he flipped backwards until he was far enough away to reassess his tactics. The commander was not going to give him such reprieve. He was upon him in lightning speed, and Tamar blocked his blow.

"Why?" Tamar asked. "Why fight for a tyrant who doesn't have your race's well being at the forefront?"

"The emperor's rule is absolute!"

"That's not what I asked." He pushed the commander back hard enough for him to hit the wall on the other side. "You would rather our race become extinct than defy a madman?"

Some of the imperial soldiers hesitated.

Gotcha'!

The other coven members, feeling the shift, went in deep to unleash their full might. He watched them dispatch the first wave and tear through the second. The commander shrieked in rage and his body shifted. The back bulged up and elongated, tearing the uniform to shreds to exposed black sleek hide. His legs shortened while his arms curved inward protruding giant pincers. The other imperial soldiers fled the scene, leaving the coven fighters amongst the Kataling.

Oh, fuck it all to hell, Tamar cursed to himself.

"Get out," he commanded the others. When none of them moved, he sighed.

Of course they won't abandon me.

He found two swords lying nearby and picked them up, swinging them to feel their weight. The Kataling commander let out another ear piercing shriek, showing off its giant fangs, before thundering towards him. He drew the swords into an X across his body as a shield which did nothing to soften the impact of the Kataling barreling into him.

On his back, he moved his head from side to side whenever it came in for a bite. Four of his coven fighters were attacking it yet it paid no attention to their efforts. It shook them off, flinging each one in different directions across the hall.

As he tried to get from underneath, its head swooped down. He felt its fangs sink deep into his side and heard himself scream. The pain was like nothing he had ever felt in his life. To not scream would have been impossible. Tears streaming down his face, he used the swords to try and pierce the leather skin, his strength fading as the Kataling let go and engulfed the other side of his torso and thigh.

There was a strange tacking sound then the Kataling's jaws relaxed. The young man looked up over the Katalings massive head and saw an older man wearing high end merchant robes standing tall holding the handle of a three prong weapon. Its tips were embedded in the Kataling. Another man came and with bare hands, pried the monster's jaws open to release him. Its body was rolled over and pushed out the way. He turned back to the first man. Eyes of silver glowed at him, dark blonde hair undone and touching the tops of his shoulders.

For some reason, he suddenly felt helpless; like the child that he was. He cried hysterically while trying to hide his face with both hands. The man knelt and gathered him in his arms.

"Shh, child. There is no need to feel that way. You did better than most." He stroked Tamar's head. "Now, it is our turn to take back what we have lost."

"Master Jaubro," the second man said. "Shall we contact the others and let them know the palace is ours?"

The man turned to him and nodded.

"We need to tend to this child's wounds immediately."

Tamar felt his body begin to shake. He was going into shock.

"It's alright. We'll take care of you."

"Jaubro," the young man said.

"Yes," the man answered with a smile. "I am your beloved Erena's uncle. The merchant workers loyal to our families hid all of us." Tamar's vision started to fade. "Sleep now."

Master Jaubro walked over to the window and looked out onto the scene unfolding at the docks. He didn't like the fact that the emperor had given chase. Vengence seethed within him about what transpired at the start of his reign. Seeing Eterenia was a blessing fueled by heartache. He wanted to come out and embrace her at the secret hideout but knew it wasn't the right time. The Kataling had turned back to its original form and the commander lay bleeding on the royal carpet.

"Make sure that one is kept alive. We may need him to rein in the soldiers."

"As you wish, Master Jaubro."

He left the window and found himself being stared at by a group of young ones. The oldest of them was maybe a hundred years old. They were bloody with eyes wide in awe at him and his assistant. Jaubro tsked.

Sending children across the galaxy to fight was asinine.

There was no doubt as to who had probably thought up such an idea. That kind of thinking was in the Strana blood, inherited through generations. It happened to have skipped one with Pridric. Chase was more like his grandfather. Master Jaubro snorted in amusement. He clapped his hands to snap the children out of their admiration.

"Come on. No time to waste. Reinforcements will be on their way and we cannot be caught slacking." That got them up. "Form a perimeter around the entrances. Let none enter."

Moments after finishing its second jump the coven leaders' ship went dark and the emergency lights came on. The navigator stumbled over to the maintenance panel screen and saw red all over the lower sector near the generators.

"Damn it!"

He turned to one of the other crewmembers.

"Can you go down and see what's going on?"

"Sure. I'll take a few others with me and a medical tech just in case."

The crewman left the bridge followed by two others. He pushed a commlink in his ear then tapped it.

"I need a medical rep to meet me in the maintenance corridor."

Durante and Tervan entered the bridge and found the navigator.

"What's the meaning of this? Did the jump go bad? Are we lost again?" Durante fired off at the navigator.

"How about letting him answer one at a time, father?" Tervan suggested.

"My apologies."

The navigator was miffed while he sat at his station to check the rest of the ship's vitals.

"Not sure what happened. Everything was fine on the first jump. Appears to be something stuck in the hull."

A ping echoed in the bridge.

"Confirmed there is indeed something puncturing the hull," the crewman said through the ship communication system. "Getting a closer look now." There was a pause. "It has a read out. Boosting a signal or something. Like a," another pause, "it's a!"

"What is it?" Durante ordered.

"It's a tracker!"

Tervan marched off the bridge and disappeared down the corridor. Durante and the navigator went pale.

"How far behind are they?" Durante asked the navigator.

"Send me the signal information," the navigator ordered the crewman.

"Coming up."

The navigator's screen changed, and a graph of data covered it. He scrutinized it for a long time, making Durante sigh with impatience.

"From my calculations maybe a little over four-teen Earth months."

"So, we don't have much time to prepare for all out war when we get back," Durante said.

"This goes south, humanity will be eaten into extinction."

My thoughts exactly.

Negotiations

Sunlight crept between the thin openings of the curtains inside Princess Adelia's bed chamber. She stirred under the light blue sheets, forcing more of the fabric to wrap around her naked body. Squinting in protest, she pulled one of them over her head. The sun was setting and had moved to her side of the castle. She usually relished in the end of daylight and coming of night. This day, she was too tired to move.

Her mother and the others had already been gone six years, leaving the rest of the covens and herself to keep the cruel and blood thirsty Commander Gallic at bay. Military forces from around the world had come flocking to the region and she was requested to attend countless meetings in the day.

Did they not understand we are nocturnal creatures?

Even Commander Gallic was peeved about it and demanded a remedy or humans face the consequences of his displeasure. They did not want to know how a sleep deprived, hungry vampire would react under stress. Count Ambrook and Marchand had taken her under their wings to teach her the ins and outs of politics. She concluded what she already knew: she despised it. How her mother was able to endure it for so long amazed her.

Beside her lay Tesul, a corner of the sheet barely covering his crotch. His tanned, muscular legs were stretched out, one slightly bent. She rolled over under the sheets and pulled it down enough for her to peek at his sleeping body. His chocolate brown hair splayed around his head, a few wisps squiggled across his face.

Open, open, open, she commanded his eyes silently.

Tesul's eyelids fluttered. Those golden irises assaulted her very being and she slid further down under the sheets. He turned his head and met her gaze.

"Did you sleep well?" He asked, his hand reaching out to caress the top of her head.

"Uhn uhn," she replied, shaking her head.

"You need to eat. Let's get you dressed."

She blushed, hearing him speak. He used to rarely do so and now only with her. Mustering up her will, she yanked the layers of sheet off and swung her legs over the side of the bed. When her feet touched the floor as she tried to stand, she slid to the floor. Tesul caught her. She went limp in his arms and resolved to stay that way. Tesul smacked the side of her buttocks.

"No. We need to get going soon."

She let out a dismayed sigh and pouted, an attempt to plead her case.

"Fine. I will."

Naked, Tesul went to the closet and flung the doors wide open. It was now full of both their attire, even though Tesul still reported to the Durante castle. He pulled out a white blouse with lace frills at the neck, black leather shorts and a double breasted black trench coat jacket. For himself, he picked a light brown suit with a white shirt and blue ascot.

"Hmmm? What, no underwear?"

Tesul stopped midway across the room, arms full of clothes.

"Did you want them?"

"Do you?" She asked slyly.

He continued towards the bed and dropped the load. Then he went to her lingerie drawer. She felt disappointed. Then she thought about everyone calling her undignified over the decades. Her undergarments picked out, she took them from Tesul and they both got dressed.

A convoy of the remaining coven leaders stopped in front of the newly acquired government building set on the outskirts of the neutral zone. The area swarmed with military personnel and government leaders with hidden agendas. Count Ambrook got out of his vehicle and surveyed the land. Hovering above, landing ramp down, was Commander Gallic's ship. From behind him, Princess Adelia, Count Marchand, and Queen Celeste emerged out of their vehicles. All of them looked worst for wear. He too was getting exhausted.

It wasn't just the odd hours of the meetings and lack of sleep on occasion. No, it was the bickering with officials about why they were here and how Gallic wouldn't be if it weren't for them. This coming from a race parasitic to themselves. Earth had seen more wars on its own soil than most alien civilizations he knew. Even before the incident that created the area where they landed centuries ago that jump started a new era of science.

"Count Ambrook," Queen Celeste purred. "How does one fare this evening?"

He checked the bags under her eyes, covered lackluster with concealer.

"As much as one can bear, my Queen."

"In that case," Count Marchand interjected. "Shall we?"

Princess Adelia straightened her posture and followed them into the building.

That' it. Good girl. Ambrook praised her.

The group was led by armed military soldiers to the conference room. A large oval table sat in the center of a theatre with seats curved around it spiraling up to the rafters. Nearly every seat was occupied except for the ones at that table reserved for the coven members. Ambrook could see the expressions of frustration and anger on most of the humans' faces. Seconds after the last of them were in their seats, the moderator began.

"Let's start with the concerns from our neighboring countries leaders." He raised a hand towards the first one on the other side of the table. "Please, go on."

The man cleared his throat and at the nod of encouragement from some of the other country leaders, he stated his case.

"With the vampires having free rein to move about the planet, we are concerned with the possible epidemic of them turning humans to increase their numbers. This has been perpetuated by the arrival of their so-called enemy who seems to have no lack of appetite for preying on our kind."

Heads bobbed in unison around the room.

Ambrook, along with Queen Celeste went slack jawed at the comment. None of the covens had turned a human in over a century, maybe more. There was no feasible reason to do so.

"And your proposal?" The moderator asked.

"I believe, restricting access to the towns and borders would alleviate this."

Count Marchand threw back his head and erupted into laughter, causing the room to become heavy with discomfort. He finally stopped and looked around at them.

"You mess with my commerce, we will have an issue."

"Is that a threat?" One of the country leaders asked nervously.

Ambrook raised a hand to his chest.

"You do realize, we have businesses around the globe and to restrict us would not only make us angry, it will tank the economy of those regions."

"We are not saying you can't run business," the original leader spat. "We don't want your kind on our soil. Surely you can get humans to run everyday operations."

"So, I should trust humans now with my money, when even you don't?" Queen Celeste asked.

The room went silent as the leaders and military people squirmed.

"What guarantee do we have that you're not going around feeding off us?"

Count Ambrook's hooded eyes scanned the room as his lips pressed thin. Before he could say anything, Commander Gallic propped his legs on the table and smiled.

"They won't touch your beloved species, but I will. I find it fascinating that you suddenly have these concerns when they strived to blend in for so long."

The country leader slammed his fist on the table.

"We have no idea the number of humans they have consumed!" He turned to the coven leaders. "Will you be truthful and tell us the numbers or have you lost count over the centuries?"

"In the last one hundred years," Count Marchand began. The humans leaned forward simultaneously like a wave crashing towards them. They waited with bated breath to hear the awful truth. "Zero."

One could hear a pin drop against the silence that followed. The government and military leaders at the table scrunched up their faces. This time, Gallic burst out laughing.

"What do you mean?" The second country leader asked.

"Zero," Count Marchand repeated.

"But that's not possible," another retorted.

"It is, and quite true."

"You feed off our kind daily. Hell, we can barely keep that monster satiated," the first said pointing to the commander.

"Yes," the commander said coyly. "Feed me."

"There's your keyword," Ambrook said.

"Feeding off them and turning them are two different things," Princess Adelia added. "I wouldn't want one of you disgusting humans as part of my coven. It would taint our bloodline."

Count Marchand winced. Queen Celeste took out a handkerchief and covered her mouth to stifle a snort. Count Ambrook rolled his eyes upward and braced for the response.

Within seconds, the room erupted into a frenzied cacophony of insults and vitriol. Commander Gallic sat back and watched in interest at the chaotic descent. His gaze met Ambrook's. At that moment, Count Ambrook feared a gate had opened and the commander was about to enter it with no mercy.

Commander Gallic left the meeting smiling, a devious grin conveying his mood. He saw an opportunity to exploit the humans' fears and the coven leaders' sense of duty. There was an obvious division since neither saw eye to eye. He thought back to his father and how the merchants had bested him despite being outnumbered. Bad planning in his opinion.

His black cloak jacket flapped with every step he took, revealing the blood red material lining the inside. As he passed one of the hallway mirrors he took a quick glance to admire his appearance. Since his arrival on Earth, his jet black hair had grown long. To keep it out of his face, he had slicked it back. The contrast with his fair skin and eyes red from constant feeding made him terrifying yet beautiful. He found it helped to lure his prey. Men and women swooned as he passed them on the street, following him to their demise.

On both sides trailing behind him were four imperial guards. Having more than that would have scared the humans more than usual and he wanted to make them feel somewhat at ease. At the exit checkpoint, their weapons were returned in quick succession. The human military staff never made eye contact, doling out their duties efficiently. He secured his short blade in the sheath attached to his waist and proceeded to the cruiser that would take them back to his ship.

Upon boarding, he went to his chamber and tossed his cloak jacket on the platform next to his bed. He sat, staring at the walls for a moment then flopped back onto the firm material. There was one thing he did agree on. Turning humans was not ideal. He had seen enough of Earth's inhabitants to conclude they were only good for feeding. It wouldn't take long to graze through the entire population.

Annihilation.

His race had conquered more than a few planets and devastated many with their appetites. They had never wiped out an entire species. He wondered what that would feel like. First, he would need permission from the emperor. That monster would love it. He was not on board with systematic culling of their home world but the emperor's rule was absolute. He touched the glowing pad on the platform opposite the other side of the bed.

"Captain!"

"Yes, Commander."

"I want a compilation of the best fare on the planet."

"Of course, commander."

"In two months time we are going to hunt until satisfied."

He touched the pad again to disconnect and let out a sigh as he rested one hand on his chest. Count Ambrook had a knowing look on his face at the meeting.

What will you do? Will you try to save the humans from my rampage? He asked.

"This is madness!" Count Marchand exclaimed while running his talons through an imperial guard coming at him from the side.

He was in a French town square of the city where he took over the vampire coven and started his business. This was the third time in four months that France had seen a massive attack on its citizens. At first, the humans blamed his coven, vandalizing his businesses and slapping huge tariffs on their goods. When it became clear that they were no match, the country begged forgiveness and an agreement to have his coven defend them.

Civilians ran in all directions, trying to get away from the soldiers pouncing on the nearest victim and sinking their teeth into adrenaline warmed flesh with rushing blood. It was an ever-moving feast for them. Count Marchand gritted his teeth in frustration as he watched his coven members attempt to deescalate the event.

"Count Marchand," his assistant called out from across the street. He was pulling his talons out of an imperial soldier who had just gotten his fangs in a young girl. "I believe this is the last of them. Should we dispatch the wounded?"

"No." Count Marchand frowned. "Take care of the human victims first. If the enemy flees and gets away, so be it. We can't fight like this and avoid casualties for much longer."

So far, the attacks were annoying in his eyes compared to what could have occurred. Large groups of people were being fed on and left on the streets, in alleys, or inside establishments like restaurants and gift shops where the entire place fell victim.

Hospitals were crowded due to intake of people brought in for anemia and weakness. They were sent home after a couple of days and were fine except for the trauma of being nearly sucked dry. In the back of his mind he felt like the commander was teasing them. That gave him a chill. The other coven leaders probably saw it the same.

After a year of fun and games attacking cities around the world, Commander Gallic was getting bored. The humans had demanded meetings to negotiate which he ignored. They began to surround his ship and plead for mercy. He didn't understand why they were so upset. The number of victims was a fraction of the population and he, nor his soldiers, had not drained any humans in the process. That, in itself, was the most boring of all. He would rather see their numbers dwindle than bounce back.

He strolled the corridors of his ship, deep in thought about what to do next. At an intersection, he heard muffled cries coming from one of the chambers. What the world leaders did not know was that he had snatched a handful, a hundred or so, of humans and stashed them on the ship for his soldiers to do with as they pleased. Less than twenty percent had died and what was left of the bodies were incinerated. Human bones weren't that great to chew on.

The ship's communication system pinged.

"Commander. There is a transmission coming through from the bridge. It is encoded."

Gallic frowned, stopping mid stride and glancing up at the bulkhead where an internal speaker was inland. He tapped his earbud.

"I am on my way."

He pivoted around and headed back from where he started then turned the opposite way. The bridge was guarded by six soldiers. They all dropped their heads and did an arm salute at their chests. The doors opened, and he stepped into the low light of the command center. Above the main viewport was a giant holoscreen.

"Open the channel," he commanded.

The screen flickered once then the emperor's image filled the space. Everyone inhaled sharply and scrambled to drop to their knees. Gallic was down before any of them.

"Master, what honor is this?" He braved a look up. "How are you broadcasting from so far away?"

The emperor smiled which terrified him.

"I was able to track the rebel merchants' ship. They are on their way back to that planet." His blood gorged eyes seemed to grow larger. "They must pay. I will take back what is mine. Including their lives."

"Of course, my master. This planet is called Earth and the human species is similar to ours yet much weaker. I have been feeding on them daily. Along with other creatures of this world."

"Why just feeding? Are they not worth devouring?"

"May I stand, master?"

"Do it."

The commander stood and met the emperor's gaze, forcing himself not to flinch.

"I was not sure if I should go about eating unrestrained. In case you wanted to negotiate with the humans."

"If they get in the way of our mission to punish the traitors, kill them. I have no need for food this far away in the galaxy."

"Then it shall be done. Your arrival, my master?"

"In less than three of that planet's years."

"I look forward to your arrival."

He got back down on his knees right as the screen

went blank. Elation and dread filled him. To wipe out the humans was thrilling. Having the emperor himself come; left him cold.

On his way back to his quarters, Gallic called his Captain of the Guard. He heard the soldiers voice answer through the earbud.

"I heard the news, commander. What do you need from me?"

"The grid you created of the cities for our feeding frenzy."

"Another attack?"

The commander grinned.

"This time we eat to our hearts' content."

"The umm," the captain cleared his throat. "Others as well?"

"Those greedy monsters would leave nothing for us!" The commander replied. "Tell them to stay in their original form and act like soldiers."

"Understood, commander."

The connection ended, and Gallic pressed his tongue against his teeth and sucked in air. The last thing he wanted was Katalings and Volshins gobbling up their meal.

He entered his chamber and pulled up the map already uploaded to his monitor. After perusing it for an hour, he decided. With one finger, he touched on the American continent. That one was first on the list. He touched the communication pad by his bed.

"Get ready for deployment. We leave at nightfall. I have sent you the selection." The captain was silent for a moment. "Did you not hear me, captain?"

"My apologies, commander. I did. I was contacting the other ships to position themselves close to the other targets."

"Hmph!" Commander Gallic snorted. "You are efficient. That was my next order. Very well, let's begin."

Small combat ships spewed from the commander's, heading straight for the American territories. It was late night on all fronts. Each ship landed in populated areas and the soldiers spilled out like a swarm of locusts. They grabbed people on the streets, taking them down where they stood. Homes, businesses, even shelters were invaded, their inhabitants chomped on by ravenous man eaters. Screams blanketed the air.

Commander Gallic stepped onto the busy streets of a large city and watched its citizens scatter in all directions. Behind him a small group of people ran into a building to hide. He casually walked into it and saw them huddled together, their eyes wide with fear. One of the females squeezed her eyes shut and turned away.

"Please, don't hurt us," one of the men said. "We have nothing against you guys. We just want to go about our lives."

"Oh?" Gallic lifted the man up by his neck with one hand, his feet dangling nearly a foot above the floor. "But, I don't want you to live at all."

He snapped the man's neck and tossed the body on the floor. While the others stared horrified, their gaze following the body as it traveled across the room, he began his feasting. Their screams were short lived.

Law enforcement throughout the country tried in vain to stop the attacks and were caught up in the fray, falling victim as well. Some were pulled out of their squad cars while trying to retreat. Others were mowed down as they fired upon the enemy. Bullets did not stop their advance. The military was called in, to no avail except causing massive structural damage as they launched missiles and sprayed the area with firepower. Nearly two hours after its start, the death toll reaching the thousands, the government relented and contacted Count Ambrook.

Ambrook Coven stirred with activity in the early hours of day. The elite fighters were preparing for assignments and the high court appointees were hammering out a strategy with the leaders. Ambrook was holed up in his office, leaning sideways in his chair, staring at the footage from multiple news outlets in the Americas. Chancellor Rayne came into the room and grimaced at the sight.

"They waited too long to contact us," he said, sitting in the chair next to him.

"Stubborn. Why are humans so damn stubborn? I don't understand."

"The one thing they feared from us, is now happening by the hands of our enemy. We should let them taste despair for a bit before sending in the cavalry."

Ambrook's eyes widened and he sat straight in his chair. Anger crept up and his assistant raised a hand.

"I jest, my lord. Please, calm yourself."

"I do not find that amusing!"

"Apparently so." The Chancellor's eyes widened briefly as he swiveled in his seat. "I am merely saying, they brought this upon themselves. They wanted us to defend them without even trying first. Now it is up to us to make it all go away?"

"I know." Ambrook breathed deep and exhaled slowly, closing his eyes. "I almost wish Chase was here to shed some light on this."

He opened his eyes and saw the shocked look from his assistant. "He had some valid points."

"That aside, what is our next move?" He reached over and changed the feed to worldwide. "Because, it seems he has started a human purge."

The view screen was covered in carnage from three continents: the Americas, Europe and Asia. Imperial soldiers, though small in number, raised havoc across the lands.

"He's hitting the areas with the largest populations for maximum effect."

"And we can't send out the ancient ones for the same reason he hasn't."

"They would eat everything."

"So now what?"

"I think it's time we had a real conversation with the humans. There's not much we can do about this." Ambrook pointed at the screen. "We'll send in members to stop the carnage for now."

"Very well. Shall I call up the other coven leaders and give them the rundown?"

Ambrook's eyes glowed as he turned to him.

"Yes. I will not be going down this road alone."

A New Fight

Count Marchand stared at the transmission coming through the relay he set up before the ship left. His assistants ran around getting prepared to go out to the landing sight. It was established that they keep the communication non-audible in case Commander Gallic was listening. He had already intercepted the one from the emperor. When the one from his people came through that morning, he was not surprised to learn about the tracker.

"So, the war has come to this," he said softly.

There was no way to hide the ship's entrance or landing. He sent a message to the human government closest to the area requesting a fully armed escort. Although, he was certain the commander would not attack without the emperor's permission, he didn't want to take that chance.

"My Lord," one of his assistants called to him. "We are ready. ETA is three hours. The docking clamps are enabled and medics on stand by at the site."

"Very good. Let's get moving."

Donning his coat from the rack by the door, he

headed out to the car parked in front of his home. His head assistant and two of his best fighters climbed in after him. They rode in silence. Along the way, he saw Ambrook and Celeste's vehicles following his. The other coven leaders still on Earth decided to stay behind and make their homes ready for welcome.

At the site, the three leaders exited their cars and went to the bunker overlooking the landing area. It was made to withstand the onslaught of any natural disaster. Celeste admired the workmanship.

"How did you ever level the surface and build that landing platform?" She inquired.

"This see through bunker is ingenious as well," Ambrook added.

"Should I be offended by all that?" Marchand replied. "What do you take me for? I always find a way to up my game." He smiled then.

Ambrook rolled his eyes.

"Yes, your pride as a scientist."

Marchand wagged a finger.

"Ah, ah. Innovator."

"Whatever," Celeste sighed.

From above came the roar of jet fighters, six in all surrounding the ship as it coasted towards the dock. It hovered, centering over the clamps as the thrusters reversed, making the ship descend slowly. The clamps grabbed hold with a loud clank. A cloud of sand and steam billowed out from beneath and the ship settled. Technicians rushed to do maintenance checks and secure the perimeter. Sharp hissing came from the pressure release as the ramp opened, extending to the dock floor. It whirred softly until fully down.

The coven leaders stood waiting for someone to

emerge from the opening. Minutes went by and still nothing. Marchand was about to get impatient and turn on the megaphone system when a figure finally emerged.

Greiger came to the edge of the ramp and looked down at the bunker. He then took in the scenery around him. The coven leaders came out of the bunker and advanced to the bottom of the ramp.

"Impressive," Grieger said. "My design?" He gave Marchand a knowing look.

"Made better with my vision," Marchand replied.

"That's debatable."

Queen Celeste nudged Ambrook and Marchand out of her way.

"Enough of the cock sizing, why haven't the rest of you come out?"

The way Grieger stared at her with an expression of fear and pity made her stomach churn. He scanned their faces, assessing their mood.

"Yes," Ambrook said. "What is the problem? Why are you hesitating?"

"Before I explain, you have to promise me," Greiger began.

"There will be no promise of anything!" Celeste shouted. "Where are my coven members? And where are my children?" Her eyes glowed with malice.

"Grieger," Ambrook seethed.

He too became angry.

Durante came to stand next to Grieger and laid a hand on his shoulder. They both nodded, and Durante took one step down the ramp.

"The battle was fierce. It probably still rages to this day." He stared at them. "Not all of us have returned."

Marchand stepped forward.

"That is not acceptable! Let my children explain it to me."

"This was Chase's idea. Tell him to come out here now!" Ambrook demanded.

Durante lowered his head. Tears brimmed Celeste's eyes and Ambrook stood rooted where he was, his face contorted. Marchand shot forth up the ramp and tackled Durante. Grieger tried to pull him off.

"Where are my children?" He screamed with rage.

Erena appeared from the dark of the ship's hangar and swung her leg around, hitting Marchand in the side of the face. The impact dislodged him from Durante and sent him rolling down the ramp. He stopped himself midway and hissed up at them, baring fangs.

"Some of the children chose to stay and fight in order to get us off the planet safely," Erena said. "They refused to run without honor. Chase, Baltise, the twins, Durante's youngest, and others did their part."

"You left them to die!" Marchand yelled.

Grieger walked down to him.

"You think they died? Did you ever have any faith in their abilities?"

"There is no proof otherwise," Ambrook said tersely.

"Exactly. So, we wait."

Celeste frowned. She stared up at Erena.

"You did not mention my son."

Erena tensed. Durante let out a heavy sigh and held out a hand towards Celeste.

"Come." She took a step, stopped, then another and glared at him. "Please."

Celeste continued up the ramp and taking his

hand, followed him into the ship.

"I'll never forgive you," Marchand spat as he stood, eyeing Erena and Grieger.

"We know," Erena replied.

Celeste entered the medical bay as technicians hit the release icon on a cryochamber near the center. She walked up to it and saw her son, sleeping with an expression of torment. Atop his chest was the infant also seemingly in pain.

"What is this?" She cried, turning to the attendant. He came and unhooked the intravenous tubes. "And whose child is this?" She pointed to the infant.

"I need you to remain calm. It will only make things worse," the attendant said.

"Who are you? How dare you..." She didn't get to finish.

Caden awoke screaming, his body arching up from the chamber. The first technician was able to grab the infant before it was catapulted out. The imperial attendant helped the other medics restrain him as his body morphed halfway between Kataling and bipedal form until it subsided. He began to cry then attacked them all, reaching for the infant who also cried. The technician holding the infant handed it to her son. She watched his hysteria lessen as he clutched the little one to his chest, slowly rocking back and forth.

"The emperor had some sort of breeding initiative that gave precedence to merchant bloodlines. His ordeal was nothing less of excruciating. I tried to make it as painless as possible." The attendant gave her a sympathetic grin.

She cautiously ran her hand through her son's hair and his body stiffened.

"I'm not going to hurt you," she whispered. "I never meant to ..." She removed her hand and stepped back from him. "I'm so sorry."

He slumped forward, unconscious.

Tervan appeared from beside her and lifted boy and child from the cryochamber as if they weighed nothing. He didn't acknowledge Celeste as he walked out of the medical bay.

"His injuries were severe," the attendant said. "As for the infant. Well, you will see soon enough." He went off to release the other cryochambers.

Celeste went after the general. Along the way, she encountered others from her coven. They clambered towards her, excited and teary. At that moment she felt guilty. Like a traitor to her coven. She had done too many wrongs to feel grateful.

The dock was covered with passengers already debarked. There were joyous reunions and heavy hearts. Lower Coven leaders had arrived to fetch their members. Erena stood before Count Ambrook.

"He would not take no for an answer. I tried to persuade them to get on the ship."

Ambrook smiled and shook his head.

"You weren't going to change his mind. I think he found something bigger than his role on Earth and decided to see it to the end."

"We have no idea if they survived. I need a bit more optimism from you," Erena chided. She looked around and met his gaze again. "Where is that impudent daughter of mine?"

"Oh," Ambrook sneered.

"You are in for a surprise as well."

Erena saw the malice in his eyes.

"Why so vengeful? This is not something we planned to happen!"

"You should have tried harder," Ambrook hissed. He turned to walk away.

"Pridric!"

Ambrook stopped. His hand clutched the ball of his decorative cane, his weight pushing it down into the sandy dirt. Grieger came up behind Erena and smirked.

"That got him." He forcibly turned Ambrook around and grabbed him by the front of his coat. "You want to blame someone? Look in the mirror. We all have to answer to our sins."

Ambrook wrenched away from him and backed up. Tears streamed down his face.

"That doesn't make it hurt any less," he cried out, his voice hoarse.

"And it shouldn't," Erena said softly.

Grieger brushed his robes.

"By the way, we brought a gift." He pointed to the four-foot cube of red slosh. "We can mass produce that."

Marchand's expression shifted from rage to elation in seconds. He nearly ran towards the two coven children carrying the cube. He caressed it lovingly, saliva forming at the corners of his mouth.

A convoy of coach buses arrived for the passengers to be loaded into. Erena rode in Ambrook's vehicle while Tervan got in with Celeste, not releasing her son from his arms.

The ride back to the De Luce castle was filled with uncomfortable silence. Neither coven leader looked at each other, making the other members nervous. At the front of the gates, the sentries walked down to greet her. One of Ambrook's men got out and opened the car door for her.

"Get out," Ambrook said, still not turning to see her off.

"Punish me all you want. This will solve nothing."

Erena got out and before she reached her entrance, Ambrook's vehicle sped off. Her secretary stood in the doorway with arms wide open.

"Welcome home, my Queen!"

Erena fell into those arms, wrapping her own around the woman. They stayed that way for a long time. Her secretary held her tighter.

"It's over for now. Rest. There is nothing dire to worry about tonight."

Exhaustion hit Erena hard. She felt her body falter and sag against her secretary who tried to hold her up. The woman's mouth was moving as if shouting yet Erena could hear nothing. Strong arms grabbed her from behind, lifting her up. Darkness enclosed.

As much as Durante wanted to ensure his coven members got home safely, he was more worried about Erena. His vehicle had pulled up behind Ambrook's and he heard their exchanged. Angered, he went to say something, but the car left. His mood shifted to despair when he saw Erena slide out of her secretary's arms. He ran forward, catching her in time.

"Thank you, Count Durante. I couldn't... she was too heavy...I."

"I know. Let's get her to bed.

He carried her through the quiet halls up to the master bedroom. Her chamber maids turned down the fresh bedding and he laid her down. He stood up and without warning, the proverbial sandman came from behind, socking him in the back of the head like a hammer. His vision blurred, and he tilted forward, catching himself on the edge of the mattress. It was no use. He was going down, his body landing atop Erena's. The last thing he saw were the chambermaids trying to pull him off and onto the other side of the bed.

For a week, the De Luce coven kept busy caring for the sleeping coven leaders while also maintaining their daily duties. Erena was the first to awaken on the eighth day. She found Durante next to her, softly breathing like a sleeping beauty. His dark hair fallen away from his face and his dark pink lips slightly parted. Not able to restrain herself, she leaned over and kissed him. His eyes fluttered.

"Wake up," she whispered. "Tavelo."

He stared up at her, searching her face then pulled her head back down for another.

The chamber door opened. Erena's Valkrie entered, her face scrunched up in disgust as she watched them disengage.

"There is something important you need to know, my Queen."

Erena sat up and addressed her.

"We will be up and about shortly."

"If you please, head to Princess Adelia's chamber today."

Erena gave her a quizzical look, remembering Ambrook's comment.

"Hmmm?"

"If you please." The Valkrie bowed low and exited the room.

"That sounds ominous," Durante said.

They waited an hour to rouse themselves enough to get dressed. Durante had left some of his attire years ago and was glad they had been recently cleaned. He took a pair of slacks and a casual dress shirt out and donned them. The chambermaids picked out a maxi dress with large floral print and white shoes for their Queen.

"We look so modern, it's disturbing," Durante said.

"I'll agree with you on that."

A commotion erupted from the hallway. Even at that distance they both heard Princess Adelia's voice.

"Where is she? Has mother awoken? Move out of my way!"

The doors burst open and Adelia entered, hunched over and out of breath. Beads of sweat peppered her forehead matting her blonde hair. She wore a long black coat over a red shirt with black vest and leggings. Her boots were not the usual platform heels that laced up. Instead, they were plain and flat. When she stood, Erena and Durante's eyes went wide with shock.

Princess Adelia, face plump and slightly pink revealed a swollen belly far into its pregnancy. Tesul came up from behind and grabbed her by the arm.

"Don't ever do that again. You could have harmed yourself and the child."

Durante stared at the werewolf. They met each other's gaze.

"Daughter? What is the meaning of this?" Erena walked over to her and cupped her face in her hands.

"This is no time for such a thing."

Princess Adelia turned her head and yanked it from her mother's grasp.

"You think I don't about how bad the timing is?" She yelled. "That I have to ready more fighters to combat that insane monster terrorizing the planet? The planet I was born on!"

Erena stepped back, surprised at her outburst.

"There's no need for you to do that alone any-more," Tervan said from the balcony.

Everyone in the room turned to him incredulous. They had not heard him come up the side of the walls, let alone across the balcony to stand at its French doors.

"I have been handling it all this time!"

"Careful, dear sister. You need to be wary of your condition."

Her eyes went red and her talons extended. Tesul smacked her across the top of her head, stunning her still. She became calm, tears forming. Erena rushed over and held her. Adelia relented, returning the gesture.

"She is under tremendous stress. It's too much for her to handle. She won't listen to reason." Tesul went around the two women and stood before Durante. "Welcome back, my Lord." He bowed his head.

"The emperor will be here soon," Tervan said. "I will take over from here."

A new meeting place for the joint deliberations be-tween human and vampire was decided since the usual one had the commander's ship sitting adjacent to it. Count Ambrook surveyed the area and approved of the darkened neighborhood with no streetlights. They had been removed after the sector was abandoned years ago from the last fight. There were so many areas like it these days.

With Commander Gallic on a rampage, country leaders unable to attend the meeting were forced to use video conferencing. Only representatives from the Americas, the United Kingdom, and Japan were bold enough to come in person. Ambrook waited for the other coven leaders to arrive before going in where the humans were already assembled.

Having hashed out the details in advance, the meeting was about logistics. He saw bright lights approach followed by the sound of multiple vehicles coming to a stop behind him. He turned to his driver still sitting in the car.

"Make sure nothing gets by you or the others."

"Understood, my Lord."

Sapienti came up next to him.

"Ready to start a war?"

"The commander did that the moment he set foot on this planet."

The coven leaders entered the building single file.

Adelia cuddled her newborn son and listened to him giggle. He was only a few days old. His tiny hands grabbed hold on a stray lock of her hair and pulled.

"Ow!"

She smiled despite that. Wearing a worn our night gown under the bundle of sheets, Adelia was bed ridden. Her hair was undone, still matted from the birthing ordeal. She was beyond exhausted and the pulled ligaments in her legs were not yet healed. Unable to do what she wanted would have drove her mad only a few years ago. Now, she almost relished it.

Her mother came into the room and reached for the infant. Adelia held him closer to her bosom.

"Stop being stubborn," her mother chastised. "You need to rest."

"He can sleep with me."

"Adelia," her mother sighed.

From the other side of the bed, Tesul gathered their son, dismissing her weak protest of strength.

"She is correct," he said. "You need to rest. I will take care of him for now."

Adelia frowned.

"This weakness is only temporary! I will be ready for battle when the time comes."

The outburst drained her. She felt her body slide down further onto the bed.

"You're not fighting," her mother said angrily. Her expression softened. "Sleep, daughter."

Adelia did as she was told and let it take her.

Erena turned to Tesul. The werewolf stopped tickling his son with one finger and met her gaze.

"I don't care what she does or how you do it. She will not see the battlefield."

"I may be able to stop that, but I cannot take away her duty to command."

"Very well." Again, Erena held out her hands. "May I? For a little bit?" Tesul set the infant in her arms. "Is this your first?" She asked. He nodded. "Protect him with every fiber of your being."

"That is a given."

After playing with her new grandson until he too fell asleep, Erena gave him back to Tesul who in turn set the infant next to Adelia. A nursemaid entered and sat in the chair next to the bed. The two exited the chamber quietly then headed down the corridor leading to her royal guards' meeting room.

Inside was Lariod having a heated argument with her son, the general. They both glanced over as she entered and abruptly stopped, standing tall to salute.

"I hope your argument was productive in finding an optimal attack route," Erena stated.

"My queen," Tervan said, bowing his head. "We were actually in opposition on who should cover the princess during her command."

"No need to worry about that," she said. They both seemed perplexed. "If she sets foot on the battlefield, I will personally string up whoever let her."

Lariod frowned. "She won't like being dictated."

"I already warned her." Erena gestured to Tesul. "I need you to coordinate with Durante's werewolves and ours for ground forces. You," she pointed to Lariod. "Need to resume your duties as guardian."

Lariod's face flushed with anger.

"I have never neglected my position!"

"I beg to differ," she seethed, turning to leave. "Make sure Tesul is up to speed."

When she was gone, Tesul and Lariod locked eyes.

Walking along the corridor back to Adelia's chamber, the two men began their dispute.

"The Queen is correct in her assessment," Tesul said.

"I have been trying to make sure her reign is not usurped!"

"Your job is to protect the Princess!"

"As is yours, if you want to be called her mate."

Tesul whirled around to face him and went for his

throat. The swordsman dodged and used his sheathed sword to block him.

"Make no mistake, werewolf. If I think for a moment your actions are detrimental to the Princess, I will end you."

Tesul's eyes glowed golden and he smirked. They resumed their walk. Lariod kept one hand on the hilt of his sword.

Commander Gallic could see the sky open from his chamber viewport as the emperor's ship pushed through the thick clouds. He sucked in air as he counted the number of ships in the fleet. The airships used on Earth were based on the planet's technology. Rugged, durable, and non-descriptive. Imperial ships were far sleeker, telling in their advanced technology. Over the years, he felt no need to use his elite group against the humans. That would end.

Military aircrafts circled the new visitors yet didn't engage. He had heard from the chatter in the relay that the humans had been given prior notice of the emperor's arrival. That bothered him. Why had they not tried to shoot the ships down? Destroy them before they could land on the surface. A thought popped in his head.

Did they think they could reason with that creature?

"Prepare my transport," he ordered his captain.

Standing silent in the corner, the captain sprung to life and headed out. The commander turned away from the window and did the same. Four of his guards stepped in line behind him, flanking each side. By the time his transport was speeding towards the emperor's ship, it had already landed in the empty field with its hangar door open.

He got out on arrival and went straight to the command center of the ship. Imperial guards watched him like a hawk but didn't attempt to escort him. The doors opened. In the center of the room against the far wall sat the emperor, his gorged eyes narrowed in anger.

"Have they surrendered?" He asked.

Commander Gallic stopped midway across the room, startled by the question, then dropped to his knees and bowed.

"They have not, my Master."

"Where are they? The tracker stopped relaying."

"Scattered about the surface."

"Then we lay waste to all of it until they come to me."

"And then?" The commander was curious.

"I will return them to our world and kill them myself. Their heads will line the palace entry for all eternity. Bring any infant offspring to me. I will choose which ones to devour."

"As you so wish, my master."

Gallic raised his head and flinched at the evil grin the emperor displayed. An awkward silence made him realize it was a signal for him to leave. He did so hastily.

Devour? Infants?

Even he had not gone that far. There wasn't much life to drain from such tiny creatures. Plus, he and his soldiers were not monsters. It dawned on him that the rumors from the royal courts were indeed true. He never wanted to believe that the emperor was eating newborns. A sickness gripped him as he walked back to his transport, making him double over. He clamped a hand over his mouth and waited until he got outside to unleash the bloody bile that rose up. One of the imperial soldiers standing guard at the hangar looked down at him with a knowing stare.

They all know this?

He staggered into his transport and leaned his head back against the bulkhead.

They watched. They waited. Every coven had spread themselves across continents ready to fight alongside humans to beat back the emperor and his fleet now made larger after combining with the commander's. In some countries, a curfew had been implemented, in others; mass evacuation into underground shelters.

Grieger and Marchand sat in a secret laboratory in France going over the inventory list of new weapons they had sent off to the front lines. They had removed their jackets and ties and were comfortable in slacks with dress shirts unbuttoned.

"You do realize, the humans will use these against each other once this fight is over?" Grieger said. "It's in their nature."

"Oh, not to worry. I will immediately relieve them of such prizes shortly after."

"They could use them on us. We have given them the means to destroy us."

Marchand leaned forward.

"Did we?" The sly look told Grieger different.

"What a clever," Grieger locked eyes with him, "deviant, you are."

"I'll take that."

"I despise you for it."

"Of course, you do. I wouldn't have it any other way."

An alert dinged from the radar mapping system. They both looked over at and saw the splat of red flash in the European sector.

"I guess it has begun," Marchand said.

"Was it really necessary to drop such a heavy payload on that area?"

"The emperor is being thorough, isn't he?"

"Still not going to send us flocking to his feet for mercy."

"Hmph."

Marchand stood and walked over to a lever on the stone wall. He pushed it down and the wall opened to a sea of battle wear and weapons. Grieger let out a snort.

"You're going to put on some fighting clothes and kill some imperial soldiers?"

"Of course. You did."

"When was the last time you actually fought in a real battle?" Grieger tilted his head while staring at him playfully.

Marchand's face scrunched up and he gave Grieger a hateful stare.

"Watch me."

Airships shot acid bombs down onto the region, disintegrating everything. Land, wildlife, humans. Count Sapienti's eldest son, Francesco, had anticipated some casualties. This would not deter his plans. Almost the spitting image of his father and similar in height, his presence demanded respect. The elite coven fighters rendezvoused with the human's military forces on the city's edge and formed a perimeter.

He counted twenty airships. The real problem was the dozens of soldiers racing out from the five battle cruisers that landed to find prey.

"Block them off," he commanded. "We can force them in an enclosed sector."

As he said that, he heard the clink of talons coming up the building's wall. He had set up a command post on one of the taller structures. Ten coven fighters were keeping guard. He turned in time to see a set of talons clamp onto the edge of the roof before a horde of soldiers leapt over to attack.

Franceso frowned and went to meet the enemy head on. The two clashed, talons sparking as they grazed together. Not giving the soldier an inch, he went low, tackling him at the legs. At first, the soldier wouldn't budge, slicing his talons down towards his neck. He bobbed his head to the side, avoiding a fatal blow but not a deep laceration on his shoulder. By adjusting his weight, it made the enemy become off kilter and Sapienti was able to bring him down. He swiped his talons across the soldier's neck, slitting his throat deep, nearly decapitating him.

Talons punched through his chest from behind. He reached up and sent his own into the unseen enemy's face. The talons made a wet, tearing sound coming out of him as the body fell backwards to the ground.

"My lord!" One of the fighters called out running to his side. "Can you stand? Should we retreat and get you to safety?" Sapienti gave him an angry expression causing the fighter to move away. "My apologies. I just...your wound."

Francesco grabbed hold of the enemy soldier and brought his neck to his mouth. He bit down hard and began sucking blood. He paused for a moment.

"I'll be fine. Clean up the others. We can't have this spot taken."

"Of course, my lord."

He fed off the cooling corpse a bit more then tossed it aside. More clicking came from the walls. He went to the ledge and looked down. A mechanical cart carrying an acid bomb dug its limbs into the building making a slow ascent.

"Give me a missile launcher," he ordered.

One of the humans came running towards him while a coven fighter dispatched an enemy soldier trying to stop him. Weapon in hand, he aimed it at the machine. It was nearly halfway up. The blast would create a giant hole that could make the top of the building prone to collapse.

But, we can still hold until then.

He shot the missile down into the belly of the machine. The explosion racked the building. Enemy soldiers were caught in the acid spray. Francesco grinned with satisfaction, his eyes glowing silver. The hole was big but not large enough to topple the building.

Perfect!

Count Marchand surfed the air atop a small jet with Grieger behind him. They approached an airship in the rear of its formation and hovered above it. The soldiers onboard looked up, bearing fangs. Marchand smiled.

"Ready to have some fun?" He yelled back at Grieger. "Let's say hello."

The two skydived from the craft into a sea of enemy soldiers. With gleeful abandon, the two cut through the masses, throwing bodies over into the valley below.

"How much farther to the launch bays?" Grieger yelled as he punched his talons into an enemy's chest.

Marchand pointed to a hatch under his feet while tearing another enemy's throat out with the other hand. They made sure every soldier was either dead or down and headed into the bowels of the airship. Rows of acid bombs sat ready to be launched at each bay, four on each side.

"Now we steer this sucker to the battleship enroute to Paris."

"You're enjoying this," Grieger said.

"Aren't you?"

Marchand gave him a wink and climbed back up to the main deck. Grieger felt his mouth twitch into a small grin.

Yes, I am.

The airship's maneuvering capabilities were limited which meant the others could not turn around to help. Grieger doubted they would even if they could. There was never any indication in the previous battles of them helping each other. It was something he and the other coven leaders had noticed after the current emperor took reign. Fires burned on the hillside ahead. Their airship crept along towards the battlefield not yet alerting the others it had been hijacked.

"And how are we going to drop these on those ships?" Grieger asked. "They move like jet fighters. This thing," he tapped the side of the bridge. "Goes one way, one pace."

"Oh, we're going to drop 'em with some new missiles I developed then-plop."

"One. Isn't that overkill? Two. What new missiles?"

Again, Marchand pointed, this time to a large bundle sitting atop two bodies crushed beneath it.

"Where the hell did that come from?"

"It was dropped after us." Marchand gave him a sideways glance. "You should be more observant, Count."

Grieger yanked the burlap off to reveal the casing. He undid the clamps and the container fell open like a blooming flower. Inside was a launcher attached to a stabilizing platform. To the side were four cartridges filled with five-foot-long blue tipped missiles. And there were one hundred of them.

"Well, I guess we do have a plan."

The scout let his vision adjust to see past the border and looked up at the sky. A bright light sparked like a sunburst followed by more. His eyes went wide as imperial ships materialized, heading directly for DeLuce castle. He grabbed the long-range communicator from the tower's window ledge. With the touch of his thumb, it connected, and he yelled into it.

"Incoming!"

Erena stopped pacing in her chamber, hearing the scout's voice come from the new PA system that broadcasted throughout the castle. She stared out at her balcony in disbelief as she too witnessed the horde of ships advancing.

"Here?" She screamed. "He's come here? To my home?"

Her eyes burned silver. In skin tight battle gear she hadn't worn in over a century, her hair pulled back in an austere ponytail, she resembled her Valkyrie. Tall, fierce, and full of bloodlust. Durante stood further in the room wearing a long blue robe cinched at the waist over a black leather bodysuit. His expression was somber, one hand raised to his lips, his fingers caressing them. His blue eyes were lit up like flames. On the balcony, their son, General Tervan, leaned on the rails watching the ships.

"I think he may be angry with us for leaving without his permission," Tervan said. "We should greet him appropriately."

"First," Erena stated. "We get my coven locked down and those unable to fight in the tunnels.

A blast from the lead ship shook the rafters. Sprinkles of dust fluttered around them. There was no mistaking whose ship it was. To confirm, the hangar doors opened for them to see the emperor walking down its ramp. He leapt from the edge into midair, his sights locked on the castle. Even at such a long distance, his blood gorged eyes were visible.

"That monster is going to land on the bailey!" Erena gasped.

Tervan pushed himself from the ledge and headed out the chamber door.

"I'll get him off," he declared.

"This is ahead of schedule," Durante said. "But, we're still prepared."

He gently pulled her hand, breaking her gaze from the chaos starting on the ground as her royal soldiers engaged with the enemy landing on her soil. She hissed loudly then followed him out.

Enemy soldiers had scaled the castle walls and entered by the windows. One group encountered a fully healed Princess Adelia, back in her usual battle garb and quite angry at the invasion. She had just secured her infant in the tunnels with the nursemaid. Knowing how close her child came to danger fueled her anger. Tesul stepped behind her along with an entourage of ten fighters.

"You dare invade my home!"

One of the soldiers hissed, "Jaubro."

Before the next wave of enemy soldiers clambered up, she plowed into the first, her talons slicing deep. Two were able to dodge around her only to be met by the giant werewolf. His golden eyes filled with malice, he pounced on them, tearing flesh with his sharp teeth.

Adelia became overrun by the second wave determined to push through and fell backwards. An enemy soldier sat astride her, his talons bearing down on hers as he tried to get them into her neck. The werewolf turned its attention to her. Four soldiers descend on him. Adelia exposed her fangs at the enemy above her and pushed harder to get him off.

A flash of silver followed by black blood swept across her gaze and the enemy soldier went still. The resistance ceased, and his body slid off at the torso. She used her legs to fling the bottom half away and stood. All around her, enemy bodies were cut in half bleeding out on the floor. Tesul was back in his man form wiping blood from his chest.

Lariod swung his longsword hard to flick the blood from its blade and returned it to its sheath. He had a few deep wounds. Nothing dire.

"You should leave the light work to me, Princess." She marched up and shoved him.

"You let some of them get away! They're going to take the castle!"

"Not on my watch." He turned to pursue the fleeing enemy soldiers. "Are you coming, beast?"

This he aimed towards Tesul.

"Stay out of my way, vampire," Tesul replied as he got in front of Lariod.

Adelia snorted.

"You're both worthless. I will show you how to destroy the enemy."

She also got in front of Lariod and followed Tesul.

"Didn't I just save you both?" He asked, mostly to himself since they were already far ahead down the corridor.

Erena and Durante arrived at the level directly beneath the bailey. Cracks appearing along the foundation became fissures. Blood seeped down, dripping onto them and the accompanying fighters. They all stared up as the entire section caved in, sending the fight and the emperor down upon them. The weight of so many bodies combined with the stones had them descend another two levels.

Grey dust covered everything in sight as they landed. Erena dug herself out from a pile of debris in time to see the emperor doing the same. Fighting could still be heard from above. Through the gaping hole she caught a glimpse of her son, holding his own against three assailants.

"You have something that belongs to me," he said, standing among the rubble.

At first, she didn't understand what he meant. Then it clicked.

"He is my child. I will not let you have him."

"I will pillage this castle and find him." The emperor sneered. "And all of you will return home for my judgement."

The emperor began to morph. From Erena's side view, she saw Durante get up from his hands and knees then speed step towards her. Realizing his intentions, she shifted her footing. They simultaneously charged the emperor before he could fully morph, knocking him through the wall and into the air outside the castle. All three went into freefall towards the active battlefield. The emperor managed to break away and went sailing farther off.

Durante landed not far from the center of the fight while Erena found herself in striking distance of Commander Gallic. He had seen her coming down and decided to greet her accordingly. His short blade barely missed her neck as she leaned back to avoid it.

"Stay still, you Jaubro whore."

Erena caught him in the side with her talons but only managed to graze him. He jumped back and eyed the emperor watching Durante taking on his imperial guards two at a time. He nodded towards him and the commander in turn got the attention of a nearby horde, doing the same. Erena caught on to what it meant a second too late.

"Tavelo! Watch out!" She turned to him.

"Uh uh," Gallic chided. "Pay attention."

Four guards attacked her from behind, forcing her to turn her back on the commander. She could see the horde of soldiers descend on Durante while the emperor charged head on. With the sound of beasts clashing, the emperor rammed Durante. He went flying into the talons of the enemy soldiers.

The shock widened Durante's eyes and blood spurted from his mouth. He still tried to fight in desperation to get them off, failing as their weight bore down, bending him forward. The talons piercing his flesh began to tear the wounds open, some protruding to the other side. Blood drenched from his clenched teeth as he yelled with each intake of breath. The emperor stood fifty yards away from him.

"You will die here, and I'll take what's left of your corpse back, so your bloodline will know their fate."

Erena screamed in agony at Durante's plight. Rage consumed her and to Gallic's surprise, broke free of her attackers. She came at him relentlessly, connecting every blow. He had no time to counter, her speed defying reason.

The emperor took a step to deliver the finishing blow to Durante then halted. Blue eyes turned red, gorged with blood, and Durante let out a shriek that stopped enemy and coven fighters cold. Erena hit the commander with enough brute force to send his body flying, landing at the emperor's feet, right as she saw Durante start to change.

Everyone's gaze turned to Durante. His shoulders split open, splattering blood, to let bloody knotted wings burst forth. His fangs grew long, his talons black, curving into claws. The soldiers lost their hold on him as his body mass expanded. He continued to grow, displaying a massive wing span. Erena stood rooted where she was, dumbfounded at the sight.

The emperor smiled.

"So, it was your bloodline after all."

Durante was no fledgling. At over four centuries old, he was a full grown Volshin. He stood twelve feet tall towering over them, resembling a dragon. The soldiers were knocked off as he rose, crushing them under his clawed feet as they fell to the ground. Two pools of black blood spread, seeping into the field.

The emperor snatched up the commander and brought his neck to his mouth. He fed off him until satiated then dropped the unconscious soldier back at his feet. He used a finger to spread the residual blood on his lips. Then morphed into a Kataling.

The Volshin flapped its wings.

Those on the battlefield went flying from the force of wind it created, their screams dissipating the farther they traveled away. Except the Kataling. Equal in size, though more squat on all fours, the force of the draft didn't stop its advance. The two monsters collided.

The Kataling went straight for the Volshin's abdomen, piercing it with its two curved front talons. The Volshin bent down and swatted it away. Before it could regain its stance, the Volshin clamped its jaws into the Kataling's side. It shrieked in pain and writhed back and forth until the Volshin could no longer hold it.

Released, it back walked, shaking off the shock and charged again. This time, when the Volshin reared its head back to take another bite, it made an evasive maneuver around behind it, catching the Volshin off guard. It tried to rip a piece of a wing off with its teeth. The translucent, leathery skin would not yield.

The Volshin twisted side to side, determined to get rid of the annoyance, and was finally able to toss the Kataling onto the nearly empty battlefield. It came up on all fours ready for another round. The Volshin flew over to it and stomped on its back, pinning it to the ground.

With eyes bleeding, the Volshin bent down, grabbed hold of one of the Kataling's limbs, and pulled. Howling, the Kataling pushed itself flat, resisting the pressure being applied. Imperial soldiers came running to its aide. They ended up being bitten in half or blown away when again the Volshin flapped its wings.

There was a wet snap.

The Kataling let out a high-pitched cry. And his body was suddenly swept from under the Volshin's feet. Commander Gallic, half functioning yet full of resolve, held the now devolved body of the emperor whose right arm dangled useless.

"Retreat!" He ordered.

"Oh no you don't!" Erena yelled, giving chase.

From the sky, twenty imperial ships appeared, weapons aimed at the castle. She stopped. Even with most of the coven in the tunnels, a bombardment of that magnitude would kill everyone. She clenched her fists. Gallic, surrounded by a full battalion, backed away for a bit before turning to board the emperor's ship as it landed. The hangar closed behind them. The surrounding ships also boarded in haste and took off in unison to the sky.

Crunching.

Erena went stiff and slowly turned to the sounds. Across the battlefield, Volshin and Kataling munched on the corpses. She felt bile rise in her throat. A wave of projectiles came whizzing through the air and she dropped to the ground, laying flat. She watched the giant tranquilizer darts hit their targets. Every Volshin and Kataling was struck with multiple rods. Within minutes, they all fell, shaking the earth before reverting to their original form.

Erena got up and ran over to Durante. He was covered in blood and barely breathing, his wounds struggling to heal.

"Stay with me!" Erena screamed, crying.

Durante stared at her with eyes still blood gorged. He managed to raise one hand and caress her cheek before it dropped. His eyes closed. She held him close, rocking back and forth, as she sat in the center of everything and nothing.

"Move!"

The gruff male voice startled then angered her. She looked up and saw Chancellor Rayne standing over her with pursed lips. She bared her fangs and hissed.

"Give him to me!" When she pulled him tighter, he lost patience. "If you want him to live, you will let me have him!"

She found herself crying more forcefully and shook her head. When her body began to feel weak, she finally loosened her grip.

"Good girl," Chancellor Rayne praised as he stuck her with a needle.

He injected the sedative and let her fall. Tervan came up next to him and stared at her.

"Was that really necessary?" he asked.

"She wasn't going to let me have your father."

Tervan nodded and bending down, scooped his mother up into his arms.

"You better make sure he lives."

He walked back to the castle.

Chancellor Rayne knelt by Durante's body. He noticed the dark bruises starting to form all along the muscles and veins on fair skin. Tell-tale signs that the count had never morphed before. From the old records he knew that the elders of the Endaga bloodline would have known.

So, why didn't they tell him, or anyone else?

He turned to his medical unit that came alongside him.

"Be careful with him. Make sure he is secured in the ship and taken straight to the blood vault in Ambrook castle."

"Yes, Chancellor," they replied and went to task.

As they wrapped Durante's naked form in soft cloth before transporting him onto the stretcher, Chancellor Rayne had a moment of envy. Regardless of form, Count Durante was a beautiful creature. Maybe even more than Count Ambrook. He chastised himself for the thought and walked with the medical attendants carrying Durante. His treatment took priority.

STALEMATE

There was a great shift in the battle zones as the tables turned. Imperial soldiers were now fighting to exit the theaters while the humans and coven fighters tried to annihilate them. The airships still intact managed to get away and hovered nearby awaiting their comrades. Fight cruisers were on standby where they landed to do the same. Marchand became agitated about the scene. It bordered on slaughter and that was not who they were as a species.

"Let them go," he sent to the coven fighters telepathically.

Like a wave, the fighters backed off their enemy, lowering their weapons. Which confused the humans enough for the imperial soldiers to make a speedy departure to their ships. When some humans tried to stop them from taking their dead and wounded, the coven fighters stepped in, forming a safe route.

The human military leader went up to the nearest coven fighter.

"What is the meaning of this? We are not letting those monsters go after they started this!" His face was flushed almost red and his jowls shook. Spittle dripped from his mouth.

"Monsters they may be, but we will not allow senseless slaughter when they are trying to retreat. This is not something out of your history's play book."

Marchand and Grieger nodded as he landed the confiscated airship. They hauled off the missile launcher and let the enemy retake their vessel. One of the soldiers walked pass, dragging another who was wounded and unconscious. He stopped near Grieger.

"We didn't want this," he whispered. "The emperor's decree is absolute."

Grieger gritted his teeth as his body stiffened.

"Not if it's wrong. You should have overthrown him centuries ago." He tried to dampen the level of rage in his tone. "Hurry up and get off this planet."

"Thank you."

The soldier continued his journey to the airship. Once all the ships were loaded, they ascended to the skies in tight formation. From below, they resembled a flock of birds migrating for the season. When they could no longer be seen, Marchand focus on the humans.

"Now, for the next objective."

He gave Grieger a nod and went further into the mass of soldiers.

"Subdue the humans. Reclaim any weapons we developed."

By the time the human general figured out what was going on from the eruption of shouting, it was too late. He was restrained by two vampires as he watched the equipment manufactured to combat the enemy were removed from the battlefield. Without them, humans would be no match for the vampires.

"You dirty sons of bitches!" He fumed.

"We should have known you would side with your own kind. What? You're going to enslave us for your sick agenda?"

Grieger turned and stared at the human with pity. Such small mindedness did not appeal to him and he grew tired of the man's outbursts. He sighed, stepping close to the general who leaned forward in defiance with his chin jetted out, and punched him in the space between the ribs and abdomen. The general's eyes widened. His mouth opened and the only thing that came out was a small squeak sound. His body went limp as his eyes rolled up in their sockets. The two coven fighters held him up until Grieger pointed down. They laid him on the ground and went to help with the extraction.

"We're going to catch hell for this," he said to Marchand.

Marchand gave him one of his signature side glances.

"What will they do? Fight us? I think they may have a new understanding once the dust settles. Our domination of this world will be complete."

"Was that the agenda?" Grieger asked, playfully.

"It became that over a century ago. Serves them right."

The two resumed overseeing the clearing of the battlefield.

Commander Gallic had a hard time carrying the emperor to his private quarters, yet he endured. He didn't trust the others to handle it after the sour taste of retreat. The emperor was heavier than normal, his body always half morphed. He reached the door and used his hip to activate the sensor. Inside, he laid the emperor on the bed. Within moments, his personal medical team arrived. Exhaustion claimed the commander. He slumped on the floor in the farthest corner of the room and fell asleep.

He woke to screams all around him.

His vision blurry, he saw movements of colors, mostly black. When his eyes focused, he reared back against the wall. The emperor held a soldier by the head, the other hand lifting him up sideways so the blood flowed more freely from the gaping neck wound. When no more came out, the emperor tossed the body against the opposite wall to join the other five. The medical team was in the corridor outside trying not to appear fazed. Their horror-stricken expressions gave them away.

The emperor wiped his mouth with the back of his forearm, smearing it more on his face. He lumbered naked over to the door and hit the sensor, sealing it shut. Some of the bodies still twitched and Gallic hoped they would recover slowly so the emperor wouldn't be tempted to drain them. He looked up and was shocked to find the emperor' eyes locked on him like hungry prey. An erection heavily gorged and straight as a rod was prominent.

For a brief moment, Gallic debated on if he should fight. Seconds later he had no choice in the matter. The emperor came at him, ripping off his already torn uniform. He was flipped over and held down by the side of his head as he felt his body being invaded. The emperor grabbed one of his legs and pulled him closer until he was in a position where his torso lay flat on the floor with his legs folded beneath him. He silently braced himself against the excruciating pain and prayed for it to be over quickly.

"This is your reward for loyalty," the emperor said heatedly.

Gallic gasped as he felt the emperor go deeper. He cried out in pain. The emperor's face came close to his and he could smell the mingled blood on his breath.

"You will submit to me."

It was not going to end soon. That was what the commander concluded in his despair. Instead of trying to ignore it, he relented, letting his body go lax. To his surprise, the pain subsided a little. The emperor seemed to hesitate mid stroke. Then he leaned back and continued his relentless thrusts. On the floor across from him, the commander caught one of the downed soldiers staring at him.

I'm nothing but a toy, he said to himself. *Better that than food.*

The moment the emperor's ship cruised out of the stratosphere of his home world and the docks came into view, he knew something was amiss. There were no Volshins in the sky or Katalings roaming the piers. The boardwalk had been repaired, reinforced with metal struts. Merchants went about inventorying cargo. Imperial guards walked around as if observing instead of enforcing law. No ships, imperial or enemy merchant came to attack or escort.

In the distance, the palace glimmered in the grey sky, majestic as it was during his father's reign. It dawned on him that the palace had fell in disrepair somehow over the centuries. Its upkeep was not his top priority and he now regretted that. Regardless of the pain and torture he endured in that place, it was still his home. And, he was the emperor.

"Keep our course steady," he commanded the navigator.

"Yes, Master."

He vowed to wipe out all who opposed him in the palace. Even if it meant his demise in the end. Losing to the merchants on Earth and not getting the two infants back made him want to abandon all reason.

On the docks, merchants stopped what they were doing to watch the emperor's ship sail towards the palace. They all braced for what may come next. The imperial guards patrolling the boardwalk slowed their pace, their gaze following the ship. Tension permeated the pier.

"That cargo will not unload itself!" The head of the Callesi merchants called out as he walked passed the dock ports. "No need to fear. The emperor's reign of terror is over."

"How can you be sure?" A female worker asked.

He gave her a winning smile.

"Oh, that's a secret."

The emperor stood at the edge of the hangar bay as the ramp opened. Below him were dozens of merchants and their workers backed by fifty imperial guards. They were not there to welcome him. He clenched his fists and made his way down. A few of the imperial guards turned their heads away as if ashamed. At the bottom of the ramp he came face to face with the leader of the group.

"You are of the Jaubro bloodline," he stated.

"That is correct." Lord Jaubro cocked his head. "You murdered my brother and his wife. Displayed their severed heads in the outer courtyard at the palace entrance."

"And this will be your revenge? To think this is enough to kill me?" He nodded at the group behind Jaubro.

The soldiers on the ship moved to come to his side. Jaubro raised a hand. The imperial guards on the ground drew their weapons ready to strike down their comrades. They stopped their advance, confused on what to do. The emperor did not give them an order.

"You should come quietly, Emperor," Jaubro suggested.

The emperor shrieked as he morphed into his Kataling form. He charged forward. A swarm of projectiles sped at him and pierced his body, covering it. He fell to the ground with a thud, his body reverting to humanoid form.

"I will not be killed by you," he managed to say angrily.

Lord Jaubro knelt before him.

"Kill you? No, no. We are going to fix you." The emperor went rigid. "It's what you father should have done long ago."

A group of medical attendants came into view and began removing the injection rods from his body.

"No! No! I won't allow it!" He tried to writhe out of their grasp as they wrapped him in metal netting.

"No! You will not," he cried. His voice faded at the end. He felt tears covering his face. "I don't want it."

Jaubro stood.

"All that unnecessary rage stemming from something that could have been avoided. All your father had to do was have your DNA altered to combat the defect. An easy fix." He nodded to the attendants. "Lock him away for now. You can begin his treatment once the drugs take full effect.

The emperor tried to force his body to obey but it wouldn't listen. He felt like a heavy boulder had been inserted inside him. His eyelids could no longer stay open yet by sheer will he kept them focused long enough to see himself being dragged into a cold dark cell in the bowels of the palace. The same place he imprisoned the Volshins and Katalings until he unleashed them to do his bidding.

"That was anticlimactic," Chase said after the emperor was removed and his soldiers disarmed. "I was expecting some bloodshed."

"I told you, we need his bloodline and he can be rehabilitated."

"Whatever you say."

"So," Jaubro said. "Are you ready to go home now? Our planet is back on the path of redemption and profit. There is no need for any of you to stay and fight."

"I think we should," Odette replied. "Plus, you need to think about Baltise, and your daughter."

Chase went flush.

"I know. My father probably won't be too happy."

"At least your father wants to see you again," Tamar said.

Lord Jaubro went and grabbed him by the chin.

"You father is not as cold as you think. He loves you. Endagas rule by their hearts." Tamar wrenched away from him. "I know you feel broken after losing your guardian in battle. Still, you must live on. Go home. Tell young Tavelo I know he'll do what is right."

"I guess it's time to board that fully stocked ship, hmm?" Olivier quipped.

"The weather will be most cooperative in a few weeks. I suggest you wait until then," Jaubro's assistant said.

"Why?" A male voice asked from the soldiers deboarding the emperor's ship.

Jaubro and the others turned and saw Commander Gallic standing with arms straight down at his side with eyes glowing.

"Fixing him would ruin him. Why do such a monstrous thing?"

"Ruin him?" Jaubro replied. "He has gone insane. The only monster in this scenario is him."

"I won't let you."

Gallic extended his talons, prepared to fight. An imperial soldier nearby struck him hard in the back of the neck. He dropped to the floor, his eyes fluttering closed.

"Take him to medical." Jaubro's assistant ordered. "He can keep the emperor company during recovery sessions."

"Ugh," Odette said, cringing.

"Now that that's over, let's have a feast to celebrate victory and your voyage home," Lord Jaubro said.

"I say we break out some of that special stash in the supply house," one of the other coven members said with glee.

"That can be arranged," Jaubro's assistant answered.

Many in the room felt their mouths start to moisten at the thought.

Returning to Earth space caused jubilant applause onboard the ship. The navigator had cut the time to four years and was praised for his skills. As the ship made its way down to the dead zone where the first ship launched, the coven members clambered to the viewpoints for a look at the landscape.

"What are those?" Odette asked as she looked out at the various territories.

Below were giant walls erected around sectors, blocking them off from the other sides. It was the same in every country they passed. All converged around the covens sitting on the outskirts of the dead zone.

"Looks like we had a falling out with the humans," Chase replied.

"Oh, for fuck's sake," she spat out. "So, they had some casualties. That's what war is. They should know that better than any species."

The ship approached the launch pad and they saw another docking station had been added in anticipation of their arrival. At the holding bays were the coven leaders along with other members. Odette could see her father as Chase did his. Both men had angry expressions.

"And we are in so much trouble," Olivier laughed.

Chase sighed heavily. Time to face the consequences.

The moment the ship was clamped down, the hangar doors opened for the ramp to extend. Coven children spilled out, running towards the crowd waiting for them. Chase, the twins, and Tamar lingered behind, not ready to be reprimanded for their bold decision.

Chase turned his head back to see Baltise coming up with their six-year-old daughter in tow. She was slightly chubby with strawberry blonde hair and blue eyes that seemed to have seen too much. An old soul. He took Baltise's hand and they walked the rest of the way together. The closer they got, the more his father's face scrunched up in dissatisfaction.

"So, this is how you return," his father said when they were a few feet away.

Chase halted before him along with Baltise and their daughter.

"You would rather chastise me than rejoice my survival, or even to ask if we won?"

His father stepped back as if assaulted, a sadness exuding.

"I wanted you to come back with the others," he snapped. "Not be some savior or martyr."

"And I am neither, so you can rest easy." Chase grinned. "We did win."

"You should have seen the emperor's face when he arrived," Odette added.

Her smile faded as her father came at her fast. He barreled into her and they both landed on the ground. He pinned her shoulders while straddling her.

"Theo!" Grieger yelled. "Stop this."

Olivier came up behind his father, talons extended. "Get off her. I won't let you harm her."

"You stupid child!" Marchand cried.

"I shouldn't have let you go!"

Odette saw the pain in her father's eyes as bloody tears fell on her chest. She too became teary eyed and reached up to hug him tight. Her brother wrapped his arms around him as well.

"Ick," Grieger said.

His mouth turned downward in disgust.

With that, Chase's mother ran up and folded him in a death grip hug. She kissed his face all over before leaning away to look at him. Then she shoved him out of the way and lifted his daughter.

"Oh, how precious. She's going to be my muse." His mother walked off with her.

Baltise held out an arm towards them in protest. Chase shook his head and pushed her arm down gently at the wrist. The two were practically inseparable and this would be the first time they parted ways.

Tamar came down the ramp and into the fray. He looked around and did not see his father. Instead, Tervan was there to greet him. They met halfway and sized each other up for longer than necessary.

"Where is our father?" He asked.

A hush fell on the masses. The returning coven children were confused by the reaction. He saw Count Ambrook's face turn pale.

"Where is he?" He yelled, grabbing his older brother by the front of his jacket.

Tervan smacked his hand away and pushed him to the ground.

"You need to listen carefully. He is barely alive. The Ambrooks have secured him in their blood vault. He will sleep until he can awaken."

Tamar felt tears brimming his eyes and a few fell. Tervan bent down and grabbed him by the collar.

They were inches apart.

"Don't you dare cry for him after what you pulled," his brother seethed.

"I know that!"

He tried to get free of his brother's grip.

Tervan's expression softened, and he let him go.

"Get up. We must go home first. I see you came back alone. I am sorry."

That was too much. The sadness hit. Tamar's face scrunched as a slow wail escaped his opened mouth. He let himself cry, tasting blood and snot trickling onto his lips, but he paid no mind. Tervan gathered him in his arms and waited for it to end.

"This turned out to be a goddamn travesty," Grieger stated.

The next coven meeting was held at Ambrook's castle. He sat in his office with wet hair dripping down the back of the chair while he stared at a spider trapping its prey on the ceiling. With swift action, the spider had it wrapped up and ready for later consumption. In a casual black suit with a white shirt, Ambrook appeared almost gentleman like; aristocratic.

He felt nothing of the sort.

What he wanted bordered on viciousness. When the battle was over, and the humans demanded an audience, the coven leaders obliged. They were met with hostility and a list of non-negotiables. The covens and many of their territories had been essentially isolated from the rest of the world. A remedy agreed by both sides, yet the economies now relied heavily on their commerce.

From outside came the sound of car doors opening and shutting. His guests had arrived. He stood and straightened out his jacket as he walked out. Chancellor Rayne was waiting for him. The two men walked in silence to the banquet hall. Erena and Celeste were present along with Marchand, Grieger, and Sapienti. Drinks had already been served. A servant set two snifters before him and the Chancellor as they sat at the table.

"Well, you look unsophisticated today," Celeste said.

He gave her a nasty look, taking a sip of his brandy. He glanced over her attire. An off the shoulder tight knit dress that barely covered her breasts and short enough to not leave much for the imagination if one chose to look.

"And, you seem to be channeling your sexual depravity." His tone dripped with malice.

The other leaders set down their drinks in astonishment.

"That is uncalled for!" Marchand admonished.

"How uncouthed!" Sapienti exclaimed.

"What is wrong with you?" Erena yelled.

"Shameful," Grieger added.

Celeste's eyes turned silver as she stared at him from the top of her teacup. Her hands shook slightly with rage. Ambrook sat back and smirked, knowing he was not wrong about her.

"I'm in a bad mood. Don't test me," Ambrook said.

The room got quiet.

Marchand picked up his drink and swirled the wine glass, watching the liquid play.

"Let's not turn on each other just yet. We have many issues to attend to."

"Yes," Chancellor Rayne said. "The first being the

new sector for the Volshins and Katalings."

"I don't see why we can't leave them be in the caves we found them in or our own castles," Celeste protested.

"Because the humans have threatened to hunt us if we are anywhere outside of the walls they built around our homes. They lived like animals in those caves. That will not continue on my watch." Ambrook took another sip as he finished.

"Does that include Tavelo?" Erena asked.

"Of course not," Grieger snapped. "He is a coven leader and one of the founding merchant families. We cannot allow him to shirk his responsibilities."

"If he even wakes up," Celeste said, shrugging.

Erena stood, knocking the table an inch sideways. "Hold your tongue."

"Ladies," Marchand purred.

"That's a loose term," Ambrook quipped.

"What is it, Pridric?" Sapienti asked. "Why are you being this way?"

"We searched," Ambrook began, "all this time for those with ancient blood, and you knew where they were, had one. Spread your legs for it." Celeste rose up from her seat, fangs exposed. "No, more likely climbed on and decided to spawn one of your own. Then you kept it secret from all of us."

Celeste crawled up on the table and swiped at Ambrook with extended talons. He leaned back, avoiding the assault. Grieger and Sapienti pulled her back off the table and into her seat. She slapped their hands away and corrected her dress that had hiked up above her waist. She wore no undergarments. Ambrook sat straight and glared at her. Erena stood with balled fists then sat as well.

"Our bloodline is in the decline. And all because we have become complacent on this planet. Breeding with humans, werewolves, and vampires."

"As is our wealth," Sapienti said. "We are intergalactic merchants and can't seem to find a remedy for this new wrinkle in human trade."

"I had to use the funds from the sale of my home within the city to have my new one built in this area," Marchand said.

"Then what is the solution, Count Ambrook?" Erena's tone was hostile as she spewed out his Earth title like venom.

He narrowed his gaze at her. Sapienti seemed to catch on to his intentions and gave him a nod. Marchand and Grieger contemplated it in their heads. Even Erena stopped being childish enough to realize his agenda.

"A slow and painful conquest."

"How about we get our affairs in order before talking about conquests?" Tervan spoke as he came into the room, surprising them all.

"I thought you would wait in the car?" Erena said.

"Oh, I wouldn't miss this. I stood in the corridor and watched for as long as I could stand it." He walked further in. "We have already shown our dominance over the humans only to expose the crumbling underbelly." He turned to Celeste. "He is correct about your decision to keep the Volshin and Kataling locations from us." She went flush, lips thin. He lifted his head to the side and glared at her. "Among other things."

"Then we should start by not keeping any more secrets from each other," Celeste chided as she brought her knees up to her chest and sipped her tea.

Tension permeated the room as they all avoided eye contact. Ambrook set down his snifter and laid his head on the table. Outside the window, a bird tried to fly through and smacked hard against the glass. Ambrook didn't flinch. He watched the blood smear as it slid down.

"I'm hungry," he said sitting up. "Who's hungry?

"What did you have in mind?" Marchand asked.

Ambrook looked out onto the glowing lights of the dark city. They all followed his stare. It had been a long time since they went hunting. The servant threw the window open and one by one, they leapt out into the night sky.

END

ABOUT THE AUTHOR

Hi there!

I'm Maquel A. Jacob. I have had a passion for the written word since the age of seven, reading everything I could get my grubby little hands on which included encyclopedias and the thesaurus. At twelve, I had my first encounter with a Stephen King novel and was hooked. I then became inspired to write my own brand of fiction, combining multiple genres to keep things interesting.

I am a HUGE Anime fan, love a great bottle of wine and rock out to heavy metal music. Green and lush Oregon is where I currently reside, spinning imaginary worlds in my head and daydreaming.

For updates, FREE short stories, Newsletters
...and more
Visit: www.maquelajacob.com
Like Maquel A. Jacob on Facebook
Follow on Twitter @MaquelAJ1

Also find me on Goodreads

ALSO BY MAQUEL A. JACOB

THE CORE TRILOGY
CORE OF CONFLICTION
SEEDS OF CONVICION
BONDS OF CONTRITION

CURVE OF HUMANITY
ORIGINS
SHADOWMEN OBJECTIVE
PURGE SEQUENCE

WELCOME DESPAIR
A COLLECTION OF SHORT STORIES

COMING SOON

CRIPPLED EARTH
CURVE BOOK FOUR

MORE OF THE CORE SERIES
AND BOOK THREE OF THE BLOOD SAGA:
BLOOD DESCENSION!

* 9 7 8 0 9 9 9 7 9 5 6 4 7 4 *